A Season to Remember

Sheila O'Flanagan

A Season to Remember

HACHETTE
BOOKS
IRELAND

First published in Ireland in 2010
by Hachette Books Ireland
An Hachette UK company

1

Cataloguing in Publication Data is
available from the British Library

ISBN 978 07553 751 34

Typeset in Galliard by Palimpsest Book Production Limited,
Falkirk, Stirlingshire

Printed and bound in Great Britain by Clays Ltd, St Ives plc

Hachette Ireland policy is to use papers that are natural, renewable and
recyclable products and made from wood grown in sustainable
forests. The logging and manufacturing processes are expected
to conform to the environmental regulations of the country of origin.

Hachette Books Ireland
A division of Hachette UK
8 Castlecourt Centre
Castleknock
Dublin 15

www.hachette.ie

To the Burke and O'Flanagan ladies,
past and present, always inspirational.

ACKNOWLEDGEMENTS

Thanks to the wonderful team at Hachette and in particular, Ciara Considine for her thoughtful editorial comments.

Thanks also to my agent, Carole Blake, who looks after every book with equal care.

And huge thanks, as always, to my fantastic readers who continue to make my writing life a joy. You can keep up to date on my news and work on my website: www.sheilaoflanagan.com where you'll also find links to follow me on Facebook and Twitter.

Prologue: The Sugar Loaf Lodge I

The Sugar Loaf Lodge wasn't really a lodge at all.

It was actually a large country house, which had been built in the late seventeenth century by a minor English earl whose family had been gifted lands in County Wicklow, Ireland. The family – the Earl, his wife and their four children – spent a single summer in the house, which nestled close to the iconic Sugar Loaf mountain, before returning abruptly to England. The reason for their departure wasn't clear, but it was generally believed that one of his children had taken ill and died in Ireland, leaving both the Earl and Countess broken-hearted and quite unable to return to their summer home.

When the Earl himself died a few years later, the property passed to his eldest son, who, having had a childless marriage and therefore nobody to leave it to, didn't much care what happened to it. He rarely visited the house, and after his death it quickly fell into disrepair. Its ivy-clad walls crumbled and the large rooms were invaded by the damp Irish air, while the once carefully tended pasture-green gardens grew wildly out of control. The local people avoided it, because rumours and legends had grown up around the derelict building, including ghost stories in which the spirit of the dead child was seen wandering sadly around the ruin. According to these stories, seeing the spirit (nobody was quite sure whether it was a boy or a girl) was meant to bring bad luck, and so generally people stayed away.

The property eventually passed to the state, which had no real interest in it either. There was a brief effort to restore it in the 1970s, but it wasn't until more than thirty years later that Neil and Claire Archer borrowed far more money than they'd originally intended, renovated it and eventually opened it as an exclusive country hotel.

Their family and friends told them they were crazy. There was no real money in the leisure business, they said. Big companies got into it for tax breaks, but for the little people it was nothing but hard slog and no rewards.

'We're not trying to become multi-millionaires,' Claire told them calmly. 'We're doing this because we want to.'

'You're amateurs,' said Neil's father, a barrister who'd wanted his son to follow him into the legal profession and who felt that running a hotel was somehow beneath Neil's abilities.

'Gifted amateurs,' Claire reminded him. 'I do have a hospitality industry qualification, you know. And I managed a hotel in England for three years.'

'Totally different,' said Alan Archer. 'Your entire livelihood didn't depend on it.'

'We've got the backing,' said Claire.

'I don't know how,' Alan said.

'A good business plan,' she told him, although the level

of debt they'd taken on terrified her. But they'd come out from under it in the end, she knew. And their hotel would be the best in Ireland.

Five years after they'd embarked upon the project, the Sugar Loaf Lodge had become everything they'd intended. Large enough for guests not to feel suffocated by each other's company, but small enough to retain a country-house warmth. With an award-winning restaurant and breathtaking spa, the Sugar Loaf Lodge was considered an oasis of peace and serenity within striking distance of the capital city. Each room was named after one of the Dublin and Wicklow mountains and was carefully decorated to reflect the ambience of an area known as the Garden of Ireland. Despite its hefty rack rates, the hotel was almost always full, and its website was regularly updated with fulsome reviews from its guests. (Well, most of the reviews were positive; Claire had been miffed to see that some people complained about the quality of the bikes that the hotel provided for cycle trips around the countryside. She thought they were fine, but apparently the guests weren't too keen on having to work hard to negotiate the hills.)

However, what people liked most about the hotel was Neil and Claire themselves, who seemed to have an almost uncanny ability to know exactly what each guest wanted or needed before they asked for it. Extra towels or blankets or pillows were provided almost as soon as the visitor thought about it; the room temperature was regulated to each guest's individual preference; and Claire always remembered everyone's name, so that they felt personally welcome. All of this meant a steady stream of repeat bookings from visitors who claimed that the Sugar Loaf Lodge was one of the best small hotels in the world.

Claire, especially, was very pleased about this. The idea of opening the hotel had been hers and she'd been the one to persuade Neil that the location of the Lodge, nestled within the Wicklow Mountains and with uninterrupted views of the rolling hills, was absolutely perfect. She'd been the one to negotiate with the council about its restoration and about the provision of a road to the building itself. She'd decided to engage an interior designer to re-create a look of stately grandeur, but with a homely touch. She'd spoken so passionately and persuasively to the bank manager that he was immediately convinced they would make a success of the hotel – although it was Neil's understanding of balance sheets and accounts that had ultimately swung the deal.

Sometimes Claire read stories of other hotel owners who'd tried and failed to achieve what they'd achieved, and she wondered if their own luck, which had helped them to avoid the pitfalls that had plagued those others, would hold. Neil, though, said that the reason they'd succeeded wasn't due to luck but because as far as both of them were concerned, running the Sugar Loaf Lodge was more than a business. It was the fulfilment of a dream. And having a dream was far more important than business plans designed to squeeze every last cent out of the hotel. You made your own luck, Neil said, and that was what they did every day.

Neil and Claire regularly turned down offers by international chains to buy the Sugar Loaf Lodge. They wanted to keep its unique identity and not lose it to corporate branding, no matter how financially attractive that option seemed. Every year they congratulated themselves on doing the right thing – even though the last bid had given them real pause for thought. It had been a substantial amount of money and they couldn't help wondering if perhaps they would be insane to pass it up.

'Let's give it another year or two.' It was Claire who decided in the end. 'Maybe by then we'll be fed up with running a hotel anyway and we'll want to hand it over to the faceless suits.'

'You think you'll ever be tired of it?' Neil smiled at her.

'I suppose one day,' she said thoughtfully. 'But right now – I love it.'

Almost immediately after they turned the offer down a sudden surge of economic gloom led to a plunge in bookings. Claire, looking at a raft of cancellations and empty rooms, felt sick inside and wondered if their amazing run of luck had turned.

People were leaving it till the last minute to book their holidays, particularly their Christmas break. Because of its wonderful location, the Sugar Loaf Lodge was usually a popular destination for Christmas, and quite often booked up by September, but this year, even as late as the beginning of December, there were still rooms available. Neil and Claire took additional ads in the newspapers and crossed their fingers while resolving that all their guests would find their expectations surpassed. Which would hopefully mean that when people were choosing their hotels for the future months, the Sugar Loaf would be high on their list of possible destinations. Always providing, they said anxiously to each other, that people would be booking any hotel in the future at all. They didn't even want to think further than Christmas!

It was a nerve-racking time. The banks were being unhelpful and the hotel staff, terrified at the possibility of losing their jobs, were gloomy. Claire called them all together to tell them that they would get through this crisis, and that with everyone's help the Christmas season at the Sugar Loaf Lodge would be the most successful ever. She said this in a strong, confident voice, which reassured the staff. But afterwards she locked herself in her office until her hands had stopped shaking.

Then she looked at the bank statements (normally Neil's job) and swallowed hard. It was because of her pig-headedness that they were in this situation. She'd been the one to insist that they could go it alone, that they didn't need branding or interference from a chain. She'd been the one to say that the success of the Sugar Loaf Lodge was built on the fact that it was a family-run business and that it wasn't logo-ed to within an inch of its life. Neil had agreed, but she knew he thought that they might regret turning down the latest offer.

The thing was, she didn't regret it. Not for the hotel itself. And not for the money that they would have made out of it. Claire wasn't someone for whom money was all that important. But she regretted it bitterly for the staff. Because unless they filled all the rooms at Christmas, and unless people spent a lot more money than they had done in the last six months, all her brave words about getting through the bad patch together would be nothing more than that – brave words with nothing to back them up. And the people who'd worked so hard for her because they trusted her and Neil to do what was best would find themselves out of work.

She looked at the bookings and felt the sick feeling again. Normally by now they were turning people away, rather than wishing that they would call. It was all going terribly wrong. And it was all her fault.

Neil was anxious too. He knew, even better than Claire, how precarious the business was. People didn't realise how quickly things could turn. There had been a time when it seemed that they could do no wrong, when people would book weekends away without even thinking about it. These days they would ring up and ask what was included and try to negotiate the price of the room or the visits to the spa or even the cost of the meals in the restaurant. Neil knew that he and Claire had pared everything to the bone, but they couldn't do anything more without compromising the hotel. It was a luxury hotel, after all. Which meant that you had to pay more. The thing was that right now, nobody wanted to pay for luxury. They either couldn't afford to or they wanted it on the cheap. And it was trying to find the balance between the two that was proving so difficult for them.

*

'What will we do?' Claire looked anxiously at Neil as they went through the bookings together. 'We're going to lose money if we don't get more people into the restaurant every night and if we're not booked up in the next week or so.'

'I know,' said Neil.

'I'm so sorry.' She started to cry. 'I thought that we had it sussed. I thought that we were the best hoteliers in the country and that we knew what people wanted. I thought we knew better than the chains and that's why I wanted to keep the hotel for ourselves. But I was wrong.'

'No you weren't,' said Neil as he put his arms around her. 'You were absolutely right. The Sugar Loaf Lodge is one of the best hotels in the country and we're good at knowing what people want and we'll give everyone who comes here the very best Christmas they've ever had.'

'And even if we do all that . . .' Claire looked at him anxiously. 'We could still end up up shit creek without a paddle.'

'All we have to do is to get through this,' said Neil. 'Anyone can run a business in the good times. Anyone can seem like a genius when the going is easy. Tough times sort out the men from the boys. And we're tough, Claire. You know we are.'

'I thought I was,' she said. 'Now I'm not so sure.'

'Of course you are.' He grinned at her and pulled her closer. 'Who was it who marched into the council offices and demanded they re-route the water pipes? Who was it who dealt with the Amazon forest of paperwork they sent us? Who was it who managed to get this hotel open for

8

business on the scheduled day even though nobody said it could be done?'

'They were things I could deal with,' she said disconsolately. 'People wanted to come to the hotel then. But now . . . everyone's hoarding their money and I can't blame them. If we had any of our own, I'd hoard it myself.'

From the first day they'd started work on the hotel, Claire had felt attached to it in a way that she couldn't quite understand. She felt as though it was more than just a pile of bricks and mortar; as though it had a living, breathing soul. She never said this to anyone else because she knew they'd think she was a bit deranged. Or fanciful. She couldn't help feeling as though the Lodge itself watched over them, like a guardian angel. And she felt as though they watched over it in return. But now she laughed bitterly at herself for being so foolish.

'You're not foolish.' The voice seemed to come from right behind her.

'What?' She spun around in the chair, startled. There was nobody there. God almighty, she thought, I'm cracking up under the strain. I'm starting to hear things. I suppose I should be grateful I'm not seeing things too.

'Everything will be fine,' said the voice.

Claire wondered if her subconscious was talking to her, trying to reassure her.

'This is only one year,' the voice said. 'The house has been here for hundreds. You'll get over it.'

She supposed her subconscious was right. But one bad year could break them. That was the problem.

9

'You're strong,' said the voice. 'You'll get through it. You won't let one bad season get you down.'

It was funny, thought Claire, how it was that all of the good times were so overwhelmed by the bad times. When the hotel was doing well and making money, they simply accepted that as a fair return. But when things were going badly, they felt utterly despondent. And even though they knew that it wasn't entirely their fault, they still wished they could have done things differently.

'We all wish that,' said the voice inside her head, and Claire could hear her own regret in it. 'Every day we wish we'd done things better. Or not done something at all! But we have to live with how things are, not how we want them to be.'

Claire smiled. Her subconscious was right. Things were the way they were. She and Neil would live with it. And regardless of how many people stayed at the hotel for Christmas, she'd make sure that they had a superb time. So that if – when – things got better, they'd remember the Sugar Loaf Lodge and they'd want to return.

'All the same,' she said out loud to herself, 'it would be just great if we could fill those empty rooms.'

She was looking at stock lists when the phone rang.

'Sugar Loaf Lodge,' she said in her most welcoming voice. 'How can I help you?'

'Hello,' said the female caller. 'I'm enquiring about rooms. I'm wondering do you have any availability for Christmas this year?'

'Yes.' Claire's heart leapt hopefully. 'We have a two-night package if you'd like that.'

'Oh good,' said the woman. 'I want to book some for our family. There's quite a few of us. I'm hoping you can fit us all in.'

Claire felt a warmth envelop her as she made the booking, and afterwards she replaced the receiver on the phone and sighed with relief. One phone call had made a difference. Four rooms. Just like that. She was still smiling when the phone rang again.

'Sugar Loaf Lodge,' she repeated. 'How can I help you?'

'I know it's probably a bit late,' said the male voice, 'but do you have any rooms left over Christmas?'

Early on Christmas Eve morning, while the staff were getting ready for breakfast, Neil walked into the traditionally decorated lounge with its panoramic views of the frosty countryside and allowed himself a small sigh of relief. It hadn't been until the last possible moment that the final available room had been booked. But it had. And so he and Claire could relax a bit. Not that there could be any proper relaxing until Christmas and New Year was over. But at least they had their full house.

At least it hadn't all come crashing down on them.

All they had to do now was make it work for the guests. And they absolutely knew how to do that. It was what they were good at.

'Everything OK?' Claire joined him at the window.

'Perfect,' he said.

They stood side by side in silence. He slid his arm around her waist.

'Ready?' he asked softly.

She took a deep breath. 'Ready,' she said.

He kissed her quickly on the cheek. And they walked hand in hand through the lobby of their hotel, both determined that this would be the most memorable Christmas ever at the Sugar Loaf Lodge.

Kilmashogue

I fell in love with Sam in an airport. Which is sort of story-book romantic in some ways but actually – not. Because I wasn't waiting for him to arrive from some distant country and realising how much I cared as I flung my arms around him; nor was I heading off myself and crying uncontrollably at the departure gate because I knew that I couldn't be with him. It was an unexpected thing, waiting to go through security at Dublin airport during the hottest day of the year; a day on which the air-conditioning had broken down and conse-quently, as we waited for our hand baggage to be screened, everyone in the queues grew hotter and sweatier and more and more bad-tempered. (So bad-tempered that in one queue a woman actually tried to hit a security guard with a bottle of water he was trying to confiscate from her. The woman was carted off by a posse of uniformed personnel, which prob-ably meant she wasn't getting on a flight any time soon.)

My own irritation quotient was going higher and higher. I'd been directed to the queue with the stupid people. The ones who – despite all of the warnings and notices – had actually packed large bottles of shampoo or matches or penknives or any one of the millions of things that you can't put in carry-on luggage any more. Our queue also contained two guys with an assortment of body piercings who were being sent back through the metal detectors over and over again.

I'd like to think that I can be a perfectly reasonable person. But I wasn't feeling very reasonable that day. Like everyone else I was hot and sweaty and getting more fed up with every passing moment. Besides, I'm not good with too much heat. I'm a crisp, cold morning sort of girl, not your lying around the pool type. Suffocating heat does my head in. And suffocating heat was exactly what we had in Dublin airport.

So not actually a very auspicious start for finding love.

In fact, as far as I was concerned, the absolute last place in the world where it might happen. But doesn't everyone say that's how it goes with love? When you're least expecting it and all that sort of thing?

He was standing behind me in the queue. Like me, his reasons for travel were business. His only luggage was a leather computer bag, same as me. He'd already taken the laptop out of the bag, ready to put it through the scanning machine. I'd done the same. And I was ready to put my shiny coral sandals through too because for some reason they always set off the scanners.

Both of us were ready. But both of us were still waiting.

When one of the piercings guys was sent back for the third time, I could hear computer-man (I didn't know his name then, obviously; didn't know he was going to be the man I fell in love with) exhale sharply and loudly. I turned to him and gave him one of those complicit little smiles –

you know, the 'are we the only competent people in the universe' sort of smiles – and he grinned back at me and asked me where I was travelling to. London, I told him, I had a meeting with some bankers there.

He shuddered and then laughed and asked me if I was a banker. Not a question I've liked answering too much ever since bankers were blamed for almost causing the end of civilisation as we know it. I accept that there were very many people who behaved atrociously, but at the time I was just someone who worked in the new business section of a bank and my job actually involved getting in corporate deposits rather than making loans to people who couldn't repay them. So I didn't feel personally responsible for what went on. Nevertheless you couldn't help but think that somehow you'd thrown in your lot with the devil and it was always embarrassing having to admit to being involved in an industry that had once been respected. (As a result of this I'd dumped my sturdy bank umbrella with its chirpy logo a few months earlier. I was afraid of being attacked on the street if I used it.)

Anyway, I told the man I was going to fall in love with that I did indeed work in a bank, but that I was an honest and trustworthy person, that I'd never lent money to anyone who couldn't pay it back (never lent money at all, I added) and that I hoped that one day the rest of the world would forgive me. I was a sinner, I told him, with a twinkle in my eye, but I had repented.

He laughed again at that and said that he'd once worked in banking himself but had left to set up his own company, something to do with price comparison sites for financial

15

products, and it was going well for him. Though, he added, the whole banking crisis thing had nearly ruined him at one point because he'd been due to get a loan for expansion and it hadn't happened and it had all been very difficult.

During that conversation, the men with the piercings had eventually succeeded in getting through security and the line had begun to move again. I put my stuff on the conveyor belt and walked through without incident. So did ex-banker-computer-man.

'Which flight?' he asked as I stood at the end of the conveyor belt, slipping my sandals back on to my feet. They were very pretty sandals, with kitten heels, which weren't all that fashionable at the time but meant at least that I could walk in them without being crippled (I'm quite good with high heels, but in a car to bar situation, not for purposeful walking).

'The eleven o'clock to Heathrow,' I told him.

'Me too.' He looked pleased. 'Fancy a coffee?'

We went to the Anna Livia lounge because both of us had passes for that. I like the lounge; at least it gets you away from the milling hordes. I've always struggled with crowds. I don't like lots of people being around me. It makes me feel claustrophobic and I get very tetchy. Which was why I'd been losing it a bit in the security queue.

Computer-man told me his name when we sat down with our coffees. Sam Thornton. It suited him.

'Holly,' I said in reply as I tipped half a sachet of sugar into my cappuccino.

'Golightly?'

I grinned. 'Gallagher,' I said.

'You could do Golightly,' he told me. 'You have a look of Audrey Hepburn in *Breakfast at Tiffany's*.'

I blushed. He was being nice, because I wasn't Audrey Hepburn material. Actually, I don't think anyone in the whole world will ever be another Audrey Hepburn. She remains for me the most glamorous, elegant woman on the planet. Even as she grew older she never lost her looks. I saw a picture of her once in her seventies. She was still stunning. All to do with bone structure, I guess. Mine isn't Hepburn-fine. Also, my hair is a very light brown, which I sometimes highlight so it's more of a dark blond. Which isn't very Audrey either.

But . . . I did have a kind of impish look about me that under certain conditions might evoke a touch of Audrey in her famous Holly Golightly role. If whoever it was who was looking at me was being generous. Which was clearly the case with Sam Thornton.

'Seriously,' he said as I stopped laughing. 'You've got a lovely face.'

Audrey was in a movie called *Funny Face* once. More appropriate for me, I thought. But still, this guy was good. He was making me feel great about myself even though I was still hot and sweaty and a lock of hair was falling into my eyes.

'Oh bugger,' I said, which made him look at me in surprise. 'Our flight has been delayed.'

And indeed, there it was on the monitor, delayed until 11.45, which was very, very annoying. Obviously, from my point of view, I would've been better off getting a flight to

City airport, but it hadn't been possible. So now I was going to be late getting into the hell on earth that was Heathrow and I'd probably be late getting into the City as well. My meeting wasn't until mid-afternoon so I wasn't under any pressure just yet, but the thing that drove me craziest about air travel was all of the time wasted faffing around airports both when you were leaving and when you arrived.

You can see my impatient nature here. Very un-Audrey. But I can't help myself. I'm an impatient kind of girl.

'Never mind,' said Sam. 'Would you like another coffee?'

It's not a good idea for me to drink too much coffee, because I get very jumpy and excitable, but we were here for a while more and there was nothing else to do. So I said yes to the coffee, and when he came back I asked him about his reasons for going to London and all about his company too, although the truth is that I wasn't really listening to him because it had suddenly occurred to me that Sam Thornton was actually the most attractive man I'd met in a very long time.

He was tall – I knew that from our time standing in the queue – and he was dark (almost Mediterranean in his colouring) and he was very handsome (think George Clooney only sexier). I couldn't understand how I hadn't noticed any of this before, but it was probably because I was too narky with the heat and the delays and everything. So there you are: I was sitting opposite a virtual sex-god in Dublin airport and he was making me laugh and I realised that I liked him a lot and then – bam! – suddenly I was in love with him.

Oh all right, maybe I was in lust with him, but it wasn't

just the sexual attraction. Sam was nice. He was a very nice guy. And that was what I fell in love with. Not the Clooney looks. (For a long time, when I was with Sam, I thought about our children. The offspring of a more-attractive-than-Clooney man and a pale-imitation-of-Hepburn woman. Would they be heartbreakingly gorgeous? Or did genetics do stupid things from time to time and would they be saddled with all of our bad points and none of the good ones? This was the way my mind worked then. Thinking of our children. Me, who'd always professed no interest in having kids whatsoever.)

Of course, as we sat in the Anna Livia lounge, I didn't want him to know that I was having fantasies about him. I kept talking to him about banking and business as though I was a serious person with serious issues to worry about. Which I probably was; after our bank had lost almost half its management staff, I'd been promoted, which was why I was the one heading off to the meeting in the City. I never felt like a real businessperson, though. I can't take it all that seriously: people trying to appear self-important and loading their conversations full of buzzwords and jargon just to make you feel inferior, which a lot of my ex-colleagues used to do. Not so smart now, I thought, a little smugly.

Sam wasn't trying any of that over-the-top stuff, though, he was simply chatting in a perfectly normal way. So was I. But keeping it businesslike too. Just so's he didn't think me a moron.

I was high on caffeine before our flight was called and had another cup of coffee on the plane, which wasn't a particularly good idea because it made me a bit giggly. I told myself that I would have to get back on track by the time I turned up in the Gherkin, that weird and wonderful iconic building where my meeting was to take place.

'Never been there,' said Sam when I told him where I was going. 'I'm afraid my meeting is in an ugly sixties block near Victoria.'

'They say those buildings have architectural merit now,' I told him.

'My arse,' he said, which made me laugh again.

'Are you staying overnight?' he asked when the plane eventually landed (we'd been in a holding pattern for half an hour at that point, which was making me irritated again).

'No,' I said regretfully. 'I'm getting the evening flight home.'

He looked disappointed. 'Pity.'

'I don't usually stay over,' I told him. 'Cost-cutting, you see. The bank can't be seen to be lavishing money on unnecessary hotel rooms. Besides,' I added, 'it's Friday; I can't even justify it by having another meeting tomorrow.'

'Why not take the weekend off?' he said.

I stared at him.

'We could go to dinner, have a bit of fun tomorrow . . .'

I continued to stare at him.

'But, you know, if you don't want to, that's absolutely fine.'

'No,' I said slowly. 'No, it would be great actually. It's just that . . .'

'What?'

'I don't have a nightie or anything.'

His navy-blue eyes crinkled. 'What makes you think you need one?' he asked.

Anyway, the truth is I'm not sure whether I fell in love with him in the airport or on the plane or later that night in his room in Claridge's. (Claridge's, I thought. The bank never put me up in Claridge's even when I did stay overnight. The comparison site company must be doing well.) It doesn't matter where I fell in love with him. That's just a detail after all. The key issue is that fall in love I did. With a thud that could have been felt on the other side of the world.

In every relationship there's a point where you start to ask questions, where you don't take everything at face value and where you want to know the bad things as well as the good things about the person you've become attached to. I was having such a wonderful time with Sam that I didn't want to ask any questions at all, but eventually I did. Casually, because I wasn't too concerned; we were taking things a bit slower than you'd expect after me falling in love with him on the day we met, but still, that was then and life isn't like a romantic movie after all. So we didn't meet every single day or even every single week, because as it turned out, Sam lived in Wexford. In Gorey, which is a little under a hundred kilometres from Dublin, making it just that bit awkward for a quick drink on a Saturday night or whatever. I'd thought that what might happen was that we'd spend weekends together. In my apartment in town or in his house in the country. I liked the sound of it and the idea of it but it didn't happen that often. He stayed with me a few times (though only Friday nights, never the entire weekend), but I never stayed with him. Which, after a while, began to rankle a little. And so I asked him about it.

Never ask a question when you don't already know the answer. My best friend, Susannah, who's a solicitor, once told me that. I retorted that you ask questions to find out answers, but her view is that you already know the answer you want to hear. And if you're not going to get that, then you're better off leaving the question well enough alone. I should've listened to Susannah. Or perhaps I should've asked the question sooner. But maybe I hadn't wanted to do that. Maybe, somehow, despite myself, I already knew the answer.

We were sitting in St Stephen's Green when I asked it.

'Why don't I ever stay with you?' I pushed my hair out of my eyes and turned to look at him. 'I know Dublin's great fun and all that, but it would be nice to do the more peaceful country thing sometimes, don't you think?'

I saw the shadow cross his face and I felt an icy hand grip my heart.

'Holly,' he said.

'What?'

'We need to talk.'

How I hate that phrase. Cormac Mulcahy, my first boyfriend, used it when he wanted to break it off with me. (We were both twelve at the time. He was a very serious kind of boy.) Dermot Doolin, my second, said the same. And the truth is that I've used it myself too on more than one occasion. So I know what 'we need to talk' means. It means we're having this conversation and it's the last one we're ever going to have and I don't want to have it with you but I'm too soft-hearted to dump you by text.

'Why?' I asked. I couldn't believe how terrible I was feeling inside. Well, I could. I loved Sam. More than anyone I'd ever loved in my life before. I'd had the wedding fantasies about him. Me in a dress that would make me look like Audrey. Him in a tux that would make George envious. I'd designed the dress myself. It was stunning.

'Well . . .' And then he told me.

It wasn't the dumping conversation; it was the other one. The one where the man you've fallen in love with tells you he hasn't been fair on you and he shouldn't have fallen in love with you because as it turns out he's already married.

'What!' At that point you realise how utterly, utterly blind and stupid you've been, and the fact that he always stays at your place and the times he hasn't been available, and a hundred and one other small things that you've noticed but ignored suddenly make perfect sense.

'I'm sorry,' he said. 'I know you must hate me.'

'Yes,' I told him. 'I do.'

'I didn't mean for this to happen.'

Oh, who bloody does?

'When I met you it was as though the sunshine had come back into my life.'

Yeah, yeah.

'I love you, Holly.'

But you're married to someone else.

'It's not working out between me and Amy.'

Amy. Nice name. Cute and girlie.

'But right now . . . I can't break up our family.'

Family? What family?

'The twins are only two years old.'

OK, one kid is bad enough. But two . . . And twins! That seems even worse somehow.

'It's not that I don't care about her,' he said.

Great. Rub it in, why don't you?

'But I don't love her in the way that I love you.'

And that was what got me. Because he said it like he meant it. Because he sounded so tortured and so unhappy. Because he started to cry.

I have conflicted views about crying men. There's a part of me that thinks it's good for them to get emotional from time to time, to show their sadness in public. There's another part of me that thinks it's fairly pathetic and un-macho.

When our bank nearly went bust, some of the guys cried. They really did. It was the strangest thing seeing them sitting at their desks with tears rolling down their cheeks. They were the tough, sexist men who'd often made my life a misery. In front of whom I wouldn't ever have dared to cry, no matter what the reason. And they were blubbing away in front of the Bloomberg screens. Unbelievable! I didn't cry back then. As far as I was concerned it wasn't something worth crying over. Though I did want to attack the lending manager who'd once made a pass at me in the lift in the full knowledge that nobody would believe me if I tried to make a big deal about it. He was a horrible man and I was glad he was losing his job. I wanted to attack him because other people were losing their job thanks to him too, not because of his pathetic pass at me.

All that stuff about the bank and the crying men whizzed around in my head when Sam started to cry. But I didn't feel the way I'd felt then, angry and bitter. I felt sad. For Sam and for me.

'I'm sorry.' He got himself together and gave me a half-smile. 'I'm sorry for not being honest with you, Holly. But the thing is – the moment I first saw you standing in the queue in your bare feet, I felt something I've never felt before. It was like an instant connection. I wasn't thinking then about . . . about what's happened since. I just wanted to keep talking to you and stay with you, and I know that was wrong but I couldn't help myself.'

I told myself that I could look at this objectively. I could decide that he'd made a decision to be nice to me and flirt with me (or whatever was going on in the queue) despite the fact that he was a married man and had no right to be nice to or flirt with girls he didn't know. I could cut him a little slack and decide that the situation in the queue was a bit different, what with the terrible conditions and the way that made people suddenly empathise with each other and comment to each other, just so's you knew you weren't the only one being driven demented with the heat and the crowds. I could decide that having coffee with him in the Anna Livia lounge was simply a friendly thing to do. Perfectly innocent on my part, though obviously not so innocent on his – especially with the Audrey Hepburn comparisons – but harmless enough.

Only it hadn't turned out to be harmless, because here

we were now with him crying and me feeling as though my heart had been ripped out.

'Do you love your wife?'

Never ask a question you don't already know the answer to. I knew I shouldn't have asked it before I'd even spoken the words.

'She's a lovely woman,' he said, neatly side-stepping it. 'She's a great wife and a great mother.'

'How long have you been married?' The answer to that question didn't matter too much.

'Five years.'

'Are you going to leave her?' Another one I wasn't sure about. I wondered if I actually liked torturing myself.

'It's all been so sudden,' he said, once again side-stepping an answer. 'I knew Amy and I were unhappy, but I didn't know why. And unhappy is probably the wrong word; it's just . . . I don't think we do love each other any more. I don't know exactly what happened. Whether it's me being away, or whether it's the twins . . .'

I would be breaking up a family with two small kids. I couldn't do that.

'I've got to go.' I stood up and smoothed down the pale skirt of my business suit. And then I walked out of the Green and left him sitting alone on the bench.

I should've left things like that. I knew I should. It's really easy to know the things you should do but not at all easy to actually do them. Sometimes it's like someone else is in your body, operating it, making you do stuff you don't want to do. Or telling you that you have to do it anyway. Which is what some part of me said when, two weeks later, Sam called and said he had to see me.

We met in the Morrison, on the north side of the city. The Morrison is on the quays of the Liffey so is only barely on the other side of town, but there is a cultural divide between north and south in Dublin. I knew why he'd picked it. It distanced him from the south. Being on the north side was, for Sam, like being in another world. (Maybe that was how he felt in the airport, which is also on the north side of the city. Or maybe it's just that airports are self-contained little worlds anyway.)

'I haven't been able to stop thinking about you,' he said. 'Every second of every day all I do is think about you. I think about you the moment I wake up and just before I go to sleep. I think about you when I'm driving in to work and when I'm driving home.'

'Do you think about me when you kiss your wife good night? Or when you're playing with your kids? Or when you're sitting down to Sunday lunch?' My voice was deliberately harsh because my heart was breaking again. I was still in love with him even though he was a traitorous, deceiving swine of a man.

'Don't make me feel worse than I already do,' begged Sam. 'Don't make me say things I don't want to say.'

There was no future in a relationship with Sam. I told myself this over and over again. I would be wasting part of my life, giving him years that could be better spent looking for someone who was available, who could love me the way I wanted to be loved. Who wasn't cheating on someone else. But the thing is – and you have to forgive me for this, because I know it's selfish and awful of me – there was a part of me that didn't care. I didn't care because I loved him so much, and because I could understand the position he found himself in.

I'd nearly got married myself. Four years earlier. With a few months to go I'd got cold feet and called it off. But I'd agonised and agonised about what I should do, and I'd even told myself that I could go along with it for the sake of everyone and get a divorce afterwards. Not rational, I know. But those thoughts had gone through my head. And so I could see how Sam might have married someone he wasn't truly in love with, because when you get on the marriage roller-coaster it's very hard to get off again. (I didn't ask him if he'd had doubts before his wedding. I truly didn't want to know the answer to that one.)

'Look,' I said. 'I like you very much, but there's no point to this.'

'I miss you,' he said. 'I miss talking to you. I know I can't expect to have what we had before, but couldn't we be friends? Maybe meet for coffee every now and then? I need to be able to talk to someone, and you're the only person I can talk to.'

'Oh, Sam . . . I don't know.'

'Give it a try?' He turned his huge dark eyes on me. 'Please?'

And so I agreed. That evening we talked and talked but there was no inappropriate behaviour, and we met for lunch a few days later and all that was perfectly innocent too; and then one evening I met him in town and we went for a few drinks and, sitting beside him in the pub, I couldn't help myself and leaned my head on his shoulder. He kissed me then and I kissed him and he came back to my apartment in Dundrum and made love to me and I knew that I could never let him go.

So that's how it happens. You tell yourself one thing and you do something else, and I wanted to believe everything he told me because, having let him back into my life, I wanted us to be a true love story. And I wanted to believe, too, that one day he'd leave Amy and his children and live with me and it'd all end up happily for everyone. Because in my little fantasy world, Amy was having a torrid affair with one of her Wexford neighbours anyway.

I was devastated when they went away on holidays, two weeks at the end of September, during which I didn't hear a word from him. I hadn't realised how closely my life had become entwined with his and how many times I texted him during the day with silly comments just to prove that I loved him. I didn't want to text him while he was away in case Amy picked up his phone and asked who Holly was. I realised that I was The Other Woman. It was a bit of a shock to see myself like that.

He phoned when he got home and he came to my apartment, where as soon as he got through the door I started to tear the clothes from his back. He did the same to me and we ended up making love in the tiny hallway, where I'm sure we could have been heard by anybody walking past the door.

'I missed you so much,' he said.

'I missed you too.' I held him fiercely. 'I love you.'

He kissed me on the mouth.

He was the best kisser I've ever known. He was the best lover I'd ever known either. I couldn't let him go.

I wasn't looking forward to Christmas. As a family it was never a big deal in our house, from the moment me and my three brothers stopped believing in Santa Claus. I was the youngest, so they had to wait for me before they could all give up the pretence of magic. I was nine years old when I asked my parents about it, and I know they weren't distraught over my loss of innocence or anything because they're both scientists and I think having to go along with the Santa Claus myth went against their principles.

We're not a very close family. It's not that we don't get on, because we do, but we don't get very emotional about being together for special occasions or anything like that. Maybe it's the scientific thing coming through, but to my parents, a date is just a date and it doesn't matter whether it's 25 December or 25 June, it's all the same to them. My mum has a little reminder on her computer for all of our birthdays because she forgot mine a couple of times and I know she felt bad about it. But I think she was equally annoyed about the fact that it's other people who make celebrating a birthday important. She likes to celebrate other things, like me finally understanding the concept of light being a wave and a particle. That was a major thing for her. They're good people, my parents. Just slightly in another world.

The year that I met Sam they were both living and working in the States and they had no plans to come back to Ireland for Christmas. Nor did it occur to them to invite any of us to be with them. Which was fine. My three sisters-in-law all asked me to their houses on Christmas Day, but to be honest, I didn't think I could face their happy family Christmases, because even though my brothers weren't too pushed about the family thing, their wives certainly were. And so it would have been a full house at Eamonn's or Christopher's or Rory's. And I wasn't really into that. (I'd spent the previous Christmas at Eamonn's and it was excruciating. Far too huggy and kissy and sharing the love for me.) I planned to have a quiet day to myself. I would stock up on booze and chocolates and I'd watch stupid movies on TV all day.

And then Sam suggested the Sugar Loaf Lodge.

'You'd leave your family for Christmas?' I was beyond astonished.

'Only Christmas Eve,' he said. 'I'd go home on Christmas Day. Around lunchtime maybe. I've got these Japanese clients in town until then and I was talking to Amy about it and saying that I thought I would have to be meeting with them and taking them to dinner on Christmas Eve and she was the one who said that perhaps I should stay in Dublin overnight and not risk coming home, especially if I had a glass of wine or something.'

'And don't you have to take them to dinner?'

Sam shook his head. 'I'm meeting them in the morning and taking them to lunch.'

The opportunity was too good to pass up. I felt a shiver of excitement mingled with guilt and told myself to lose the guilt. After all, if Amy had really wanted him to come home she would've insisted on him dumping the Japanese clients.

'Why the Sugar Loaf?' I asked.

'They do a great Christmas Eve dinner,' said Sam.

I crumbled. I couldn't help it. I said yes.

My three sisters-in-law were intrigued by my revelation that I would be staying in a hotel over Christmas with my boyfriend. Naturally I didn't say that it was only for one night. And that my boyfriend was married. Nobody knew about Sam's marital status.

'Why didn't you tell me about him before?' asked Tara.

'A boyfriend! Taking you to the Sugar Loaf. I'm impressed,' said Blanaid.

'You lucky thing,' said Katy over the sound of my nephew Keith beating up his little sister. 'I wish someone would take me to a bloody hotel for Christmas.'

And so, at two o'clock on Christmas Eve, I drove up to the gates of the Sugar Loaf Lodge. I leaned out of the car window to buzz reception from the keypad by the locked wrought-iron gate at the beginning of the long driveway to the hotel. The receptionist told me that I was very welcome and said the porter would meet me at the entrance to the Lodge. As I pulled to a halt outside the hotel, a sharply dressed concierge welcomed me and said that he would bring me to reception while my car was being parked. I'd never had my car parked for me before and I was a little bit embarrassed about it. After all, when you think of valet parking you think of Mercs and Jags and cars like that. Not my trusty Ford Fusion. But it didn't seem to bother the concierge so I tried not to let it bother me either.

He left me in front of a polished walnut table where a stunningly beautiful woman, glossy and shining, smiled at me and welcomed me. If this was the standard of looks at the Sugar Loaf Lodge, I was going to have to up my game and Audrey-fy myself as much as possible. I was offered a glass of mulled wine, which I decided against (I didn't want to start on the slippery slope to drunkenness before Sam arrived), and then the porter showed me to my room, which looked out over the valley and was called Kilmashogue.

The view was wonderful. The sky was china blue and the green valley was lush even in the depths of winter. It was probably even more beautiful in the summer when the trees were also green instead of stark and bare like they were now, although there was a certain beauty about that too.

I devoted a good few minutes to looking out at the scenery and thinking how lovely it was before I turned my attention to the rather more materialistic beauty of the room. Kilmashogue was one of the Sugar Loaf Lodge's junior suites. It had a bedroom, a bathroom and a separate sitting room, in which the hotel management had placed a tabletop Christmas tree complete with two foil-wrapped presents underneath. The tags on the presents said 'With the compliments of the Sugar Loaf Lodge' and I was, childishly, itching to open them. There were two Lir chocolates on the table as well and I popped one of these into my mouth straight away.

It was very luxurious. The robes in the bathroom (which had toasty under-floor heating) were thick and warm. The towels were huge. The marble was white and shining. In the bedroom, the king-sized bed was festooned with cushions and pillows and the duvet looked soft as a billowing cloud. I couldn't have asked for a more romantic bolt-hole. I was ecstatic. Now all I had to do was await the arrival of my lover.

He'd told me that he wouldn't be there before four, which was fine by me. It gave me time to get ready for him. I undressed and had a long, hot shower, using the hotel's Molton Brown products instead of my supermarket buy-one-get-one-free Herbal Essences. I padded around the room in my oversized robe (a bit too big to be comfortable, to be honest, but great all the same), then I dried my hair, spending ages twisting it into long, loose corkscrew curls. I hardly ever did this because it took for ever and the results could be hit and miss, but this time I managed it and I was delighted with the effect. (I'd had my highlights done, so I was more blonde than brown.) Then I spent a long time doing my face and my eyes because I wanted to look utterly gorgeous and dramatic for Sam. Most of the time he saw my chic but casual look, or my laid-back business look. I rarely went all-out vamp for him. But I wanted to tonight. It was more make-up than I usually wore, but what the hell – it was Christmas. When

I was finally styled to the best of my ability, I changed into my dress and shoes.

I'd blown an absolute fortune on the dress, which was a figure-hugging fuchsia-pink Herve Leger. It was criminal how much I'd spent, especially since it was a colour I hardly ever wore. And I'd spent a fortune on my shoes too, which were cripplingly high Louboutins. I'm not actually a Herve Leger or Louboutins girl, no matter how well I can manage the heels in short bursts. But I love how confident they look. And that was who I wanted to be tonight for Sam, who was leaving his family to be with me.

It was a quarter to four. I had a bit of time to spare but I wanted to see him arrive, so I meandered down to the lobby and sat on one of the crimson-upholstered armchairs. Then I got up again and took a newspaper from the reception desk. I'm not good at sitting staring into space.

I opened the paper and began to read snippets of news, but I couldn't concentrate. I kept looking at my watch and checking the time, which was passing with excruciating slowness. There was an article in the paper about my former boss in the bank who'd got a ridiculous pay-off for being incompetent, so I read that with some interest. Then I made myself read all of the letters to the editor, before looking at my watch. Four o'clock. I checked my phone to see if there had been any texts that I'd missed, but I already knew there weren't. I deleted a few old messages just to look busy and then I put the paper down and kept my eye on the door. It was still light outside because the day had been

35

utterly cloudless, but I could see traces of dusk in the sky. I hate December really. Such short days and such long nights. I don't like long nights.

At a quarter past four I got up and walked around the small lobby area. I stood by the long windows and looked out at the valley below. I could feel the chill of the cold air outside on the glass. Already frost was beginning to form on the ground and on the bare branches of the trees. It was stark yet beautiful in contrast to the Sugar Loaf Lodge, which was warm and comforting. I moved away from the window. The management had set up a hot-chocolate station in one corner of the lobby and were dispensing frothy drinks to the residents. I love chocolate but I didn't want to end up with marks around my mouth or stains on my expensive dress. I tugged at the hem as I sat down again. It was just that little bit short for comfort. I wasn't used to wearing very short dresses. (Not dresses at all, to be perfectly honest; I'm not entirely at ease showing my legs. Though today they were exfoliated, waxed and fake-tanned, so they looked great. I'd had the tan done in a salon so's there'd be no telltale orange streaks.)

The lobby, which was actually more like a big drawing room, was quite full now. There was a group of older women who were chatting happily to each other. One of them glanced at me from time to time and I couldn't help feeling that she was thinking dark thoughts about the shortness of my pink dress. I knew I looked great but I was beginning to wonder if it was quite right for the Sugar Loaf Lodge, where most of the guests seemed to have gone for a more conservative look. The four older women were wearing grey trouser suits and different-coloured blouses, although I did hear one of them talking about changing for dinner, so perhaps they'd let rip a bit then.

Sitting side by side on a nearby sofa was a couple who weren't speaking to each other. This didn't automatically mean that they were having a row but, for the entire time I'd been there, they hadn't uttered a word. I wondered if that sort of silence was awkward when you'd been together for a long time. Or whether it was inevitable. After all, when you've been married for twenty years, what the hell is left to say? A waiter approached them and placed two glasses of champagne in front of them, which made them both perk up and smile at each other. Maybe they were having an affair too, I thought. Maybe they weren't married at all and their silence was just because both of them were thinking of kinky things to do when they got back to their room.

I shook my head. I was losing it now. There were some things outside the bounds of possibility, and kinky sex for this conservative couple was a step too far.

I glanced around me, thinking that perhaps Sam had somehow managed to enter the hotel unseen and walked by me to the bar. It was off to one side of the lobby and (unusually for an Irish bar) currently empty. With the exception of the champagne-swilling couple, most people were tucking into the hot chocolate, and that was probably having an effect on bar sales. I wondered how good an idea that was for a hotel, to keep its residents away from the alcohol!

Not all of them, though, because then I saw a man walk through the lobby, ignore the hot chocolate and go straight up to the bar and order a drink. A drink was what I wanted too, I thought. Something nice and frivolous and Christmassy. Something to ease the tension I felt because Sam was late, and something that would put me in the mood for a great night alone with him. But I couldn't order anything yet. I had to wait for him. I wondered what had delayed him.

Oh, I was really wondering if he was coming at all. You knew that already.

I checked my phone again, but still no texts or missed calls. I wandered around the lobby, trying not to look as though I was waiting for someone, but naturally I couldn't help looking at my watch and my phone every couple of minutes. And then, finally, the phone beeped with a message and I was shaking as I looked to see who it was from.

It was Susannah, telling me to have a great Christmas and a fantastic time at the Sugar Loaf Lodge. She knew about Sam but not about him being married. I wasn't able to tell her that, even though she was my best friend and I knew I should tell her everything. I texted back to say that everything was fantastic and wonderful and very, very romantic. I didn't say that I was still waiting for Sam and still waiting for the romance to start.

I went back to the room. I'd been waiting in the lobby for nearly an hour and I was conscious that if I was looking at other people and wondering about them, they'd also be wondering about me. I didn't want to give them fodder for thought, and besides, I reckoned that waiting for Sam was like waiting for the enigmatic watched pot to boil. He'd probably arrive as soon as I was safely back in the comforts of Kilmashogue.

I took off the Herve Leger and hung it on a padded hanger in the wardrobe. I put on the robe instead. Sam would be just as turned on by seeing me in that as seeing me in the pink dress. I turned on the TV and flicked through the channels. My choice of viewing was two carol services, an episode of *The Simpsons*, a programme about the Blasket Islands, *It's a Wonderful Life*, celebrity something-or-other, a quiz show and four different news channels all giving bulletins about Santa's progress from the North Pole.

Sam was over an hour late.

I was trying not to think about what that meant.

What it meant was that he wasn't coming. He texted me at half past five:

Oh, babes, so so sorry. Had to come home after all. Bit of an emergency. Have a great time. Call you asap. Sx

I hated when he called me babes.

I opened the minibar, took out a half-bottle of white wine and knocked back a glass in a few gulps. Then I curled up on the big bed, hugging my knees beneath my chin, and rocked slowly backwards and forwards. What sort of a fool was I to think that a man would leave his wife and children on Christmas Eve to have a bit of sex with me? Because that was all it was, wasn't it? He couldn't possibly love me. If he loved me he wouldn't have left me here on my own. On my own on bloody Christmas Eve in a bloody hotel where I'd stick out like a sore thumb. The girl on her own. Sad, pathetic and dumped. I hated Sam Thornton. Hated him.

And then my mind started doing a rationalisation thing and saying to me that something had obviously happened to make him go home and that no matter how much he might want to leave her he couldn't possibly do it now and that maybe after Christmas it might be different and when I talked to him I'd understand. I lay on the bed, conflicting thoughts and emotions spinning around my head, for over an hour. I think I might even have fallen asleep at one point, which was unbelievable really because I was too miserable to sleep; perhaps it was just that my thoughts drifted into thinking that maybe he'd turn up after all and that kind of calmed me down. Plus, the bed was very, very comfortable.

So what was I going to do? I couldn't leave the hotel and go home. I just couldn't. I would be totally and utterly humiliated, and done for drunk driving too because I hadn't eaten all day and the glass of wine had gone straight to my head and I was feeling woozy. But I couldn't stay here either, because I would still be totally and utterly humiliated although without the drunk-driving record.

I looked at my watch. (I felt as though I'd spent the whole day looking at my damn watch.) It was after six o'clock. Sam and I had had a reservation for the restaurant at seven. I didn't feel hungry, but my stomach rumbled. I would have to cancel the reservation even though the meal was included in the stay. I suddenly thought of the bill. Sam had made the reservation on his credit card but they'd taken an impression of mine when I'd checked in. I'd told them that my partner would be arriving later. But he wouldn't, would he?

So now I was going to be stung with the cost of the worst Christmas in my whole life. Because even if I waited until I sobered up and told them that there was a domestic emergency and I had to go, I'd still be left with the bill. And I'd be going home to my empty apartment with its quota of M&S frozen dinners. Which was an OK option, I supposed. But not quite what I'd expected.

Fool, fool, fool.

That was what I was. That was what I'd been ever since the day in Dublin airport. Foolish and stupid and selfish too, to ever think that I could carry on an affair with someone. And now I was being punished for it and my foolishness would be known to everyone. Because if I stayed at the hotel they'd all know that something had happened to me. That I'd been dumped at Christmas. That someone didn't love me enough to be there for me at the most special time of the year.

No matter how Sam felt about Amy, he obviously loved her enough not to do that to her.

Which was a good thing. Made him not so much of a traitorous, cheating bastard. A man who couldn't leave his family at Christmas wasn't all bad, was he?

I couldn't understand why on earth I was trying to find positive things to think about him. Was it to make me feel less awful about myself?

My stomach rumbled again. I still wasn't hungry. But I

wondered if I'd become the sort of woman who ate when she was miserable. I poured the rest of the white wine into the glass and drank that instead. I switched on the TV and watched an episode of *ER*. I'd seen it before. Twice. But I watched it again anyhow.

By eight o'clock I was starving. I thought about ordering room service, and then I told myself that I wasn't going to hole up in the room by myself. It was too lonely and miserable and depressing. Instead I would go back to the lobby and order a sandwich and read my book. And I would look good doing it.

So I did a repair job on my make-up (I'd cried when I got the text from Sam, and although my mascara was supposed to be waterproof, I've yet to find one that doesn't smudge with tears) and I restyled my hair and I put on the Herve Leger dress, because the way I looked at it I wasn't going to ever wear it again anyway. Christmas Eve had been flagged as dressing up in the Sugar Loaf Lodge night, and the pink dress was my dressing-up dress.

I put on the Louboutin shoes and made my way back to the lobby. I suppose most people were at dinner, because it was deserted. I sat down near the windows and a waiter came rushing up to me.

'Any chance of a plain ham sandwich?' I asked. His eyes widened slightly. I suppose everyone else was tucking into their pumpkin soup and quails' eggs or whatever and ham sandwiches weren't in big demand. But he just said 'Certainly, madam' and asked if I'd like tea or coffee with that and I said tea, and a few minutes later he bustled over with tablecloths and napkins and cutlery and I was all set up for my gourmet meal.

In fairness to him, he didn't ask why I hadn't gone to the restaurant for my all-inclusive dinner; he simply put the plate with its delicate triangles of bread and ham nestling in a forest of mixed green salad and some shoestring chips in front of me.

'Anything else, madam?' he asked.

I shook my head.

'Kilmashogue?'

This time I nodded.

'Enjoy,' he said.

Well, that was Christmas Eve dinner. Not as good as the restaurant but an improvement on last year, when I'd gone on the lash with some of the people from work and we'd stopped off at AbraKebabra. The ham sandwiches were far, far better than the Eastern Spice kebab. I guess everything is relative.

People started to return to the lobby after dinner. They arrived in dribs and drabs and began ordering drinks. The waiter had cleared away my sandwich and was now dealing with one of the family groups. I thought I should order a drink for myself. The wooziness from the wine had worn off and I wanted more alcohol. It would make me look less alone. (Why I thought that, I just don't know. Yet someone in a bar sipping an alcoholic drink looks as though they've a reason to be there. Someone with a juice looks lonelier. It's a weird thing.

43

But true.) Anyway, I decided to go to the bar to order my drink.

I asked for a cosmopolitan. The bartender did a good job of mixing it. I brought it back to the lobby, near the piano and the open fire. I could hear the clicking of my Louboutins on the marble floor as I walked.

'Do you mind if we sit here?'

It was the couple who'd been sitting in silence earlier. I glanced around the room. It was full of people now and the only free seats were the two armchairs opposite me.

'Not at all,' I lied.

'Only I thought you might be waiting for someone,' said the man apologetically.

'Not right now.'

That was a good answer. I'd been waiting for him all my life and I'd been waiting for him all day too, but I wasn't waiting for him right now.

'It's lovely here, isn't it?' The woman smiled warmly at me.

'Yes.'

Were they trying to strike up a conversation with me? Well, why not, I supposed. They weren't talking much to each other!

The man signalled for the waiter, who took their order for a beer and a glass of wine.

'Can I get you anything?' the waiter asked me.

'Another one of these.' I drained my cocktail glass.

'Certainly,' he said.

'Have you family with you?' asked the woman.

'No.'

'Neither have we,' she said. 'I'm Bridget, by the way.'

'Andrew,' said her husband.

'Nice to meet you.'

Now leave me alone.

'So how long are you staying?' asked Bridget.

Did she really give a shit? Or was she one of those nosy people who have to know everything about everybody?

'Oh, just till tomorrow,' I said.

'You mean, you're only overnighting?'

Not in theory. It hadn't been possible to book for a one-night stay. The Sugar Loaf Lodge package insisted on two nights so that you were there Christmas night too. I'd told Sam that I might stay on after he left, although I hadn't really planned to. So pretty much we were shelling out a fortune for our one night of illicit love. Which wasn't even happening.

'I'm not sure,' I said eventually.

The waiter returned with the drinks, which was good. It changed the subject.

Andrew and Bridget started talking. Bridget did most of it. Mainly about their family. Four grown-up children (fair play to Bridget, she wasn't a stunner or anything but she didn't look like she had four grown-up kids). They seemed to be very proud of them, but I guess all parents are proud of their kids. I wondered how proud my mother would be of me, waiting in a hotel for a married man who hadn't turned up.

They asked about my parents and I told them about the

fact that they were in the States. Their eyes widened and they said it was a shame that they were away at Christmas. Then Bridget asked me if that was why I was here all by myself.

I smiled non-committally and allowed her to think that it was. Allowed her to think that I was an only child whose work-obsessed parents had left her all alone. Allowed her to feel sorry for me for the wrong reason.

'Join us for dinner tomorrow,' said Bridget enthusiastically.

'Oh, no,' I said quickly. 'It's your Christmas. Enjoy it.'

'We wouldn't mind,' said Bridget.

'Well, it depends,' I said. 'My friend might be here tomorrow.'

'Oh!' She beamed at me. 'How nice. I hate to think of you on your own. But in that case you should both join us.'

It was becoming a nightmare. They kept talking and talking and talking (perhaps the champagne they'd had earlier, as well as the beer and the wine, had opened the floodgates of conversation) but I suppose their company made it look as though I was part of it all. As though they were my friends. In fact there was one moment when Bridget had gone to the loo and I was sitting opposite Andrew when I thought that people might think that we were the ones who were together. And then I thought, no. He was too old for me. Too boring. And too married.

There was music. And dancing. I didn't want to dance, although Andrew asked me. I told them that I'd been stupid and had too much to drink. I walked to the bar, a bit

46

unsteady on my high heels now. I ordered another cosmo-politan. I watched the dancing. The four Golden Oldies were doing most of it. They'd hauled some guy (it might have been the man I'd seen earlier but I wasn't sure) on to the dance floor and were making a show of him. He didn't seem to mind too much. I bet his wife was cringing, though.

I finished my drink and ordered another one. I asked if it could be sent to my room. They said no problem. A girl had started playing the piano and people began to sing. Jingle Bloody Bells. I walked across the marble lobby in my shoes, but when I got to the glass corridor leading to the rooms, I took them off. I didn't need to pretend here.

They'd done a turn-down service in the room while I'd been away. The cushions had been moved from the bed and another Lir chocolate had been left on the pillow. There was a little Christmas card too, from the management and staff of the hotel.

But nothing from Sam. Nothing at all.

It was about two o'clock in the morning when my mobile rang. I groped around in the dark and knocked it off the bedside locker. I turned on the light. A missed call. From Sam.

I hesitated. Should I ring back? Or would that cause him problems? Though surely not if he was ringing me. The phone buzzed again and I nearly dropped it.

'Hello,' I said.

'Holly. How are you?'

'In bed,' I told him.

'Sweetheart, I'm so, so sorry. We had a crisis at home.'

47

'Oh?' I didn't really care about his crisis. I was having one of my own.

'Amber fell down the stairs.'

She was the older of the twins by nine minutes. Sam said that she was far more adventurous than Luke, her brother.

'Is she all right?'

'She bumped her head and so we had to bring her to Temple Street hospital. She's fine but you can never be too careful.'

Of course you can't. Not with your child.

'I'm glad she's OK. I wish you'd been able to call earlier.' I cringed. His child had been hurt and I was sounding petulant.

'It was too difficult,' he said. 'And I've got to go now. Amy's just gone to bed and I'm outside, leaving carrots for the reindeer.'

I thought of him standing in the frost, with his phone in one hand and carrots for mythical reindeers in the others.

'Good night, so,' I said.

'Happy Christmas,' said Sam. 'I'll call you tomorrow.'

I thought about tomorrow. I thought about him coming downstairs and opening the presents under the tree with Amy and Amber and Luke. I thought about Amy cooking Christmas dinner. I thought about them together as a family. I thought about the fact that he'd been there for them tonight. And that he'd be there for them tomorrow too.

I powered down my phone and switched off the light.

*

48

I wished that Santa Claus was real, and that he could bring you the person you loved for Christmas. Because that was all I wanted. Someone to tell me that he loved me and cared for me and that I was the most important person in the world to him. I wanted Sam to tell me all those things. But I knew he never would.

Next year, I promised myself as I lay back on the super-soft, super-smooth pillows, next year I'll do things differently. Next year I won't make an eejit of myself with a married man. Next year I'll stay at home with the M&S frozen dinners or I'll go to America and go out somewhere cool and sophisticated with my parents and we'll have a Christmas that's just another day. Maybe by next year I'll have met someone else, someone who'll love me and want to be with me and who doesn't have to spend Christmas Eve leaving carrots out for the reindeer.

And tomorrow . . . my heart ached about tomorrow. But I would get through it. That would be my Christmas present to myself. Getting through the first day of my life without Sam.

Kippure

Andrew and Bridget set out for Wicklow on Christmas Eve. The lock on the car door had frozen in the chill northerly wind, and Andrew needed to use a kettle of warm water to thaw it out before he could insert the key. He turned the heat up high in the Ford Mondeo as he drove along main roads lined by hoar-frosted fields, although the warm air did nothing to dispel the chill inside the car. Bridget was huddled into the passenger seat, looking straight ahead of her, her fingers busy plaiting and unplaiting the fringe of the grey wool scarf around her neck, and Andrew couldn't help feeling that she was regretting having agreed to this trip. That she would have preferred to be at Alannah's with their daughter and grandchildren instead. He was pretty certain that the idea of spending Christmas alone with him this year was something she felt she had to endure rather than enjoy. He supposed he couldn't blame her. He wished that she was chatting away beside him as she normally did, instead of sitting in silence, but he knew that she'd said everything that mattered already. So he continued to drive carefully, watching out for patches of ice on the road, hoping that it would be worth it when they got there but feeling all too certain that he'd made a terrible mistake.

The concierge who greeted them at the steps of the Sugar Loaf Lodge told Andrew that the valet would park his car. Andrew wanted to say that he'd park it himself, but the concierge had already held out his hand. I always dreamed of having a Mercedes-Benz, Andrew said to himself as he handed over the keys. Which would have been a far more appropriate car to have parked by a valet. But I guess there's no chance of that now.

Andrew's first car had been a Ford Anglia. He'd bought it second-hand from Ferriter's Garage on the Dublin Road, shortly after he and Bridget had moved into their new house in the Tipperary town of Kilcannagh. It hadn't been possible, back in the mid 1970s, to buy a house and a car at the same time. The bank simply wouldn't lend them the money. Besides, a car wasn't an immediate necessity. Andrew was easily able to walk the three miles from their two-bedroomed bungalow to the food-processing factory where he worked as an accounts clerk. In fact he enjoyed the walk along the twisting road that led out of town and to the factory. (In the summer, anyway, when the birds were singing in the trees and the air was warm and balmy; it wasn't quite so pleasant in the cold and dark of winter.) But almost as soon as he and Bridget married, he started putting money aside so that he would eventually have a

51

deposit for the car. He knew that one day they'd need it. And when Bridget announced, a few months later, that she was pregnant, he congratulated himself on his forward planning.

Andrew was a man who believed in forward planning. He didn't like to leave things to chance. He knew that he was a bit of a plodder and fairly predictable, but he told himself that there was nothing wrong with that. He reckoned there'd be plenty of women who'd like the security of a man like him.

Marrying Bridget had been part of his plans from the moment he'd first seen her at the Saturday-night dance in the local GAA club. She'd been wearing a mid-length denim skirt, tan boots and a white cheesecloth blouse. Unlike many of the girls in the club, her eyes hadn't been smeared with bright blue eye shadow, nor was her face a startling shade of bronze due to the over-generous supply of foundation that seemed to be essential for most of Kilcannagh's single women. She looked pretty and natural with hardly any make-up at all, and Andrew had been struck by her wide smile and intelligent gaze. He knew that he wanted to go out with her. He was fairly certain, even then, that he'd marry her. And so, even while other guys were zeroing in on the girls with shorter skirts or brighter eye shadow or tighter blouses, Andrew went over to Bridget and asked her to dance with him.

Bridget Moran was a teacher in the local primary school and something of a forward planner too, because she liked Andrew but there was no point, she thought, in bothering with him if he was simply looking for a bit of fun. Bridget was twenty-three and thought she was getting a bit old for the Saturday-night dances. Most of her friends were already engaged; some were even married. It was time, reckoned Bridget, that she settled down too. It never occurred to her for a moment that there was a life beyond Kilcannagh or that she didn't have to get married yet. In the 1970s, getting married was almost mandatory. If you hadn't got a husband by the time you were in your mid-twenties, you risked being on the shelf for ever. So Bridget wasn't prepared to waste time with someone who wasn't serious about her. Fortunately Andrew was also ready to settle down. He was two years older than her and he thought it was about time he started a family.

Six months after they met, Andrew and Bridget got married in Kilcannagh parish church. The reception was a quiet ceremony in the local hotel. Even though she wasn't an extravagant person and didn't like a lot of fuss, Bridget would really have preferred somewhere with a bit more glamour for her wedding reception; but Kilcannagh wasn't a glamorous place and the faded hotel was the only real option. (It closed down a few years after their marriage, and Bridget wasn't really surprised.)

They went to Galway for their honeymoon. There wasn't a lot of glamour in Galway either at the time, but they liked being alone together and both of them quietly congratulated themselves on having found the right person. And when Bridget told Andrew she was pregnant, he was truly delighted.

Bridget planned to keep working after the baby was born, because they needed the money. It was OK to be a married working woman if you were a teacher, she told Andrew earnestly. It was only if you had a different sort of job that people looked at you as though you were slightly mad (and selfish) to want to do anything other than stay at home with your kids. One day, she agreed, she'd give it up to be a stay-at-home mother. But not quite yet.

Andrew had known that a car would be necessary so that Bridget could take the baby (a beautiful little girl they'd named Alannah) to her mother's each morning and pick her up after school. Bridget's parents had a small farm six miles outside town, too far for her to push the pram every day, even though Bridget, like Andrew, was used to walking. They got the car a month before Alannah was born. Andrew had planned ahead again, thinking that it would be good to have it in plenty of time so that he could get Bridget to the hospital when she went into labour.

The Ford Anglia was pale mint green with cream-flecked upholstery. When Andrew first got behind the steering wheel he felt like a million dollars. He decided that one day, when he'd saved enough money, he'd buy himself a brand-new car so that when he got into it he'd know that nobody else had ever driven it before. If he was really lucky it might even be a Mercedes-Benz! He knew that day, if it even existed, was in the far-off future, but it was a nice dream to have. Right now, though, the Ford Anglia was his pride and joy and he cared about it almost as much as he cared about his baby daughter.

Supporting his family was, clearly, more important than any car. Being an accounts clerk wasn't exactly exciting, but it meant a steady wage, which was important at a time when jobs were hard to come by, especially in a small town like Kilcannagh. There was potential to do better in the accounting department at the food-processing plant, and Andrew decided to study at night for a qualification that would push him to the front of the queue when possible promotions were being discussed.

It was a good idea. Shortly after he qualified he was moved to a more senior position, and Bridget became pregnant again. Both she and Andrew decided that the time had come for her to give up her teaching job. Even though she would have liked to stick with it a bit longer, she felt it was unfair to expect her mother to take care of two children. Besides, she wanted to be home with them herself now.

The loss of Bridget's wages, which had been an initial worry, didn't matter because of Andrew's new salary. In a minor stroke of luck, the man that Andrew directly reported to decided to leave the company shortly after Anthony was born, and Andrew was promoted again. Bridget congratulated him on his foresight in studying at night and the two of them had a celebratory drink in Morrison's bar. (It was a rare enough occurrence for them to visit the bar, neither being big drinkers and both having had experience of people in their families for whom alcohol played too important a role.) They enjoyed the night out together but both of them agreed that relaxing at home in front of the TV was a better way of spending the evening. And a lot cheaper too!

Andrew took delivery of the two-year-old sky-blue Mark II Cortina a couple of weeks before Bridget gave birth to their third child. Kevin was just ten months younger than Anthony and he hadn't been planned. But, as Andrew said philosophically, you couldn't get the planning right all the time. And they'd done pretty well until then. Besides, they both agreed, Kevin was an adorable child and it didn't really matter that he'd come along sooner than they'd expected.

Bridget liked the extra room and comfort of the Cortina. She liked its extra power too. Although Andrew always drove the car when they were together, she enjoyed being behind the wheel. She'd learned to drive on the farm's tractor when she was in her teens, and Andrew would sometimes have to remind her that she wasn't driving one when she was behind the wheel of his precious Cortina. A little less brute force and a little more finesse would go a long way, he'd say anxiously as she crunched the gears. Bridget usually laughed when he criticised her driving. She could get from A to B without an accident, she said. That was the essence of travel, wasn't it?

She used the Cortina at weekends to visit Tipperary town and do the sort of shopping she couldn't do in Kilcannagh. And she drove to Dublin from time to time too, to check out the big department stores of the capital. When she was there she would meet up with her only unmarried friend, Tess Doolin, who'd taught alongside her in Kilcannagh primary school for a couple of years before announcing that she couldn't bear the stifling nature of a small town any more and getting a job in the city.

Bridget liked meeting Tess, who always had stories about the buzzing pubs and nightclubs she went to every weekend. But although it all sounded very cosmopolitan and exciting, it also seemed a little sad, because while Tess seemed to meet lots of men at places with names like Sloopy's and Zhivago's, she hadn't ever met someone like Andrew and there was no sign of her getting married and having a family of her own.

Tess once asked Bridget if she had any dreams. Bridget looked at her friend in surprise and said that she dreamed as much as anyone, she supposed, when she fell asleep at night. Tess shook her head and said that she wasn't talking about those sort of dreams.

'Don't you have anything you really and truly want to do?' she asked. 'Something mad or bad or exciting.'

Bridget thought about it for a while.

'Not really,' she said eventually. 'I like my life. I've got a good husband and a great family. I don't want anything else.'

'I'm going to Italy,' Tess told her. 'I have a dream of walking through the streets of Rome and eating ice cream with the heat of the sun on my back.'

Bridget looked at her in amazement.

'You could always go there on holidays,' she said. 'You can get package tours to places like Rome. Although I think they're quite expensive, especially for people on their own.'

'You really haven't a clue, have you, Bridget Holohan?' Tess's voice was pitying. 'You're a middle-aged woman and you're not even thirty-five. When was the last time you did anything frivolous? Or spent money on yourself? Or simply had a good time just for the sake of it?'

Bridget couldn't help thinking about what Tess had said. It wasn't possible to be frivolous when you had a husband and a family. And it certainly wasn't possible to spend money on yourself when it was needed for household expenses and school uniforms for the children and a million and one other things.

So that they would always be on top of things, Andrew would pay his wages cheque into their joint current account each month, then transfer ten per cent of it to a deposit account, which they called their Rainy Day Account. Bridget did the same with her children's allowance money. The concept of having some savings for a rainy day was something they both agreed on. They were surprised that more of their friends and family didn't think the same way. Bridget was particularly annoyed when she heard Andrew's younger sister refer to them as the most frugal, penny-pinching couple she'd ever met. She said nothing in response to Noeleen, who (like Tess) was now living in Dublin and apparently spending a fortune on clothes and make-up and nights out in the pub.

Anyway, for Bridget there was no time for clothes, make-up or nights out in the pub, because she was pregnant again. She hadn't told Tess this because she'd felt that her friend would be even more judgemental than she apparently already was. She didn't quite know why Tess seemed to disapprove of her being a careful housewife, but it was clear that she did. Tess seemed to disapprove of Andrew too, although Bridget remembered that on their wedding day she had commented that he was the best-looking man in Kilcannagh and that Bridget had been bloody lucky to get him.

A few months after Killian, their fourth child (a planned pregnancy this time), was born, Andrew was promoted to chief accountant at the food-processing plant. The promotion meant that the family could finally buy a bigger house, with four bedrooms and a large garden. It was a practical move, Andrew said, because the two-bedroomed bungalow wasn't suitable for a family with one girl, three boys and their assorted books and toys.

Bridget loved the additional space, although keeping up with the mortgage payments as well as all the other household expenses stretched her budgetary skills to the limit. They'd decided to upgrade the car too. Andrew chose another Cortina, a year and a half newer than the last one. It had been owned by a man who hardly drove it anywhere, so the mileage was extremely low. Danny Ferriter told Andrew he was getting a bargain. Andrew agreed, although there was a part of him that would still have loved to buy a new car (he kept looking at the brand-new iridium-silver Mark II on the garage forecourt). But he'd changed his mind about ever wanting to fork out for something brand new. A new car was a complete waste of money because it plummeted in value the moment you drove it out of the garage. He'd stepped aside from the silver Mercedes-Benz Danny showed him too. Even though it was second-hand, it was more expensive than the Cortina, although it was very beautiful and tugged at his heart.

Bridget sometimes got letters from Tess, who'd gone to Italy as she'd promised and was now living in a three-roomed apartment near Rome. Tess had sent her a photograph of the apartment, which looked to Bridget as though it had been built at least a hundred years earlier and might collapse at any moment. The shuttered windows and wrought-iron balcony were very pretty, she conceded, but that wasn't going to help when the whole thing subsided into a pile of rubble. Nevertheless there was a part of her that envied Tess the freedom to do whatever she wanted whenever she wanted. There were times when Bridget thought, as she cooked and cleaned and ferried the children around, that not a single moment of her life was her own any more.

During the remainder of the 1980s, as the Irish economy plunged into deeper and deeper misery, Andrew worked hard to help keep the finances of the plant under control. He was very conscious that it was one of the major employers in the town, and he felt responsible for the jobs of everyone who worked there. He was absolutely devastated when management, in a cost-cutting measure, made the decision to let some people go.

It was ironic, Andrew thought, that the hard times for the company had actually worked in his favour. He was putting in extra hours and being well paid for them. As time went by, he briefly thought about trading in his car again, but he didn't want it to appear as though he was able to afford the luxury of a new car when other people had lost their jobs. Besides, the Cortina was a great piece of automotive engineering. He hadn't had a moment's trouble with it from the day he'd driven it home from Ferriter's.

The economy, and the food-processing plant, limped on into the nineties. And then, almost overnight, it turned a corner. New technology was introduced and new products were created. The orders began to flow again and they were starting to hire people once more. Andrew's salary increased regularly and he was eventually able to replace the old Cortina. Danny Ferriter suggested that this time he might like a brand-new Ford. Or perhaps something a bit more stylish, he said. A BMW or a Mercedes.

Andrew didn't think of himself as a Mercedes man any more. Nor was he a BMW person. He couldn't see the point in spending all that money on exclusive brand names when so many other cars were just as good. Danny told him that it wasn't just a means of transport; that there was also the issue of style and comfort. And a touch of luxury too, he added, opening the door to a forest-green Mercedes 280CE coupé and inviting Andrew to get into the driver's seat. Luxury that the chief accountant of one of the town's biggest employers deserved.

There was no doubt, Andrew thought as he sat in the car, that the Mercedes was very luxurious, but he didn't need it. No matter what Danny said, it certainly wasn't necessary for him to drive around in such a car, even if he was an important person in the town. Andrew hated people who showed off. And driving this car around Kilcannagh would very definitely be showing off. In the end he bought a year-old Ford Focus. With the money he saved by not indulging in the Mercedes, he bought Bridget a five-year-old Fiesta, because she was spending a lot of her time running the children around the country for their various pursuits and she needed a car of her own.

*

61

As her family grew older, Bridget went back to work. She hadn't imagined that she'd ever want to work outside the home again, but the children were getting more and more independent and she realised that she was a little lonely. She didn't go back to teaching but instead took a part-time job as a guide at a heritage centre where a lot of tourists came to discover their Irish roots. She was good at directing them to the best places to find what they needed, and always celebrated when someone came back to her and told her that they'd unearthed evidence of where their ancestors had come from. She added most of her salary to the Rainy Day Account, but the one treat she did allow herself was a regular cut and colour at Bernadine's Hair Salon in the main street, because she thought that grey hair was very ageing and hers was no longer the natural soft brown that it had once been.

From time to time she still got letters from Tess Doolin. Tess had married an Italian engineer ten years earlier but had separated from him shortly afterwards. In her letters to her friend, Bridget asked what had gone wrong, and Tess had replied that they had both wanted different things. Bridget couldn't understand that – surely, she thought, you should both know the things you wanted before you got married. Surely that was the point. She didn't say this to Tess and she was glad that she'd kept her own counsel, because one day she received a letter in which Tess said that what Salvadore had actually wanted was a wife at home and a few mistresses around town. She'd discovered he was having an affair, she wrote, and she hadn't been able to live with him after that. But, she added, it didn't matter. She was a free woman again and was going to go on a round-the-world trip. Which was a long-standing dream. And then she asked Bridget if she'd ever come up with a dream of her own that was a bit more exciting than being able to say that she'd got married and had children and managed to keep her Rainy Day Account intact for twenty years.

Bridget had wondered if there was a bit of a sting in Tess's words. Especially about the Rainy Day Account. She'd told her about it a long time ago and Tess had got excited, saying that when Bridget turned fifty she should take all the money out of it and do something mad. Bridget had pointed out that it was for emergencies, not doing something mad, and that they had dipped into it from time to time, especially to help with the children's college expenses. When you had four children, she wrote in response to her friend, there were always unexpected demands on your financial resources. There was no time for thinking of mad things to do with your money.

They used a large chunk of the Rainy Day Account for Alannah's wedding. It was, as the neighbours remarked to each other, an unexpectedly lavish affair for the Holohans (Noeleen's judgement of them as frugal was shared by many others; some, a little more harsh in their views, suggested that they were miserly), but Andrew had wanted a great day for his daughter and Bridget had always expected that they would foot the entire bill for Alannah's big day. They held the reception at a new four-star hotel near Tipperary (built to take advantage of a number of tax breaks that the government had introduced to get the economy moving). The hotel had all the glamour that had been so sadly lacking at Bridget's own reception, which made her feel very happy indeed. And which was why, she reminded herself as she watched the bride and groom posing for photographs, she hadn't dipped into the Rainy Day Account before like Tess would have wanted and squandered it on mad things for herself.

The economy took another leap forward and the processing plant was bought out by a multinational company, which invested in modernising the plant and equipment. Andrew had been concerned when he'd first heard of the buyout, but his job was secure. New businesses had opened in Kilcannagh, and the food-processing plant wasn't as essential to local employment prospects as it had once been. There were more houses in the town, more people and, consequently, significantly more cars. Lots of them were massive SUVs, which made driving down the narrow main street on a Saturday almost impossible as they took up so much space.

Andrew didn't allow himself to be lured into SUV ownership. He thought they were ridiculous vehicles for people who lived in the semi-detached houses that had sprung up on the outskirts of the town. He was perfectly happy with his latest acquisition, an almost-new cobalt-blue Mondeo with interior accessories and leather trim. He enjoyed driving it, especially on his regular trips to Dublin, where he had to make presentations to the multinational parent company about the Kilcannagh plant's financial health. The meetings in Dublin took up an entire day and he would stay there overnight.

Andrew always felt a sense of achievement whenever he checked into the hotel and took out his company credit card. He would look around at the other men in business suits, carrying briefcases and talking urgently into their mobile phones, and tell himself that he was part of their world. He sometimes wished that he'd been a bit more dynamic when he was younger and taken more chances with his career. Maybe he could have been the MD by now instead of remaining as the chief accountant. The current MD, Jason Carrick, was actually younger than Andrew. He was in his late thirties and had a masters in business studies. Which was all very well, Andrew thought from time to time, but it didn't mean he knew everything.

Andrew had never really wanted to be the MD. But he did sometimes think that although his life hadn't passed him by, he'd never really taken it by the scruff of the neck like other people had.

He met Gerry Laughlin in the hotel bar one evening. He'd come back to the hotel after a meeting at the company's head office and had settled in to watch an international soccer match on TV. Andrew wasn't big into soccer, but he knew enough to maintain a casual conversation, and happily exchanged views on the two teams with the man who'd sat down beside him. When the match finished, they started to talk about their work. Gerry was a financial adviser, and he told Andrew that he'd achieved fifteen per cent returns for his clients over the last year. Andrew was impressed by this, but, he told Gerry, he was happy enough knowing that his money was safe in the bank. And in a few bank shares too, he added. I'm not a total idiot, I know that I need to take a bit of a risk to make more money. Gerry agreed with Andrew that it was good to be conservative but that sometimes it meant you were left behind. He gave him information leaflets about his company and its funds, which Andrew took up to his room and read while he was in bed. The returns were excellent, he thought, and the risks were more limited than he'd thought. Perhaps it would be good retirement planning to talk to Gerry Laughlin again.

People were certainly better off these days, Andrew thought the following morning as he checked out of the hotel. More confident, too. The businessmen in the hotel looked much the same as businessmen all over the world, in their sharp suits and shiny shoes, and the women, of all ages, were somehow smarter than they'd ever been, with their glossy hair and their perfect teeth and their unbelievably high-heeled shoes. Andrew glanced down at his own suit, which he'd bought in Tipperary. It was well-made and hard-wearing but it wasn't as stylish as the one Gerry Laughlin had been wearing the previous night. And he doubted that Bridget – unlike the woman he'd overheard talking to a friend over breakfast – would ever spend eight hundred euros on a handbag just because it was by an apparently must-have designer.

Their simple lifestyle had never bothered Andrew before.

He dismissed as bitchiness Noeleen's occasional comments about their frugality. But for the first time in his life he couldn't help thinking that perhaps he and Bridget were missing out. Perhaps they deserved more than simply knowing that they'd done their best for each other and their children. Perhaps they should have embraced the whole concept of having a great lifestyle, as everyone else in the country seemed to have done.

When he got home to Kilcannagh, Andrew thought about it a bit more. Somehow designer suits and expensive lifestyles didn't seem quite as important when he was back in the house, where Bridget was busy making jam. For Alannah and the kids, she said. They loved her home-made jam. Andrew didn't think Gerry Laughlin's wife (if Gerry was even married) would be making jam. But maybe at this stage of her life Bridget shouldn't be either. No matter how much Alannah and her family liked it.

He rang Gerry Laughlin the following week. He'd decided to move the rainy-day money into one of Gerry's top-performing funds. He was looking forward to it doing well so that when he retired in a few years' time, he and Bridget would be able to have the good life that they hadn't bothered with until now. Maybe, he said to Gerry, he'd even splash out and buy himself a brand-new Mercedes-Benz. After all, he remarked, if the fund kept on making the kind of money that Gerry said it would make, he'd easily be able to afford it. And he wouldn't even care that it would lose value as soon as he put the key in the ignition.

He didn't tell Bridget what he'd done. But he made plans. They would go on a world cruise. Or buy a holiday house in the sun. Every second person in Kilcannagh seemed to have a holiday home in Spain or Portugal or Bulgaria or Turkey. Bridget had remarked on this one day, wondering how they could all afford it. After all, she'd said, it's not something we could do, and you earn a good salary, so how the hell did Marge and Eamonn Murphy manage to buy a villa in Malaga when he's a self-employed plumber and she doesn't work at all?

Three weeks after he'd invested the money with Gerry, Andrew walked into the office and knew that there was something wrong.

'What's going on?' he asked Jason Carrick.

'Profitability,' said Jason.

'We're doing all right,' Andrew told him. 'Down a bit, but OK.'

'The company as a whole isn't OK.' Jason leaned back in his leather swivel chair. 'There's a significant downturn in the market. Part of it is due to all these celebrity chefs banging on about processed food. The ready-meals division is suffering.'

Andrew nodded slowly. Although the plant produced frozen curries, pasta and TV dinners, he'd never actually eaten a ready meal in his life. Bridget was a good cook and always had a substantial dinner waiting for him when he came home.

'And the rest is because of the economy. People are tightening their belts again, and our export sales have fallen.'

Andrew was sceptical. Sure, there were rumblings about a slowdown. But he couldn't really see that it would affect them that much. People had to eat, after all.

'We need to be thinking about the future,' said Jason. 'We need to think about rationalising again.'

'Rationalising?' Andrew looked concerned. 'You mean redundancies?'

'Last resort,' said Jason. 'See what you can do on cost-cutting measures first. I need a plan for the group meeting at the end of the month.'

Andrew went back to his desk and called up the spreadsheets. The company was already being run in a very cash-efficient manner. He wasn't sure where he was meant to trim costs. He rang the group accountant, Miles Morrissey, to ask him what was going on.

'They're looking for an excuse to make cuts,' said Miles. 'You know what these multinationals are like. But we're profitable enough, aren't we?'

'Yes,' Andrew replied. 'I've been looking at the numbers, though. The group as a whole has a lot of debt.'

'Refinancing is up to the treasury department,' said Miles dismissively. 'We just do what we can.'

But Andrew really couldn't see what the Kilcannagh plant could do. He found a few small savings but he knew they weren't enough. He went back to Jason to give him the bad news.

'Head Office won't be happy,' said Jason.

'Head Office can think of something else,' Andrew told him in return.

Head Office did think of something else. They decided to close down the Kilcannagh plant. A group email was sent to everybody, but Jason had called them all together to give them the news first.

'I'm really sorry,' he said. 'It was the only thing they could do.'

Andrew was utterly shocked. He couldn't believe what he was hearing. The plant had been his life for over thirty years. How could it be that in the space of a couple of weeks it had gone from being a profitable company to something that was being culled? It didn't make sense.

Miles said it was because the banks were putting the squeeze on companies like theirs, cutting back on loans. The food-processing plant had quite a number of loans and the banks were reluctant to renew them.

'But those loans are for sound business reasons,' Andrew protested.

'Doesn't matter,' said Miles. 'Head Office wants to streamline everything. And this plant is surplus to requirements.'

Andrew still couldn't believe how quickly it had happened. For the first time since he'd left school, he didn't have a job. Realistically it didn't matter as much to him as to the guys who had young families and big mortgages, but he suddenly had the feeling of being on the scrapheap with nowhere to go. And despite his long service to the company, he was only getting statutory redundancy.

'What will you do, Jason?' he asked.

'I'm moving to Head Office,' said the MD succinctly. 'They've offered me a management position there.'

Bridget was equally shocked. She couldn't believe that the parent company had closed down the plant just like that. It was going to wreak havoc in the town and surrounding countryside.

'Maybe it won't be that bad.' Andrew tried to sound philosophical. 'After all, there's been growth in new industries over the past few years. Hopefully the lads will find something.'

'And what about you?' Bridget was worried for the younger men in the company too, but she was more concerned about Andrew, who'd given his whole life to his job.

'I'll get something,' said Andrew. 'Eventually.'

'I'm sure you will,' she said, although she doubted it very much.

It was as though, with the closure of the Kilcannagh plant, somebody had knocked over the first domino in a chain. Quite suddenly the only news was bad news. Companies were closing and jobs were being lost everywhere. It was like the eighties all over again. Talk of recession gripped the country and people were terrified to spend any money in case they were the next person out of work.

Even though she couldn't help being worried, Bridget

didn't feel as though she was in the middle of a catastrophe. Andrew had received his redundancy money. She still had her part-time job in the heritage centre. Things weren't that bad. She wished that the media would tone down the doom and gloom a bit. There was no need to terrify people, she thought. No need to make them think the worst all the time.

Andrew, though, was feeling extremely worried. He knew that the fund in which he'd placed his rainy-day money must have fallen in value. Gerry had given him the usual guff about values going down as well as up, and then had laughed and said that nobody had ever lost money on his funds. Except, he added, people who tried to cash in too quickly. But you're a long-term investor, Andrew. You'll be fine.

Only he wasn't fine. He was out of work, and although they weren't yet struggling, it would have been nice to be able to dip into the Rainy Day Account. But right now he couldn't even get in touch with Gerry, whose phone seemed to be permanently engaged and who wasn't answering his emails.

There was a level on which Andrew had always expected the bad news to come. From the moment he'd embraced the idea of getting a bit more out of life, of making his money work harder; from the moment he'd visualised the feeling of sliding into the brand-new Mercedes-Benz, there had been, at the back of his mind, a feeling that he wasn't entitled to this sort of thing. That he and Bridget were plodders, and that they shouldn't expect anything more than a plodding lifestyle. All the times he'd come up to the company head-quarters in Dublin and stayed overnight in the hotel; all the times he'd told himself that he belonged there among the businessmen and their suits and their briefcases, he'd always felt a bit of a fraud. Because he wasn't smart and shrewd like them. He was simply an accountant, who looked at the figures and warned about the worst-case scenarios. He was a glass-half-empty kind of person, and he'd made the basic mistake of thinking that perhaps his should be half-full. And now he wasn't even sure if there was a glass in front of him at all. Because the headline in the paper said 'Missing Millions' and the story was about Gerry Laughlin, who, it seemed, had left the country, taking his clients' money with him.

Andrew didn't know what to do. He sat in the study (it had once been Alannah's bedroom, but when she'd got married, he'd put a desk and a PC in it and taken it over for himself) and looked at the statements that Gerry Laughlin had sent him. According to the figures in front of him, the returns on the fund were excellent. But the newspapers were now saying that this had all been a lie, that Gerry hadn't actually invested the money at all and that it was an elab-orate pyramid scheme. Andrew couldn't believe that he'd been caught in a pyramid scheme. He was far too sensible for that. He was a cautious investor. He didn't take risks.

And yet he had. He'd gambled their rainy-day money. And now there wouldn't be any round-the-world trip or brand-new Mercedes-Benz or stays in luxury hotels, because their nest egg had gone and everything that Andrew had believed in had gone with it.

Andrew hadn't told Bridget about Gerry Laughlin. She still thought that their rainy-day money was safely tucked up in the bank, waiting for the day when they might need it. She still thought that he was looking after her as he'd always done. And he didn't know how he was going to tell her otherwise.

A part of him harboured a vague hope that it would all come right. That he'd get a letter telling him the fund was down in value but that it did actually exist, and that Gerry Laughlin hadn't conned him out of his lifetime's savings by pandering to his ego. Because Andrew realised now that that was exactly what had happened. For once in his life he'd wanted to step outside himself, stop being cautious Andrew and be part of the club of people who talked about their financial adviser and knew that their money was working for them instead of simply sitting there. He'd been suckered in by financial glamour and he'd ruined everything.

Bridget tried not to let her shock show on her face. She knew that Andrew was devastated. She knew that he thought he'd let her down. The truth was, he *had* let her down. His job was to keep her and their family secure. And he hadn't done that. What he was telling her now was that all the careful saving, all the years of being frugal and sensible, all the times they'd denied themselves little pleasures had been for nothing. Because there was nothing left.

'I'm sorry,' he said. 'I thought I was doing the right thing.'

She nodded slowly.

'And now I'm on the scrapheap.' His voice was rasping. 'I've got no job and no prospects and no savings. I've made a mess of things, Bridget.'

She wanted to say that he hadn't, but she couldn't help feeling he had.

She said instead that it didn't matter. That they would have left the money to the children anyhow. That they still had the money she was earning from the heritage centre and that they'd be fine. Money had never been important to them. So what difference did it actually make that they didn't have the Rainy Day Account any more?

But both of them knew that it made a huge difference. They might not have intended to spend the money, but knowing that it was there had always been a security blanket for them. Now that the blanket had been pulled away, neither of them was sure how to cope.

Tess Doolin sent her an email saying that she was coming back to Ireland for a visit the following year and she hoped they'd meet up. Tess was now living in New Zealand. She'd married a man fifteen years younger than her and they ran a farm together. Bridget found it vaguely amusing that Tess had left Ireland to chase dreams of sun and romance and a more exotic life but that she had, in the end, returned to her roots. She'd

75

been a farmer's daughter and now she was a farmer herself, and one who was coming home, even if only for a short stay, after spending most of her life away. Perhaps it wasn't possible to escape the person you'd always been, thought Bridget. Perhaps it always came back to haunt you in the end.

Towards the end of November, Andrew received a cheque in the post for €2,500. There was a letter enclosed with it, from his ex-employers, saying that they had miscalculated on the redundancy payment owing to him. Andrew frowned. He'd checked the redundancy payment himself and it had seemed perfectly correct. But someone called J. Dylan Jones had signed a letter saying otherwise. Andrew didn't know J. Dylan Jones. He was one of the international vice presidents and he'd never had anything to do with the Irish company before.

It was a mistake, Andrew concluded. There'd be a phone call telling him that in the next day or two.

But nobody called. Andrew took the cheque out of his wallet and looked at it disconsolately. It wasn't his money. He knew that.

He rang Human Resources and spoke to a girl named Cathy Cunningham. Cathy told him that the calculations were correct. Andrew said OK and hung up.

He told Bridget about it the second week in December. And then he told her what he'd done. She looked at him in astonishment.

'You've what?' she said.

'I've booked us into the Sugar Loaf Lodge,' he said. 'For Christmas.'

'Why on earth did you do that?' she demanded. 'That's one of the most luxurious hotels in the country.'

'I know.'

'We can't afford it. Not now.'

He winced. When they could have afforded it, when the money he was supposed to be managing had been in the bank, he never would have dreamed of spending it on a couple of days in an expensive hotel. Bridget was right. He'd been stupid again.

'I'll cancel it.' He sounded defeated.

'No,' she said suddenly. 'Don't.'

Almost immediately she regretted saying it. But the expression in Andrew's eyes was enough to tell her not to change her mind again.

All the same, she thought, as they walked up the steps to the beautifully restored country house, while someone else parked their car, this wasn't going to be a good Christmas. Neither of them wanted to be here. Neither of them would be able to enjoy it.

The lobby of the hotel, with its roaring fire and carefully decorated Christmas trees, was very welcoming and very Christmassy. A waiter brought them each a glass of mulled wine as they stood at the walnut desk where the elegant receptionist was checking them in. Bridget hesitated before accepting the wine, but then took the glass in its silver holder and sipped it cautiously. As the warmth of the alcohol radiated through her body, she could almost feel herself physically relax. And, strangely, she thought she heard someone whisper 'Welcome' in her ear.

'You're in Kippure.' The receptionist, whose silver name-badge said 'Sarah', smiled at them. 'One of our executive suites.'

'Suite?' whispered Bridget to Andrew as they followed the porter along a narrow corridor.

'It was all that was available,' he whispered in reply.

The porter unlocked the door and showed them into the room. He wished them a pleasant stay and then left them alone. Bridget stared at the luxurious furnishings and the rich drapery as she took off her shoes and buried her toes in the thick mink-coloured carpet.

'It's like something out of a magazine,' she said. 'I didn't think that the likes of us could actually stay in places like this.'

'Why shouldn't we?' asked Andrew. 'We should have done it before.'

Bridget said nothing. She walked through the room into the big bathroom with its two sinks and massive sunken bath. It was surreal. And yet not, she told herself. Because people stayed here all the time. People who thought that underfloor heating, oversized bathrobes and sunken baths were the norm. But not the norm for her and Andrew. She'd been brought up on a farm, where the welfare of the animals had always come before the welfare of the family. And Andrew had been raised in Kilcannagh town, in a two-up two-down house with an outside toilet. They weren't the sort of people who came to flashy hotels. If they still had the rainy-day money, they wouldn't have spent it on this hotel. She knew they wouldn't.

'Let's go downstairs,' said Andrew, 'and have a drink.'

They sat near the big open fireplace with its crackling log fire. Andrew ordered two glasses of champagne and Bridget looked at him questioningly.

'Why?' she asked. 'Why are we doing all this when we can't afford it?'

'I don't want to talk about it,' said Andrew. 'Not now.'

The two of them sat in silence and waited for their drinks to arrive. Bridget was feeling overwhelmed both by the luxury of the hotel and by Andrew's uncharacteristic behaviour. She was worried about him. Worried about the fact that he'd also behaved uncharacteristically by handing over the rainy-day money to that con artist Gerry Laughlin. Worried that he was shelling out stupid money on an unnecessary Christmas break. And worried about the future too, now that he was out of work and likely never to work again, because there was no way anyone would employ someone of Andrew's age when they could get a young graduate with a sackful of qualifications to do the job instead.

I've always worried about the future, Bridget thought as she waiter arrived with their glasses of cool champagne. All my life I've worried about making sure we had enough to get by. About the rainy day. And now it's come, and we don't have the shelter that I thought we'd built up. And Andrew is blowing the unexpected windfall that would have kept us going for weeks, for no good reason at all.

'Happy Christmas, Bridget.'

She clinked her glass against his and smiled. But the smile barely reached her eyes.

The girl in the pink dress distracted Bridget from her own thoughts. She reminded her of Alannah. She had the same groomed look as her daughter, her hair carefully styled, her face smooth and flawless thanks to cleverly applied make-up. And the dress (though showing a bit too much leg, Bridget thought critically; Alannah would never have worn one so short) was well made and clearly expensive. It struck Bridget, for the first time, that the generation of people to which Alannah and the girl in the pink dress belonged was a generation who felt that lavishing money on themselves was a perfectly reasonable thing to do. Who were entirely comfortable with the idea of spending time in expensive hotels.

Alannah had been surprised when Bridget told her what she and Andrew were doing for Christmas. She'd expected them to come to her house as they'd done for the past two years.

'Your father wants to treat me,' Bridget had said. She hadn't told Alannah about the loss of the rainy-day money. She couldn't bring herself to let her daughter know that Andrew had made a mess of things.

'Well, you certainly deserve a treat.' Alannah had smiled. 'I've always said that you two are far too stick-in-the-mud for your own good. It's about time you got out and enjoyed life.'

80

It was the second time Alannah had spoken to her about enjoying life.

'Oh come on, Mam.' Alannah had laughed when Bridget told her that there was no need to keep telling her to enjoy herself, because she did already. 'You don't really. You and Dad are like two little squirrels hoarding everything away for the dark winter that never comes.'

'Don't be so silly.'

'Brian says that Dad is a typical accountant,' Alannah said. 'He's excited by the numbers but not by what they mean. And what's the point of money if you don't spend it?'

Bridget had wanted to shout that they didn't have any money now, that somebody else was spending it, but she stayed silent.

The girl in the pink dress ordered a drink and looked at her watch. Bridget wondered about her, who she was waiting for and why she'd come to the Sugar Loaf Lodge for Christmas. Why had anyone, she asked herself, as she looked around the lobby, when they could have been sitting at home in front of the TV and not spending a fortune on an overpriced few days just because it was Christmas?

Dinner in the Michelin-starred restaurant was amazing. Designer food, Bridget thought, but that didn't take away from the intense flavour of the tiny cup of pea soup and the baked cheese to follow, or the perfectly roasted goose with chestnut soufflé accompanied by delicately cooked vegetables. They had the creamiest of crème brûlées to follow and then some petit fours and proper tea, all of which was perfect.

She had to admit that it was wonderful to be waited on, not to be hopping up and down to check on the status of the turkey or the roast potatoes or the vegetables. (Not that she'd be doing this on Christmas Eve anyway – they usually just had a couple of chops and potatoes – but Christmas Day was different. Even when they spent it with Alannah, who was quite happy for her to help with the cooking.) When the waitress brought a pot of tea made with leaves and not bags, she sat back in the chair and smiled at Andrew. It was the first time she'd smiled all day, and he felt the tension in his stomach, which had stopped him really enjoying his meal, ease ever so slightly.

Then Santa arrived, doing his ho-ho-ho thing, which enchanted the children and made the adults smile. He wished Bridget and Andrew a happy Christmas and gave them a present from the sack over his shoulder. It was a half-bottle of red wine, a Cabernet Sauvignon, which Bridget knew that Andrew liked. Santa moved through the room, stopping to talk to everyone, including, Bridget noted, a man who was eating on his own, his head buried in some kind of computer notebook throughout the meal. She wondered if he was actually with the girl in the pink dress. If it was a row between them that had left her alone in the lobby while he ate in the restaurant. She wanted to tell him that it was stupid to row. But she knew better than to interfere.

She and Andrew left the restaurant very shortly after Santa's visit. There were only two seats left in the drawing room, opposite the girl in the pink dress, who seemed to have stayed there all through dinner and who now had a rose-red cock-tail in front of her. Andrew asked if she'd mind them sitting there and she said no. He said he thought she might have been waiting for someone and she said no to that too.

Bridget thought the girl looked miserable. She thought about asking if she'd rowed with the man in the restaurant, but she knew that Andrew would be horrified if she asked such a question. Besides, she wasn't the sort of person who talked very much to strangers. She'd always been someone who let them start talking first.

Yet she couldn't let the girl sit there in silent misery. Not on Christmas Eve. She started to talk to her about her own family instead, saying that this was the first time she and Andrew had come away for Christmas, and that it was strange to be in a hotel and not at home. She knew that the girl probably didn't want to listen to her, but suddenly she couldn't seem to stop. She talked about how life now was so different to how it was when she and Andrew were first married. How it was easier, but maybe that was only an illusion. She talked about her children and how much she loved them and how proud she was of them. And she said that they probably worried about her because children usually did about their parents, but that there was no need really, because no matter what happened she was a survivor. She'd been brought up tough. She always would be tough. She knew that Andrew was listening to her, and she also knew that the girl probably wasn't, but she didn't really care, because it was a relief to articulate the thoughts that had plagued her over the past few weeks but which she simply hadn't been able to discuss with her husband.

The girl, when she did finally speak, told them that she was here on her own because her parents were abroad, and Bridget realised that she hadn't rowed with the man in the restaurant after all but that she was actually all alone for Christmas. Which made her ask the girl, whose name was Holly, if she'd like to join them for dinner the next day, even though, as she spoke, she realised that she wasn't making her a very good offer, because for the past couple of months the atmosphere between her and Andrew had been so strained that nobody could have put up with it. Holly thanked her politely and said that she might not be staying for dinner, it depended on whether a friend was arriving later, and Bridget, unable to stop herself, said that the friend should eat with them too. Holly smiled politely.

'That's very kind of you,' she said. 'The arrangements are up in the air at the moment. He's got work commitments.'

'At Christmas!' Bridget looked surprised.

'You know how it is,' said Holly. 'Your life isn't your own any more.'

Bridget nodded, although the truth was she didn't really know that. Andrew had never let work commitments come ahead of his family. Which had been a good thing. He'd always put them first. Put her first. He'd always done his best. Which, she supposed, was what he'd thought he was doing when he'd met with Gerry Laughlin and broken the habit of a lifetime. That's what he'd told her. He'd wanted to make them secure. He'd wanted to give her things he thought she deserved.

What neither of them had realised was that he'd done that already.

She was still very angry about the money. She hoped that evil things would happen to Gerry Laughlin. But quite suddenly, she wasn't angry with Andrew.

Because she loved Andrew. She always had.

The girl in the pink dress sipped her cocktail.

And Bridget slid her hand into Andrew's.

He looked at her in surprise. She squeezed his hand. And she saw relief flood into his eyes. Seeing his expression made her feel better than she had in weeks. She squeezed it again. The girl in the pink dress checked her watch.

When the music started up, Andrew asked Bridget to dance with him.

She got up and put her arms around him.

'I'm sorry,' he said.

'I know.'

'I blew it all.'

'No,' she said. 'You didn't. He did.'

'I should never have—'

'Maybe not,' Bridget interrupted him. 'Maybe not, and maybe I'll never quite get over it. But if I let it eat away at me, eat away at us . . .' She leaned her head on his shoulder. 'There are more important things than money, Andrew.'

'People usually only say that when they have plenty of it,' he told her wryly.

'I know. But the truth is that we're not the sort of people who need plenty of it. It was good to have, I can't say it wasn't great to be able to help out the kids when they needed it too. But they're adults now. They can make their own way.'

'I wanted to be able to give you things,' said Andrew. 'I wanted us to kick up our heels. I wanted . . .'

'What?'

'I wanted to buy a brand-new Mercedes-Benz and not care that it would depreciate as soon as I drove it home.'

'We can sell our house and downsize and have enough money for a Mercedes-Benz *and* for kicking up our heels,' said Bridget.

He stopped dancing and looked at her.

'Or we can hang on to the house and cope. It's not like we have huge expenses, after all. And I'm still working; you seem to have forgotten that.'

'No,' he said. 'Only I always thought that your job was extra.'

'We're all right,' she told him. 'We really are. We always will be.'

'Would you really sell the house?' There was a sudden lightness in his tone. 'Just for a Mercedes-Benz?'

'Actually,' said Bridget, 'I would.'

They danced some more, then Bridget went to the ladies'. Andrew sat down again, feeling as though a weight had dropped from his shoulders. He smiled at Holly, who'd ordered another cocktail. He asked her if she'd like to dance and she told him that she'd had too much to drink and that her shoes were too high and that she wasn't half as good a dancer as Bridget.

'You two are so lucky,' she said shakily. 'You're happy together. That's great.'

When Bridget returned, she and Andrew said good night to Holly and returned to their room. Bridget rang Alannah, who wanted to know what the hotel was like and if they were having a good time; and Bridget started to tell her about the suite and the food and Santa and the girl in the pink dress. Alannah interrupted her to ask if she was actually a bit drunk, because she was blathering. Andrew took the phone from her and said that they'd had champagne. He said it in a proud way, and Alannah replied that she hoped they'd enjoyed it, and he said yes, they had, they should drink it more often.

After they'd finished talking to their daughter, Andrew told Bridget that he was going to fill the sunken bath and that they were going to get into it together, and Bridget looked at him in astonishment and then giggled and said OK.

While he was running the bath, she rang for room service. Ten minutes later there was a knock at the door and a bottle of champagne was delivered to them.

'More champagne!' Andrew looked at his wife in amazement.

'Why not?' she asked defiantly. 'Why not? We haven't drunk enough champagne in our lives. We kept putting off kicking up our heels. We were too worried about the rainy day, and d'you know what, it's sort of come and gone and we're still here!'

Andrew opened the bottle and poured the golden liquid into the perfect glasses.

Bridget started to speak again. 'We did everything right and we've had good times together, but . . . but . . .'

'What?' He was looking at her anxiously.

'Maybe we forgot to smell the roses a bit. And I know there aren't many roses to smell right now,' she added hurriedly. 'I know that it's tough. But so fecking what? We have each other.' She took a slug of her champagne. 'I kept thinking about it downstairs when I was talking to that poor girl, Holly. I don't know what's going on in her life, but tonight she's here on her own and she's unhappy. I feel grateful that I have you and you have me, and that we're still together. And I want us to enjoy ourselves for the next couple of days.'

Andrew smiled. 'You're really embracing the kicking-up-your-heels now.'

'Yes.' Her tone was suddenly fierce. 'Yes, I am. I felt sick when you told me you were blowing the money on this stay, but you know what, I'm really glad you did. And I know that kicking up our heels doesn't always mean spending a fortune, but it does mean . . . well, maybe grabbing the moment a bit more. And not always worrying about tomorrow.'

'Worrying about tomorrow kept us going all our lives,' Andrew pointed out.

'I know. It was the right thing to do. But maybe not the right thing to keep on doing,' Bridget said. 'You've opened my eyes with this stay, Andrew. To a different way of doing things.'

'We won't be able to do this on a regular basis,' he said in alarm.

'But when we can,' she said, 'we should. It's not just about being responsible. It's about getting joy from life. I've always worried about the future. But this *is* the future. And we have to embrace it.'

She kissed him. She'd never kissed him in a hotel room with a glass of champagne in her hand before. It felt decadent and lovely and very, very erotic.

Andrew suddenly remembered the bath.

'Afterwards,' murmured Bridget.

Andrew laughed. Afterwards was a good time. A good time for everything that wasn't right now and perfect. Afterwards they could worry about everything they needed to worry about. But now . . . now it was Christmas, and his wife was taking off her linen dress to reveal a body that was still in good shape because she'd always been busy and active.

Afterwards, he thought, he would think about the best way forward. Which wouldn't be selling the house to buy a car. If they downsized, they wouldn't have to worry . . . He stopped himself. Maybe they would buy a car. Or maybe they'd go on a round-the-world trip like Bridget's friend Tess. Or do something else together. Anything really. It didn't matter. All that mattered was that their time had come. They were kicking up their heels at last.

And it was worth it.

Carrigvore

(Featuring Andie, Jin and Cora from *Anyone But Him*)

The piano catches my eye every time I walk into the marble lobby leading to the bar. Which isn't surprising, because pianos are part of my life. It's a Steinway baby grand and it's in a corner of the room, near a window overlooking the rolling gardens of the Sugar Loaf Lodge. The first time I saw it, I wanted to play it. That happens to me a lot. I get this urge, like an unbearable itch, to touch the keys of a piano I haven't played before. I need to know what it sounds like, how each note will resonate in the space around it. Even after years and years of teaching piano and hearing kids butchering some of the world's most beautiful musical pieces, I still get an indescribable thrill from playing myself.

Playing the piano was a refuge for me when I was younger. And a refuge for me as I was growing up. Even now, although it's my job, sitting in front of the piano is still my refuge and what I do when I need time to myself, time to be calm.

And right now, I really, really need to be calm.

I should have been calm already, of course, because I'd come to the gorgeous Sugar Loaf Lodge the previous night with my mum and we'd had a fabulous Christmas Eve dinner in their superb restaurant (not normally my sort of thing;

I'm more of your bangers-and-mash sort of girl myself, but it's nice to take a walk on the posh side occasionally); we'd also had a lovely evening afterwards in the bar over a couple of glasses of wine. We don't often spend time alone together in such glamorous surroundings, and both of us enjoyed ourselves tremendously. It's nice to be looked after, which is what the Sugar Loaf does so well.

Not that I knew anything about it previously. I realise it sounds as if I'm doing myself down a bit, but decamping to luxury hotels isn't part of my normal life. It's part of my sister's – less frequently now than before, but you can't take the luxury gene out of the girl – and she was the one who came up with the idea.

'You and Mum could take the two-day Festive Package at the Sugar Loaf,' she told me when she phoned. 'It's great value this year. Liam and I will join you on Christmas Day for dinner.'

Jin and I don't often see eye to eye on plans, especially ones that involve Ma, but it seemed to me that this was quite a good one. Christmas has never been the same for her since Dad died. We all miss him, naturally, but his absence hits Ma most this time of year. There's so much emotion washing around the place that it's impossible for her not to tear up when remembering past Christmases, when we would all gather around the tree and Dad would solemnly pronounce that Santa had been because the glass of milk we'd left for him had been drunk and the carrots for the reindeer had been eaten. (She reminds us of that every year. And every year it makes her cry.)

Ma and I had spent the last few Christmases at Jin's

gorgeous house in Malahide, but they weren't total successes for a variety of reasons, not all of which were Jin's then-husband Kevin's fault. Ma tended to drink too much and get maudlin, while I felt like the awkward living-on-her-own daughter who was only invited because otherwise she'd be a lonely singleton eating cold turkey slices and Mr Kipling mince pies by herself. Not that I didn't appreciate being asked. I didn't want to be a solitary saddo overdosing on supermarket party food. But I couldn't help comparing Jin's life with mine, and although I didn't want her lavish lifestyle, I always felt inadequate when it was shoved in my face. So what with Ma's sadness and my edginess, they had never been comfortable times.

There had been vague talk this year of Ma doing everything herself in our family home at Drumcondra, because Jin doesn't live in Malahide any more, but neither of us was too keen on that. We both agreed it would be even more emotional to have Christmas at home, despite the fact that the house has changed beyond recognition from the times of Santa and reindeer. Actually, both of us feel like visitors when we go there now.

This is because Ma redecorated it completely and turned it from the faded but comfortable home we'd been reared in to somewhere far more contemporary. She did it during her fling with the gorgeous Jack Ferguson, and in the process she also dealt with her grief for Dad, who'd died at an unfairly young age. Neither Jin nor I totally approved of her road to recovery at the time; the home decor was fine, but the sexy toy boy to accompany it wasn't, and as far as we were concerned, the idea of our mother walking around the streets of Dublin with someone twenty-five years her junior was embarrassing beyond belief. Kevin, Jin's soon-to-be-ex-husband, was equally scandalised. (Isn't it strange to think that people can still be scandalised in modern society? It's amazing that we allow all sorts of weird behaviour by so-called celebrities but are far more conservative when it comes to people we actually know!)

Jin and I hatched multiple plans to split Ma and the toy boy up, justifying our actions by telling ourselves we were doing it for her own good, but the truth of it is that Jack Ferguson was the best thing that could have happened to her and we were wrong to meddle. In fact, the relationship did wonders for her. Wonders for all our family, because Jack also helped me with my decision to end my four-year affair with one of Kevin's employees. And he helped Jin realise that there were more important things in her life than the luxury Kevin had been providing for her. All in all, his time with us shattered our preconceptions about ourselves and each other and shook us out of the particular ruts we were in. We still couldn't see, however, what it was that had attracted him to Ma in the first place.

Later, he confided in me that he loved the easiness of being with her and the lack of demands she placed upon him; and when I learned more about him and his background, I understood – although I still think he was actually looking for a surrogate mother, and Ma fitted the bill perfectly. However, not being a psychoanalyst, I've probably got that all wrong, and maybe he genuinely did think that Ma was both comforting and sexy at the same time. (I really don't like using the words sexy and Ma in the same sentence. I accept that she's not an ancient crone and that she's perfectly entitled to a fulfilling sex life, but I just don't want to know about it!) Jack was actually quite sweet about me and Jin making such a mess of things with our ridiculous plans, one of which was me throwing myself at him in an effort to seduce him, thus proving to Ma that he was fickle and childish and not worthy of her. Not surprisingly, it failed. Jack told me afterwards that it was touching that Ma's two daughters cared enough about her to want to meddle in her life.

I liked Jack a lot. But I was very afraid that he'd end up breaking Ma's heart. And that was why I went against my better judgement and interfered.

In the end, though, nobody's heart was broken. Jack, who was from the US, eventually returned home to take up a job in his family business, and Ma settled into widowhood again, although this time with a great deal more zest and enthusiasm than she'd had before. But there were no new men in her life after Jack, and she continually told us that she didn't really need one. Maybe some day, she said. But not yet.

Jin (who'd also thrown herself at Jack, for entirely different reasons, none of which had anything to do with splitting him up from Ma) was sorry to see him go too, though she was far too preoccupied with the details of her divorce to worry about him very much. Unlike me, Jin isn't cut out for the simple life. She likes her luxuries and Kevin had provided them. Their house near Malahide was an absolute mansion, which intimidated me every time I set foot in it. So I can only imagine how she felt the morning after she left him when she woke up in my one-bedroomed flat. (I'd spent the night on the sofa so's she could crash out on the bed.)

It had been a complicated, messy time for everyone, but the thing was that we emerged stronger at the end of it. Ma was a bit of a celebrity among her friends for touting 'the young fella', as they called him, around with her for a while; Jin regained a level of control over her life and returned to modelling; not, obviously, catwalk stuff – she hadn't been that sort of model anyway – but she was appearing in store catalogues again and she looked great as a kind of yummy-mummy character in casual skirts and tops or a serious businesswoman in the career collections. Meantime I got on with things as I'd always done. I continued teaching music and used it to dull the pain after I'd finally told Tom that we couldn't carry on our relationship any more. It was the hardest thing I ever did and I wouldn't have been able to cope without the music.

However, I stopped feeling sorry for myself. That was the big thing. For much of my life I'd felt sorry for myself. Sorry that I wasn't as pretty as Jin. Or as popular. Sorry that I'd missed out on a place in an orchestra. Sorry that I'd ended up teaching music instead of playing it for a living. And then I was sorry for myself because I'd fallen in love with a married man. During the whole time we'd been together, even when we were at our happiest, I'd regretted the fact that I didn't have the kind of boyfriend I could show off to my friends and I hated that I spent so many of my nights alone. I was sorry, too, that he would never be able to leave his wife . . . he had good reasons for staying with her, but I resented them all the same. It's funny how, when you're having an affair, you can make everything seem reasonable, even the man you're having the affair with telling you that there can be nothing more.

Tom and I had tried breaking up before but it had never worked. After Jack, though, it did. Because Jack had made me see that I deserved more than being in the shadow of another woman, and that Tom's wife deserved more than a dismal marriage. Whether Tom and Lizzie stayed together or parted, the decision couldn't be because of me. That was what I told Tom, and at first he didn't believe me. He tried to contact me and get back together. But this time I stood firm. This time it really was over. And although I'd never felt so miserable about anything in my life before, I knew that I'd done the right thing.

The greatest difficulty after Tom was in realising that I had to go out again. To move on (as the relationship magazines and self-help books I bought by the truckload told me). I'd been so closed and insular during my time with him that I'd lost touch with many of my friends and allowed my social life to narrow to practically nothing. But the truth is, you've got to make an effort with everything. Even getting out there. Which is what I've really tried to do, although so far the results haven't been all that great. Despite the fact that he was a married man, everything had been easy with Tom. And I simply can't seem to recapture that easiness with anyone else, no matter how I try.

The first person I went out with after Tom was Dominic. He was a neighbour, living in the flat over mine. He was divorced with two kids, which, in the end, was the problem.

Having split up with someone who was married, I felt awkward about dating someone who'd been married before. Actually, I felt almost as guilty as I had when going out with Tom, even though as far as Dominic's ex-wife was concerned, everything really was totally over and they'd been living apart for years. I really liked Dominic. In other circumstances I think we could have made a go of it. But the scars from Tom were still too raw, and even caring, thoughtful people like Dominic can only take so much neurosis in a woman. He eventually stopped asking me out. At first I was relieved. Then disappointed. I decided that I was hopeless with men, went out and got drunk with some of the people from the music school and slept with a cello teacher from Budapest whose last name I couldn't even pronounce properly.

Obviously I'm not proud of that. But it was probably a good thing to sleep with someone else. And Victor was good in bed, I think. I don't honestly remember that much about it. I returned to my flat feeling bad about what I'd done but also relieved because I reckoned it meant I was moving on; and I bumped into Dominic, who was doing exactly the same.

I think I'd thought that sleeping with Victor would make it easier for me to fall for Dominic. But it was too late for that. He was moving out. A town house, he told me, on the other side of the city. Nearer his ex-wife and his children. I didn't know what to say.

'All the best, Andie.' He smiled at me. 'I hope you have a great life.'

I thought we'd keep in touch. But we didn't. And I

didn't sleep with Victor again either. There were one or two further half-hearted efforts with men I didn't really want to get to know, but they all fizzled out. So the fact is that for the past few months my life has been a man-free zone. Which is partly why I was happy to do the Christmas thing with Ma. I wasn't sure that it would be good for me to sit on my own with the telly and a tube of Pringles on Christmas Eve. I might descend into self-pity after all, and I was utterly determined that I wouldn't do that.

There was no time for self-pity at the Sugar Loaf Lodge, and that was fine with me. Ma and I participated in all the activities that were going, including dancing, which she loves but I'm not great at, though I did play the piano for a little while, which people seemed to like. It's only since Jack that I've been able to play in public and not get embarrassed about it. He made me do it during the party at which I was supposed to seduce him. I still don't play much in front of people I don't know. It would've been different with an orchestra. But I'm a private person at heart. I like pouring my soul into the music. I've done a lot of that during my man-free months.

In contrast to me, Jin bounced happily into another relationship a few months after leaving Kevin. Liam Donovan is my ex-brother-in-law's polar opposite. He's the most relaxed man I've ever met in my life. He works in the Department of Finance and hobnobs with government ministers and international bankers. Where Kevin would have been abrasive and confrontational, Liam is urbane and conciliatory. Yet he's also good at getting his own way. He's absolutely perfect for Jin and it's an awful shame she didn't meet him years ago. Liam lives three kilometres from the Sugar Loaf Lodge, and Ma and I are expecting her to move in with him any day now, though I know Ma will be a tiny bit upset; not because she doesn't like Liam, just because one of her daughters will be living outside Dublin. She's a city girl to the core. To be honest, she thought Malahide was the country, and it's less than ten kilometres from the centre of town!

So it was also because of Liam and Jin that we agreed to the Sugar Loaf Lodge. Jin had already said that she wanted to spend Christmas Day with Liam and he'd suggested that maybe we'd all like to come to his house, but, despite her new-found acceptance of relationships, Ma didn't quite feel comfortable about being looked after by Liam yet. So – in his diplomatic way – he came up with the idea of us staying at the Sugar Loaf Lodge and himself and Jin joining us there for Christmas dinner. When Jin phoned and I told Ma about it, we agreed that it was an excellent plan.

And it had been, until about an hour earlier, when I'd gone for a walk in the extensive gardens. I'd left Ma chatting with a woman around her own age who seemed to be staying in the hotel with a group of friends. I'd asked if she wanted to join me on the walk and she'd said no, that she was going to toast her feet near the huge fire in the corner of the lounge. I wanted to be outside for a while – I love walking in cold, crisp air. It resonates with music for me; each crunching step over frosted grass is like the swish of a brush on a drum. Birdsong, the rustling of evergreens, the sound of trickling water – all of these things form sonatas in my head. I never listen to an MP3 player when I'm walking. The music is inside of me all the time.

And until the moment I saw them, the music was beautiful. A playful gavotte scampering around my mind. Cheerful notes running into each other. Amusing but serene. Which abruptly changed into a minor key when I turned the corner. Because they were there. Tom and Lizzie (I always think of her as Lizzie because that's the name he had on his mobile for her, even though he used to refer to her as Elizabeth). She was pushing a pram. It was one of those desperately expensive ones that are built for off-road walking or maybe even mountain trekking. The kind that you don't ignore. Not being good at babies, I couldn't tell how old the one in the flashy pram was. Old enough to be propped up and looking about, anyway. There were plenty of blankets wrapped around it, and it wore a Christmassy red hat with a white bobble on it.

I stared at them in complete amazement.

The reason why Tom and Lizzie's marriage had gone through such difficulties was because she couldn't have children. Every time she got pregnant she miscarried. It sent her into a whirlwind of depression and Tom into my arms. When we'd split up the last time, Lizzie had just lost another baby. Tom had said that he couldn't go through it again. He'd begged me to stay with him, because there was no way he and Lizzie could carry on. It had taken all my self-control to say no.

I couldn't avoid them. The pathway was narrow and they were walking straight for me. Even as I debated whether I'd look like a total crazy person if I just turned around

100

and began running back to the hotel, I caught the flicker of recognition in Tom's eyes.

I took the deepest of breaths and held it until they were opposite me.

'Andie?' There was an inflection in his voice as though he were asking a question.

'Tom?' I put the same into mine.

'How amazing to see you here.'

I thought he sounded like someone on a particularly terrible afternoon soap.

'You too.' So did I.

'Elizabeth – you remember Elizabeth? – and I came for a walk in the gardens,' he said. 'We wanted to get an appetite before dinner. We live close by, moved here a few months ago. Lizzie, you know Andie Corcoran, don't you? Jin Dixon's sister.'

We knew each other. We'd met before I'd started the affair with Tom, and once or twice afterwards, too. I smiled at her and she smiled back. Not much of a smile, though. Tom always said that she didn't know about me and him, but it was hard to truly believe that. She'd seen us dancing at some work function once, and she must have registered the way he was holding me and the way my head rested, for a millisecond, on his shoulder.

'And this is . . .' I gestured awkwardly towards the baby.

'Tuyen,' said Tom.

'It means angel.' Elizabeth bent down and tucked the blanket more closely around the baby.

'You adopted?' I could see the baby's features now, its smooth face and almond-shaped eyes.

'From Vietnam.' There was a light in Tom's eyes that I'd never seen before.

'Congratulations.'

This time Elizabeth's smile was brighter.

'Thank you,' she said. 'We'd waited so long and we didn't think . . . but then we got our chance.'

'I'm glad things worked out. I'm very happy for you.'

'And you, Andie? How are you?' I wondered if Elizabeth could hear the underlying concern in Tom's voice.

'Great,' I said robustly. 'I'm staying here for Christmas. With my family.'

'Is Jin here?' he asked.

I nodded.

'How's she been since the divorce?'

'Working,' I replied. 'And happy.'

He couldn't ask too much more. After all, he'd been a barman employed by Kevin. We should only be the merest of acquaintances.

'Are you staying for dinner?' I asked.

'No.' Tom shook his head. 'It's cooking in the oven at home. No luxury country hotels for us. We just came up here for the walk.' He laughed and so did Elizabeth. And I felt a band of jealousy tighten around my heart.

'Well,' I said, 'I'd best be going. I want to get as far as the lake.'

'OK,' said Tom. He looked at me hesitantly. 'Um . . . happy Christmas.' Then he leaned forward and pecked me on the cheek. The touch of his lips and the scent of his aftershave made me dizzy.

'Happy Christmas.' I moved away from him and smiled,

frozenly, at Elizabeth. 'Have a great New Year too, and I'm so pleased for you and Tuyen and everything . . .'

'Thank you.' She linked her arm proprietorially with Tom's and began to walk down the pathway again. I counted to twenty before I turned back to look at them. But they'd already disappeared from my view.

There was no reason I should have been so upset by seeing Tom again. I was the one who'd broken off the relationship; I was the one who'd made sure it had stayed broken. But seeing the result, seeing him with her and their baby and so clearly happy at last, had totally unsettled me. It wasn't fair, I thought as I stood beside the dark waters of the lake, that I was the one on the margins. That I was the one without a family of my own. It wasn't fair that he could go back to playing happy families when my heart was as broken as it had ever been.

'Andie, are you going to stand there staring at the piano all day?' My mother, already in the lounge waiting for me, sounds impatient as her words splinter my thoughts.

'I . . . sorry . . . no . . . did you want a drink?' I have to drag my mind back from the image of Tom, Lizzie and their baby and the melancholy music that seems to have enveloped me. 'I thought we were going to sit by the fire and wait for Jin and Liam.'

'Yes, but you can do that with a drink.' Ma looks at me as though I've lost my mind.

I walk away from her and to the bar and order a Bacardi and Coke. While I wait for the barman to fill a glass with white wine for my mother, I take a large swig of my Bacardi. It doesn't settle me, but I don't really expect it to. Alcohol never has the effect it does in the movies, where someone downs a whiskey or a brandy and feels instantly better. When I gulp back a drink, I feel instantly worse.

'Is everything all right?' She's managed to nab comfortable chairs close to the fire.

'Absolutely.'

'Are you sure?'

'For heaven's sake!' I put my drink down on the table and look at her impatiently. 'We're in one of the nicest hotels in the country on Christmas Day. Why shouldn't everything be all right? And why shouldn't I be sure that it is?'

I take another gulp of Bacardi and look around the lounge. I don't know if I'm expecting to see Tom and Lizzie again; whether deep down I think that maybe they're really staying in the hotel and that they'll pop up just when I'm least expecting them. But there's no sign of them among the guests, who are all getting into the spirit of the day. Some of them are sporting party hats; others look quietly elegant and one or two ever so slightly frazzled (like the dark-haired girl in the red jumper and the tailored trousers, whose eyes are positively tortured. She reminds me of myself in the days before I dumped Tom. And she reminds me of how, quite suddenly, I'm feeling again).

My mother is looking at me curiously, and I know that I have to pull myself together. I study my watch.

'Jin and Liam are late.' It sounds lame.

'Probably having sex,' says my mother equably. Since Jack,

she's been much more outspoken about everything. It freaks me out. Just as I don't want to think of my mother's sex life, I don't want to think of my sister's either. I glower at her.

'What?' The return look she gives me is one of injured innocence.

I'm about to lecture her on the appropriateness of speculating on what Jin and Liam are up to when they arrive. For a moment, as they walk towards us, Jin is the centre of attention.

My sister is one of the most stunning women in the world. Even if she never did quite make it to the top of the modelling tree (and we both agreed that that was a good thing, because she's not naturally stick-thin; she has a few curves in the right places and so she would have to starve herself to wear designer clothes), she still has model features. And she can wear clothes in a graceful way that simply passes me by. When she was married to Kevin, she spent an absolute fortune on designer gear. After she left him, she kept most of it, but whereas previously she wouldn't have dreamed of wearing something from the previous season's collection, now she mixes and matches quite happily. And she looks, as I said, stunning.

'Hi, Ma.' She stoops to kiss our mother on the cheek. 'Happy Christmas. Same to you, Andie.' I get a hug. Then she shrugs her coat from her shoulders and sits on one of the high-backed armchairs. 'Are we late?'

'No,' says my mother. 'It's lovely to see you. And you too, Liam.'

I like Liam in a way that I never liked Kevin. First of all, he absolutely adores Jin, and it's kind of life-affirming to see

105

two people so very much in love. Kevin, I think, saw her as an acquisition. She was his trophy wife. The younger second wife, which didn't help things when their marriage came under pressure. I never thought he respected her as much as he did Monica, the first Mrs Dixon. But I'm making judgements without knowing the full facts. However, Liam both loves and respects Jin, and in the six months they've been together, he's always treated her like a princess. Which is perfect, because that's exactly how Jin likes being treated. A more impoverished princess than she was when she was with Kevin, though, because although Liam earns a respectable salary, it's nothing like the squillions that Kevin brought it.

Nevertheless, they are an almost nauseatingly happy couple, and Ma and I had discussed the possibility that they might announce their engagement at the Sugar Loaf Lodge this year. Ma thought it would be romantic. I thought it'd be a bit sentimental, but then Jin goes for the whole sentiment thing, so I wasn't ruling it out. I was glad that Jin had found someone like Liam. She's the sort of person who needs a man in her life.

Me – well, I'm used to being single now. At least, I should be.

I can't believe I'm thinking about Tom again. I can't believe that meeting him has knocked me so badly. I'm over Tom. I have to be, don't I? Because of the baby. It suddenly comes to me in a lightning flash of realisation that I hadn't been over him after all. Not really. I'd always had something to fall back on. The fact that he and Lizzie didn't have a child. That they weren't a real family. And that maybe one day he would leave her and it would be nothing whatsoever to do with me at all. But that he'd find me and tell me that he loved me, and in the end, like all great love stories, we'd be together.

But we won't. And today is the first day I've really believed it.

Jin looks more beautiful than ever as she sits opposite me, totally unaware of the thoughts colliding in my head. She has left her old life behind her and she really has moved on, and I bet that she doesn't think for a single second of Kevin and what he's doing now (not remarried, but apparently squiring a younger version of Jin around town. Tacky, I think).

'Oh, listen, Liam and I have some news, and we were going to keep it till after dinner, but I absolutely can't.' Jin smiles at me and Ma as she reaches out and takes Liam's hand. I glance at her hand too, expecting to see a diamond sparkling on her finger, but she's still wearing the small ruby she bought herself the day she moved into her rented apartment. (Kevin is paying for that. Everyone says she let him off quite lightly, because she could've probably got the palatial house in Malahide, but she said she didn't want it.)

Ma looks at her expectantly and I think I look expectant too, but I'm having to clamp down on a spurt of jealousy. I absolutely do *not* want to be jealous of my sister, who has found happiness with someone who loves her. And who'll look radiant at her second wedding, which will be as tasteful as the first, I'm sure, even if not quite as glittering.

'I'm pregnant.'

At first I don't realise what she's said, and then I do and I know that I'm crying.

Jin and Kevin broke up mainly because, like Tom and Lizzie, they didn't have children. Although in this case the reasons were entirely different. Kevin, with two of his own from his marriage to Monica, was utterly adamant that he wasn't having any more. Jin, however, had grown obsessed with the idea of a baby of her own – that, in fact, was why she'd thrown herself at Jack. She'd had a mad notion of getting pregnant by him. (She was pretty stressed at the time; she's not really the sort of woman who'd jump on a guy to get pregnant. Honestly.)

'Oh, Jin, darling. How wonderful.' Ma is hugging her and kissing her and I'm rapidly wiping the tears from my eyes while Liam looks quietly pleased with himself.

'Is this what you wanted?' I ask, and everyone looks at me a bit crossly because it's as clear as anything that it is. Liam confirms that he's delighted at the news and then Jin says that they'll probably get married after the baby is born but the thing is that she doesn't feel she needs to be married to Liam for him to love her. But, she adds, she wants to be married to him as a statement of their commitment to each other. Which could all have been very corny and senti-mental but actually wasn't.

'Are you happy for me?' she asks, turning to me, and I say that I truly am while clamping down on that green-eyed monster that has a hold of me still.

*

Dinner today is a buffet, and we join the happy throng, who are attacking the carvery as though they haven't eaten in a fortnight, even though most of them were in the posh restaurant last night. The girl in the red jumper is ahead of us. I'd thought, as I watched her earlier, that she was here on her own, but now I realise she's with someone. I'm a bit confused by this, because I'm nearly certain he was in the restaurant last night too, but by himself. Maybe, I think, they've had a row and this is turning into their worst Christmas ever. Because for all the enforced jollity, it's a shocking time for rows and arguments and families falling out, never to speak to each other again for years.

I wonder what Tom and Lizzie are doing now. If they've taken their turkey and ham out of the oven, and if he's carefully carved them and told her he loves her and . . . I cannot believe I'm thinking like this. I was better, I really was. And now . . .

'Are you all right, Andie?'

I know Ma is worried about me because I can see it in her eyes. I don't want her to worry. I'll get over this. I will. I swallow hard and fix a bright smile on my face.

'Just getting sentimental,' I tell her. 'Don't mind me.'

After dinner, people play charades. Ma is good at this. Our team, the four of us plus a friendly couple called Andrew and Bridget, are neck and neck with the four women of Ma's age and the guy who earlier on that evening I saw helping his wife/girlfriend out of the restaurant. She was totally pissed; her hair was falling around her face and she was unsteady on her high-heeled shoes. But he led her away with a tenderness and concern that made me want to cry. The way I'm feeling right now, everything makes me want to cry. Even beating the team calling themselves The Golden Girls by a single point.

Jin and Liam leave at midnight. Jin says she's tired, which she's putting down to the pregnancy (in her day she was an all-night-party person). Liam hugs me and Ma and tells us that it's been a wonderful Christmas and that he hopes we'll have many more together. We agree that it was fantastic and we congratulate them again on the baby. When they go, Ma flops into one of the oversized armchairs and smiles.

'I'm so happy for her,' she says. 'It means so much.'

I nod.

'And it proves that eventually everybody finds what they want.'

I'm about to pull her up on this and tell her that it isn't true. Some women desperately want babies but they remain childless, unable even to adopt like Tom and Lizzie. I wonder if that woman will be me one day. I honestly haven't worried about the baby thing before, but today has made me think differently. About me and moving on and what I want from my life. I still don't know, to be honest. I don't know if I'll ever want a baby or if I'll meet a man I could even consider having one with. I don't know if I'll ever find someone to love. Or someone who loves me back.

'You will,' says Ma, and for a moment I think I must have spoken out loud. She leans forward and takes my hand in hers. It's a long, long time since she's done that. Not since I was in primary school, I think, and Ursula Gordon told me that she wasn't going to be my best friend any more. I'd come home crying my eyes out and Ma had hugged me and sat me down beside her and taken me by the hand and told me that Ursula Gordon didn't deserve to be my friend and that one day I'd forget all about her. Which was true, because I haven't thought about her in years!

'You'll find the right person, Andie,' says Ma. 'And when you do, he won't be taken by someone else.'

I feel as though a bolt of electricity has shot through me. Ma doesn't know about Tom. She's never known about him. I went to enormous lengths to make sure she didn't find out.

'What sort of fool do you take me for?' she asks, still gripping my hand. 'I know you. I know my daughters. I always knew there was someone but that he wasn't the right person. I didn't know why for a long time. And then I guessed.'

My lips are dry and I'm finding it hard to swallow.

'And then I did find out and I was angry for you, sweetheart, but I knew that you'd have to do it your own way.'

'When did you find out?'

'A while after I met him.'

Me and Tom had bumped into Ma and Jack one evening in a Chinese restaurant. It had been horribly embarrassing and I'd worried she'd known who Tom was, but I was certain she hadn't.

'He was vaguely familiar. I wondered about him. I

111

wondered why you never talked about him or brought him to see me. The way I looked at it, there was only one reason.'

All the time I was worrying about her, I didn't ever think that she was worrying about me.

'Jack told me,' she says. 'I asked him and he told me.'

'He was supposed to keep his big mouth shut.' I sound truculent.

'Not his fault.' Ma grins. 'I can be very persuasive.'

OK, I don't want to know how she persuaded him.

'Why didn't you say anything?'

'Your life,' she tells me. 'I didn't want to interfere.'

That's obviously a dig at how I tried to interfere in hers.

'I saw him today.' The words come slowly. 'He was with his wife and their child. They were walking in the gardens.'

'Oh, Andie.' Her fingers tighten around mine. 'I'm so sorry.'

There's a strength coming from her that I've never felt before. I can feel it flowing through her fingers to mine, spreading along my arms and through my body. A few seconds earlier I thought I was going to cry again; now I know that I'm not.

'It's all right.' I know my smile is faint. 'I'll be all right.'

'Are you sure?'

I can still feel the strength as I nod.

'Yes. I am.' This time my smile is more solid. 'Seeing them was a good thing. It's drawn a line in the sand, taken the safety net away.'

She nods.

'Really,' I tell her as I slide my hands from her. 'Really, I'll be OK.'

I get up and walk over to the piano. The lounge is a third full. People are talking in muted tones, most of them tired from the jollity of the day.

I lift the lid. I touch the keys. And this time when I start to play I can feel a burden being lifted from me and I know that Ma is right. That some day I'll spend Christmas with the man I love and with a family of my own. And for the first time since I met him, I'm not thinking of Tom as the music spills from my fingers.

Keadeen

Grace was the eldest. She was also the organiser. She was the one who, for the last five Christmases, had booked the hotel and told Phil and Carmel where they were going. They'd been happy to leave it up to her and she was happy to be the one they'd left things up to. Last year they'd stayed in the Radisson in Galway; the year before that it had been the Sheraton in Athlone; and for the three previous years they'd gone to a small, family-run hotel in Cork, which had closed down after the proprietor had been diagnosed with heart trouble and decided (as his wife told Grace on the phone) that running a hotel was far too much bother for someone with a dicky ticker.

The Sheraton and the Radisson had both been lovely, but this year would be Gill's first Christmas on her own and they felt she'd be happier staying somewhere quieter and more intimate. Grace had suggested the Sugar Loaf Lodge and, as usual, they'd all agreed. She'd booked the rooms back in August, a month after the funeral of Gill's husband, Iggy. They hadn't said anything to Gill for a few weeks, but when they told her, she was pleased. She'd often said that the Golden Girls' Christmas trip sounded like great fun.

Well, Grace thought, it *was* fun. She worked hard to make sure that it was. She sometimes wondered if the others appreciated exactly how much effort she put in on their behalf: researching hotels, checking the facilities, making sure that they had the appropriate entertainment laid on, and a host of other little details – but she doubted it. Carmel and Phil just assumed that she'd organise their trip every year and they always fell in with whatever she decided. They never helped out with the research and never offered any suggestions. (Not that Grace would have welcomed their intervention, but still, it meant that the success or failure of every Christmas was entirely her responsibility.) Gill, naturally enough, had been only too happy to let someone else look after her this year. Despite having been a rock all through Iggy's illness, she'd been struggling a bit since his death. But she was doing her best, Grace knew. She was trying to be cheerful for everyone else's sake.

Even if it was a bit of an effort for her, Grace was glad that Gill had come along. Four was a much better number than three. It meant two rooms, for starters. There'd always been an issue about rooms before; whether they should all try to share, or have single rooms (almost impossible at Christmas), or whether one would have a room to herself but they would split the cost . . . Honestly, Grace thought, sometimes she'd needed the skills of Ban Ki-moon to work it all out. But she always did. They always agreed with her plans. Women invariably came to an agreement, she told herself as she bagged a table in the bar for them after dinner on Christmas Eve and ordered a gin and tonic. Women together were so much better at getting on with life than men; so much better at sorting out their differences. Most women, anyway. Not all of them. She was about to allow herself a few minutes of frustrated misery, but the barman arrived with her drink, so she put on her enthusiastic face again. She didn't mind really. There was no point in getting upset.

Her mobile phone buzzed. It was a message from Phil, saying that they would be down in a few minutes. Richard, Gill's son, had called just as they were about to leave the room. That had delayed them.

Grace knew that Richard had asked Gill to join his family for Christmas. But she'd been firm about wanting to be with her friends. He'd been affronted and she'd soothed his feelings. She'd been soothing them ever since.

You always had to soothe your children, thought Grace, as she sat back in the comfortable armchair and sipped her gin and tonic. You always had to make allowances. Though they weren't so good at making allowances for you. At least not until you were old enough to be a worry. And then they were on to you all the time. That was what Carmel often said. Grace's own experience was somewhat different. But then that was her own fault. As Melanie had pointed out over and over again.

Melanie was Grace's only child. They hadn't seen each other in months. But Melanie saw Len, Grace's ex-husband, every bloody day.

Grace Bellew had first met Len Geraghty exactly fifty years earlier. He was twenty and she was eighteen. Carmel, who had been Grace's best friend ever since they started primary

116

school together, had introduced them. Len worked with Carmel's brother, Tom, in Boland's Flour Mills and the two of them cycled the two and a half miles from their homes near The Coombe to the Mills every day. For a short while, earlier in her teens, Grace had wondered if she and Tom would get together. It would have been convenient, she thought, and fun to go out with her best friend's brother. But they never quite hit it off. She once heard him call her 'Carmel's opinionated friend', which was annoying. So after that she stopped thinking about him as a potential boyfriend. (It was important for a girl to have a boyfriend, even if you weren't thinking about getting married. There was a cachet about having a boyfriend that all of them, including Grace – despite the fact that she didn't think much of most of the boys in her area – desperately wanted.)

Grace met Len at a Christmas party. It was the first proper Christmas party she'd ever been to, held in a hotel and not somebody's house. She wasn't actually a guest, though. Carmel worked at the hotel, and because casual staff had been needed for the event, she'd asked Grace if she'd like some extra work. She'd said that there were jobs for Tom and Len too, in the kitchens. The money was good, and although the boys had no chance of seeing the style that was at the party (which was really the only reason Grace agreed to go), they all wanted the money.

And the style was wonderful. The party was hosted by Mrs Victoria Afton-Forde, whose husband was a surgeon at one of the top hospitals. The Afton-Fordes were, as Grace's mother described them, West Brits, descended from English people who'd come to Ireland centuries before and

117

been given vast amounts of land. But everyone liked Victoria Afton-Forde, who, despite being rich and glamorous, was also fun-loving and generous and wasn't above herself at all. Grace knew that Victoria was an older woman – she had grown-up children, after all – but she didn't look half as old as her own mother. In fact, on the night of the party she looked stunning, wearing a long silk dress in deepest scarlet, with painted nails, impeccable make-up, and her shining golden hair pinned up in an elegant style. Grace ached to be like Mrs Afton-Forde, but unfortunately she didn't know any prospective surgeons or people with money, so she wasn't sure how she'd manage to achieve the other woman's social status. And her confidence. Grace couldn't help wondering if it was the money that made you able to tell people what to do in a way that made them do it. Or whether it was something inside you. And how was it, she wondered as she deftly cleared away empty bottles, that all the men at the party looked so damn handsome? Surely having money didn't mean you got all the good looks too?

Len Geraghty didn't have money and he wasn't exactly handsome, with his dusty blond hair, blue eyes and freckled, open face; but he was hard-working and kind and, unlike Tom Cantwell, he didn't seem to think of her as opinion-ated. Len was a relaxed sort of man who seemed to like being with a woman who had opinions of her own and who would make decisions for him.

That meant he was the only male on Meath Street inter-ested in Grace Bellew. Most of them preferred to be the one in charge. None of them really wanted to go out with a girl who was bossy and headstrong and who talked constantly about getting a job and making money of her own.

Grace didn't see herself as either bossy or headstrong. She was independent. She wanted to do better for herself than her own mother, who had been weighed down by the responsibility of rearing six children without much help from a husband who'd never recovered from being shot in the leg during the civil war that had followed Irish independence in 1922. Mamie Bellew would never have been able to host a Christmas party like Victoria Afton-Forde. It wouldn't even have occurred to her that it was something she'd be able to do.

But times were changing, Grace knew that. And she was looking to the future. Women like her were getting a better education, getting jobs and making lives for themselves. They were earning money of their own and not being dependent on men for everything. Grace thought this was a good thing. Even though her own mother worked hard, she still depended on her father. Not for money any more, because Charlie couldn't work. But for a sense of herself. For being a married woman. Grace thought this was ridiculous, but at the same time she understood it. Times were changing, but not everyone could change with them.

She would sometimes sit in the bedroom that she shared with her three sisters and think of the type of future she wanted. Successful, she thought. One in which she was an important person. Maybe even glamorous, like Victoria Afton-Forde, or like the Hollywood actresses in the films she saw with Len when they started dating. Her favourite actress was Natalie Wood, in *West Side Story*, which she saw five times.

119

(Only once with Len, though. She also went with Carmel, with two of her sisters, and with one of the girls from the office where she'd got a job as a telephonist.) She thought that Natalie was wonderful as the doomed Maria. She took to wearing her hair in the same style as Maria and draping a peach organza scarf over her head. It was a look that suited her and softened her rather hard face. Len told her that she was pretty. And witty. And bright. He sang the words to her as they walked home from the cinema together. Which made her laugh. Len always made her laugh. She couldn't help liking him even though he had no ambition.

Carlo Ginelli, whose parents owned the fish and chip shop around the corner, told her that she looked pretty too. When Grace came first into the chipper wearing a pastel pink knitted cardigan over a tight skirt, her organza scarf around her head and her eyelashes lengthened by the black block mascara that she'd bought out of her wages that day, Carlo gave her his best smouldering look, along with extra chips, and told her that she was the prettiest girl ever to come into the shop.

Grace had known Carlo for years but she hardly ever spoke to him. She considered herself head and shoulders about someone who worked in a chipper, even though Carlo had turned into a heartbreakingly handsome man, tall and spare, with olive skin and dark brown eyes. Not unlike Richard Beymer in the musical, although thinner. At work he dressed in a grey T-shirt and old trousers. But when he was out he wore dark suits, white shirts and narrow ties. He was a much snappier dresser than anyone else in the neighbourhood. And far more handsome than most of them too.

120

There was a certain frisson in being called pretty by Carlo Ginelli. But she wasn't going to let that turn her head. She wasn't going to let any man turn her head because she had plans of her own and they didn't include head-turning men.

She knew she was clever. She seemed to pick things up more quickly than any of her friends. She could finish crossword puzzles that other people had abandoned; she was good at mental arithmetic and problem-solving. She was quick and efficient in her job as a telephonist, and because of this she was moved, after a few months, to working in the administration department. She was just a clerk but she knew that she could be more. The chief clerk was a thin, mean-spirited man named Robert Cassidy, who wasn't half as quick and clever as she was. Grace wanted to take over from him one day. She knew that Robert Cassidy earned twice as much money as she did. But he didn't deserve it. When she became chief clerk, she'd certainly deserve it. And maybe she could even become the head of the company. It wasn't totally impossible. Unlikely, right now. But not impossible.

In the meantime, though, the move to administration meant an increase in her salary, which she kept secret. She already gave the bulk of her wages to her mother. She wanted to keep the extra for herself. She saved some and spent the rest on make-up and clothes, enjoying the way powder, mascara and lipstick could soften her face and make her seem more vulnerable on the outside, despite telling herself that she wasn't one bit vulnerable inside. The men in the office liked the women to appear a little bit soppy, and even though she had plans to take them on, she thought it better to appear unthreatening at first. Len liked her appearance too, although he didn't seem to realise that it was down to the make-up. He didn't seem to notice that she used it at all.

Sometimes she thought about breaking up with Len, because she'd been going out with him for a long time and people were expecting them to announce their engagement any day now. She didn't want to get engaged to Len. But even for someone who was thinking about having a business career, there was something reassuring about having a boyfriend to take her places. Having a boyfriend still mattered. Every girl she knew was going out with someone. Grace was a confident person. But she wasn't confident enough to be the only girl on her own. Her friends already gave her a hard time for caring about her job so much. If she said that she wasn't bothered about men or getting married or starting a family, they'd think she was a total misfit altogether.

Although he knew that she was going steady with Len, Carlo Ginelli flirted outrageously with her whenever she came into the chipper – especially when she changed her look from Natalie Wood as Maria to Anita Ekberg in *La Dolce Vita*, and shortened the hem of her skirt by an extra inch. Grace sometimes flirted back, enjoying the sensation of quick-fire chat with a boy while knowing that it wasn't ever going to come to anything.

She was so utterly determined that it wasn't going to come to anything, she really didn't know how it happened one night that she was talking to Carlo as the chipper closed, and that she walked with him all the way to the Grand Canal afterwards. She thought Carlo was a bit of a joke,

122

really. He talked such rubbish about how lovely she was and how sexy. He said 'sexy' in a sultry voice that should have made her laugh but suddenly, that night, made her melt. Grace knew that she was far more intelligent than Carlo Ginelli, so she couldn't explain, even to herself, how she'd found herself making love to him beneath the bridge at Harold's Cross. How she'd turned to him and let him kiss her. How she'd wanted to slide his greasy T-shirt over his head. And how she simply hadn't been able to stop him when he'd undone the button of her above-the-knee skirt.

Afterwards, she told herself that she would never do such a thing again. She didn't want to get a reputation, after all.

She and Len had originally talked about 'saving' themselves, but Grace hadn't been entirely sure what she might be saving herself for. She had no intention of marrying Len Geraghty. But after the night with Carlo Ginelli, she felt a desire ignite within her. A desire she'd never felt before. And so when, on the way home from the Metropole the following week, Len led her into a darkened laneway and began holding her close to him and kissing her as he always did, she responded as she'd done with Carlo, pressing herself against him and sliding her hand beneath his thin blue shirt so that her fingers were moving slowly over his skin. Len had gasped and pushed at her light jumper. She knew he couldn't keep it together any more. Nor could she. Nor did she want to.

But, she told herself afterwards, she was dicing with danger. And exciting though that was, she had to be careful. She didn't want to ruin her life, after all. And there was still the issue of her reputation.

Unfortunately, Grace hadn't been careful enough. A few

days before her nineteenth birthday, she realised that she was pregnant and she knew that the future she'd promised herself had suddenly changed completely.

She sat in her room and cursed and swore and wondered what she could do about it. Getting rid of it was an option, but not one she was comfortable with. It wasn't that she was afraid, as so many of her contemporaries were, about the sin and the Church. What she was afraid of was getting an infection and dying. She'd read an article about it in *Woman's Own* magazine. It had sounded terrible and had scared her even more than the thought of having a baby.

There was only one thing she could do. She told Len, allowing the tears to trickle down her made-up cheeks and then sobbing convulsively so that he put his arms around her and told her not to get upset. That everything would be all right. He'd make sure of it.

He insisted that they would get married. He'd always intended to marry her, he said. It would just be a bit sooner than they'd originally planned. She didn't say that she hadn't originally planned to marry him at all. It would have seemed ungrateful.

Her mother had called her a slut. But when Grace told her that she was getting married to Len, her expression changed to one of quiet resignation. She'd asked her best friend to make the wedding dress and had also given Grace some money towards the small wedding, which had been held quickly and without fuss the following month.

*

Melanie was the most beautiful baby in the world. She was born with a heart-shaped face, dark eyes and a tiny tuft of black hair that stuck up on the top of her head. She had rosebud lips and the cutest smile in the world. Len was utterly besotted by her. He kept touching her face, smiling at her, kissing her on her smooth, soft skin. Grace told him that she'd grow up to be a daddy's girl, and Len laughed and said that was perfectly all right by him. No matter how many children they had in the future, she would always be special.

Grace herself had already decided that one baby was enough. She hadn't liked being pregnant one little bit. And she never wanted to give birth again.

Len left Boland's Mills and started work in a factory on the Airton Road in Tallaght. This was convenient for him, as they'd finally bought a house, a three-bedroomed semi-detached home on the Greenhills Road. Grace was over the moon with the space both inside and outside. She loved having a garden. She spent hours sitting in it every day, playing with Melanie and sometimes having tea with her neighbours. Every woman in the estate was a new mother. Except for Phil Mallory at number 21, who worked in a city-centre office and went there on her motor scooter every day.

Grace wondered if Phil could get her a job at her office. Naturally she'd had to leave her old job once she'd become pregnant. But now that she was married and Melanie was a year old, she didn't have to be chained to the house and baby any more.

125

She asked Phil about it one Saturday, when she met her in the corner shop at the top of the road. Phil looked at her and frowned.

'Don't you have a baby?' she'd said.

'Yes.'

'Then I can't see how you could possibly work for us.'

Grace gritted her teeth. 'I can get someone to look after her,' she said, although at that point she had no idea who.

'But why would you do that?' Phil was genuinely puzzled. 'Why would you give your baby to someone else? And who would you give it to anyway?'

Grace didn't have an answer to that. She looked at the other woman with frustration. Phil shrugged and paid for her groceries. Then she put them in the basket on the front of her scooter and went home.

Grace went home too. Len was in the garden with Melanie. The baby was lying on his chest. They were both smiling. She stacked the groceries in the kitchen cupboard and blinked back hot tears. Her life was over before it had even begun. She was in the same boat as her mother. She was twenty-one and her responsibilities were to her husband and her daughter.

She wished she hadn't been so bloody stupid when she was supposed to have been the intelligent one all the time.

Melanie graduated when she was twenty-one. She'd been the first member of the extended family to go to college, and both Len and Grace were very proud of her. It was unfortunate that there'd been no work for her when she qualified, because it meant that she'd immediately headed off to the States on a student visa, but there was no work for anybody that year. Len had been made redundant from the Tallaght factory and was doing nixers on the side. Actually, the nixers (plumbing, electrical work, building – Len was good at anything physical) were bringing in nearly as much as the factory work and, crucially, they were tax free. But it wasn't secure employment. And Grace knew that Len needed security. He hated being unemployed. Hated thinking that, at forty-three, he was on the scrapheap. Grace told him that he wasn't on the scrapheap, that everyone was in the same boat, and Len looked at her tightly and said that she wasn't, which led to a bit of tension in the house, because he was right.

Grace herself was working. She'd been working ever since Melanie had started secondary school.

She'd met Malachy Gorman at an open day at the school Melanie was to join when she moved up from primary. All the parents and children had been invited along to look over the school and see what it had to offer. Grace had been astonished at the facilities: the science and language labs were bang up to date, the geography room had display cabinets and overhead projectors, and the classrooms themselves were bright and modern. She couldn't help comparing it all to her own education in the run-down city-centre school, but she was truly grateful that Melanie would have opportunities that she hadn't. It was important that Melanie would get to use her brain. She was an intelligent girl, and Grace – who hadn't tried again to find work while her daughter was still young – had used the time to coach her and give her extra lessons at home so that she would be well placed to grab any opportunities that presented themselves to her. Grace was determined that things would be different for Melanie. She nurtured her daughter's inquisitive nature, encouraged her to think about the world and her place in it and endlessly repeated that there was no need to rush into having boyfriends or getting married – that both of these things were unnecessary for clever girls like her.

Malachy Gorman spoke to Grace when they were both in the science lab looking at the racks of beakers filled with fluids with labels like Hydrochloric Acid (Conc) and Potassium Sulphate.

'I'm not convinced that a posse of teenage girls should be let loose in a room with dangerous acids,' he remarked.

And Grace, who had been wondering what Hydrochloric Acid (Conc) was and what on earth Melanie would do with it, turned to him with an irritated look on her face.

'Why shouldn't girls learn about acid?' she demanded. 'Do you think they're more likely to do unsafe things with it than boys?'

Malachy looked surprised. 'No. No. It's just . . .'

'You're all the same.' Grace snorted. 'Sexist.'

She'd recently read *The Feminine Mystique* by Betty Friedan and wasn't in the mood to give a man the benefit of the doubt.

'Hardly,' said Malachy mildly. 'I'm here, amn't I? Practically the only man in a gaggle of women.'

He was right about that. The parents at the open day were mainly mothers.

'Why are you on your own?' asked Grace.

'My wife's an invalid,' said Malachy simply. 'Too many stairs to be negotiated here, so I came.'

'I'm sorry.' Grace felt bad about snapping at him.

'Don't be.' He grinned. 'I like spirit in my women. Kathleen is very spirited. You wouldn't even realise that she had mobility problems.'

'Well, I *am* sorry,' repeated Grace. 'I shouldn't have made judgements. But I so want my daughter to do well . . . I want her to have opportunities.'

'If she's anything like you, I'm sure she will,' said Malachy.

Grace laughed at that. She told Malachy that the only opportunity she'd had in her life was to get married. But that she hadn't done much by way of anything ever since. She wished, she told him, that she'd had a proper job, but nobody liked taking on married women. Even though things had changed in the last few years and places like the civil service now allowed women to stay on after they got married, the culture wasn't to give married women jobs. It was to keep them at home, cooking meals for their husbands. Ireland was an antiquated country, she said, no matter how much people liked to think otherwise.

Malachy listened to her with interest and asked her what sort of qualifications and experience she had.

She said that was the point really. She'd no qualifications and had gained no new experience over the last thirteen years, even though she'd done well in the office job she'd landed after school.

'But you run a household, don't you?' said Malachy.

'It's not hard.'

'You manage the income and expenditure. You make sure that meals are on the table, that laundry is done, that bills are paid.'

'Yes.'

'It's the same as running a small business,' he said.

She stared at him and he grinned.

'That's what Kathleen tells me. And she's right. I look after her because of her illness. But she looks after everything at home. You must do too.'

Grace thought of the pile of ironing that was waiting for her after the visit to the school ended. She supposed he was right. But she probably wasn't the best housekeeper in the world. And ironing sheets wasn't exactly a great intellectual challenge.

'I'm looking for a secretary,' said Malachy. 'Would you be interested?'

She'd wondered, for a time, whether he was looking for something more. Len had wondered that too and had been dubious about her taking the job. But Grace had been determined. Melanie was supportive. And in the end Malachy had only wanted a secretary who was competent and efficient, which Grace turned out to be.

The company grew and expanded during her time with it – all the way through Melanie's secondary education, while she was at college and for a few years afterwards, until Malachy retired and it was taken over by a rival. Grace was sorry to see Malachy go. She would have stayed with the company, but it simply wasn't the same without him. Besides, she'd had an offer from one of Malachy's clients to come and work for them in their accounts department. Which she did.

That was when Len had been made redundant. Grace told him that it didn't matter, because she was being paid more than he'd ever earned in the factory anyway. She was glad that she'd done something for herself, which, in the end, had been for the family too.

Melanie came back from the States in the early 1990s. She had grown into a stunning woman, with her dark hair highlighted, her teeth whitened and her skin glowing with health and vitality. West Coast living, she'd told Grace, who was utterly astonished at her daughter's beauty. And worried by it too.

As far as Len was concerned, no man was good enough for Melanie and when she arrived home one day with her boyfriend, Cian, and a massive engagement ring on her finger, Len's first reaction was one of antipathy towards the man who had stolen his child, even though he knew that he was being ridiculous. Grace was equally restrained in her delight, which surprised Len because he knew that she liked Cian. But, she told him afterwards, she wondered whether getting married meant that Melanie would be devoting less time to her career. Melanie was working in an investment bank, and although neither Grace nor Len knew much about banking, they did know that Melanie had a great job and was on an astonishing salary. Cian

131

worked in the bank too. Neither of them was short of money or struggling in the way that Grace and Len had when they'd first married. And although Grace and Len had put money aside to help pay for Melanie's wedding, their daughter told them not to be silly, she and Cian could afford it themselves.

They compromised on the cost in the end. It was a wonderful wedding.

Melanie had a baby almost straight away. They'd started trying at once, she told Grace in the hospital, cradling baby James in her arms. Being in her thirties meant that there was no time to waste. Not like your day, she'd said, when most women had their first child before they were twenty-five. Or like you, before you were twenty-one. Grace told her that she was lucky to have had a life before having a baby, and Melanie had frowned and asked if Grace regretted having her. She'd sounded agitated and Grace had rushed to say that the day Melanie was born was the happiest in her life. No question. Just as she was sure that the day James was born was the happiest in Melanie's. Her daughter smiled and they hugged each other. And Grace sighed with relief.

Len had to go to hospital himself shortly afterwards. He'd been diagnosed with an enlarged prostate and they wanted to run some tests. Nothing serious, Dr Jackson had said cheerfully, just routine. Just precautionary.

Len didn't have a serious disease, which was a relief. But the results were a shock to him all the same.

There had been a part of Grace that had always known this day would come. That one day the truth would emerge. She'd known it from the moment she'd first set eyes on her beautiful daughter, whose dark eyes and pouting mouth were so very clearly a genetic inheritance from Carlo Ginelli and not Len Geraghty. And now they'd proved it. She'd hoped that somehow Len wouldn't find out. But the doctors investigating his prostate problems discovered that he was infertile. So there was no chance, no matter how remote, that he could ever have been Melanie's father. No need, as it turned out, for Grace to have been adamant about birth control for so many years.

Grace and Len had forged a marriage based on together-ness, not passion; on doing the right thing. He'd given her moral support when she'd told him that she wanted to work when no more children had come along. She'd given him financial support when he was unemployed. She had always deferred to him in public while sometimes arguing vociferously with him in private. She thought that he didn't try to achieve his full potential. He thought that she was too restless. She was often impatient with him. He didn't understand her need to be involved in so many different things. But they were married, and she wanted it to work; so when she complained about him it was always in the exasperated way that all women complain about the men in their lives. And when he told her enough was enough she would nod and agree with him. Because he was a good father to Melanie, who truly was a daddy's girl and who utterly adored him.

Melanie was shocked. And angry. She wanted to know who her father was. How Grace had known him. Where he was now. She wanted to know if he knew about her. She wanted to know everything about him. She wanted to know who the hell Grace thought she was keeping this information from her. And from Len. Who she called Dad.

Len told her that he wanted a divorce. Grace stared at him in utter amazement.

'We're been married for over thirty-five years and you want a divorce?' She tried to make a joke of it.

'You married me under false pretences,' said Len.

'No I didn't,' Grace told him. 'You were far more likely to be Melanie's father than anyone else.'

'But I wasn't, was I? And you knew it.'

'I didn't!' she repeated. 'I absolutely didn't. You were the one, Len.'

'The one what?' he demanded. 'The one who believed everything you told me. The one who believed your life would be ruined if I didn't marry you. The one who was played for a fool, that's what I was, Grace Bellew.'

'So I didn't tell you the whole truth,' she said. 'But it

was years ago, Len. And you can't throw away what we've had over all this time.'

'Can't I?'

'We love each other!' she cried.

'Do we?' he asked. 'Do you really love me, Grace? Did you ever?'

'Yes!'

'More than him?'

'I didn't love him,' she said.

'But you had sex with him.'

'It was . . . passion,' she said.

'And with me it's not.'

'You're my rock,' she told him.

'You don't need a rock,' he said.

It had happened nearly fifteen years ago and yet she still felt a raw pain whenever she thought about it. She supposed that it was the same pain as Len had felt when he'd found out about Melanie's father. Although she knew that in his case it must have been far, far worse.

What was most difficult for her was the fact that Len and Melanie had grown even closer afterwards. She hadn't expected that to happen. After all, she was Melanie's mother. Her blood relation. She was the one who'd carried her for nine months and given birth to her and suffered for her. Len, when it came down to it, wasn't part of her at all. But Melanie said that she and Len had been far closer than she and Grace had ever been. That Grace might have given birth to her but that Len had always been there for her.

Who was it, she demanded, who'd been at home to give her dinner when she got in from secondary school? Grace had wanted to yell at her that it had to be Len because he was unemployed at the time and she was working, but she knew it was a waste of time. Both Len and Melanie felt betrayed by her. And now she felt abandoned by them.

Carlo Ginelli had emigrated to Canada in the 1980s. He was married and living in Vancouver. He had five other children. Melanie, when Grace gave her this information, decided not to contact him. He might be her father, she said, but he wasn't her dad.

Len always went to Melanie's for Christmas. She made it into a big traditional occasion. Her three children, James, Aoife and Brendan, all loved Grampy Len (who they cheerfully called Grumpy Len whenever he complained about anything. Which, to be fair, he hardly ever did, except to amuse them). And although they met Grace throughout the year, she knew that they never had as much fun with her as they did with him. They called her Grandma. But they were polite, not affectionate. As Melanie was too.

Grace had never been good with Christmases. She'd always thought the family stuff was highly overrated. Early on in her marriage there had always been a big debate about whether she and Len would go to her parents or his; or invite her parents or his to their house. Len always wanted to go to his family, where Christmas was noisy and traditional. And he never wanted them to come to their house, because Grace was hopeless with the little touches that he liked – the mistletoe over the kitchen door and the Christmas carols CD playing on repeat in the background. Grace shoved up the tree and arranged cards on the sideboard, but that was pretty much that as far as she was concerned.

The first Christmas after the divorce, Melanie rang Grace and asked her what she was doing for the day.

'I don't know,' Grace had told her. 'I haven't decided yet.'

'Do you mind if I ask Dad here?'

'Of course not,' said Grace.

'I know he could go to his sister's, but I'd like him here.'

'That's fine.'

'You'll be OK, won't you? You'll have somewhere to go? You talked about going to Aunt Maud's before.'

Grace's older sister had moved to Australia with her husband twenty years previously. Grace had mooted the idea of going to Sydney a few times, but Len hadn't been interested. She didn't really blame him. She wasn't especially close to her brothers or sisters. It could have been awkward.

'That's a good idea,' said Grace, even though she had no intention of visiting Maud.

Instead, she asked Phil Mallory, who she'd got to know quite well, what her plans were. Phil's husband had died young and she'd never remarried. There had been no children either. Phil said that she didn't have time for them. She ran a travel agency.

Grace and Phil had gone to Tenerife for Christmas. They'd had a great time.

In all the years that followed, she and Phil had spent every Christmas together. Carmel had joined them after her husband had died. And now Gill was part of the group too. They'd stopped going abroad for the holiday season when air travel had become so stressful. Much better, they all agreed, to come somewhere lovely like the Sugar Loaf Lodge, which you could get to in under an hour, and be pampered and cosseted straight away.

She wished, though, that she had someone. That was the only thing. The understated luxury of the hotel, the fun and laughter of the games and the dancing, the superb dining and the fabulous surroundings didn't entirely compensate her for the fact that her daughter preferred to be with Len than with her. It wasn't that she actually wanted to spend Christmas in Melanie's house. It was that she would have liked to have been asked.

'Hi, Grace!' Carmel sat down beside her. 'The other two will be down shortly.'

'Good,' said Grace.

'Everything OK?' Carmel had seen the faraway look on her friend's face as she'd been sitting alone.

'Absolutely perfect,' Grace told her as she placed her glass on the table and gestured to the barman.

138

Carmel asked him for a vodka and orange. Grace requested a tonic without the gin this time.

'We were just saying that it's been great so far.' Carmel leaned back in the chair 'The bridge this afternoon was fun, wasn't it?'

'I enjoyed it,' agreed Grace. 'There's dancing later this evening. I've already had my eye on one or two men who might be able to hoof it with us.'

Carmel grinned at her. 'And I bet they have their eyes on you too.'

Grace laughed.

'You look so lovely,' Carmel said. 'That trouser suit is fabulous on you. You wouldn't think you were a day over fifty.'

'What a compliment.' Grace smiled.

'It's true,' Carmel looked at her appraisingly. 'You look younger now than you did twenty years ago.'

'It's nice of you to say that,' Grace said. 'But we both know you're talking rubbish.'

'Ah no,' said Carmel. 'I've always thought . . . well, Grace, being a single woman suits you.'

Grace frowned. It was a long time since she and Carmel had talked about her broken marriage. When Len had insisted on the divorce, it had been Carmel that Grace had turned to and Carmel who had supported her. As she'd done all of her life. From before Len to after him. Never judging her, just being there for her. A true friend.

'I should never have married him,' said Grace ruefully.

'You did what you had to do back then,' said Carmel.

'I lied to him,' Grace reminded her. 'I lied to him for thirty-five years.'

'As you said yourself, it was a sin of omission,' Carmel said.

'I always knew, though.'

'So did I.'

The two of them shared a complicit smile.

'I just wish she didn't blame me so much,' said Grace. 'I wish she understood more.'

Carmel nodded sympathetically.

'But you can't make people do what you want, can you?' Grace sighed. 'I did my best. I always have done.'

'And you can't keep beating yourself up over it,' said Carmel.

'I don't.' Grace sat up straighter in the chair and her expression hardened. 'I did for a while, and then I realised that it wasn't doing me any good. Or anyone else.'

'You're a strong woman,' Carmel told her. 'Isn't that what the business supplement called you?'

'A strong leader,' Grace corrected her.

'And you are,' said Grace. 'You are for me and for Phil and for Gill. And you are for the company too.'

Grace smiled at her friend. 'Thank you,' she said.

'I know you get upset at this time of year,' said Carmel. 'It's natural. Everyone does. You think about the past, about the mistakes you made and how you should've done things differently. And you think about your family and compare it to other people's and it always comes up wanting. But you have to remember that you did make a success of things, Grace. You really did.'

Grace nodded slowly as she took the tonic from the tray the waiter had just brought over and added half of it to her glass. Carmel was right.

When she'd moved to the accounts department in

Malachy's client's company, she'd set up new systems straight away. She'd saved the company a vast amount of money. And eventually she'd been made the CEO. It had been a huge honour. The first woman CEO. And then, later, the first female chairperson. Who had negotiated some tough deals to keep the firm ahead of the competition, and who had brought it unprecedented success.

And unprecedented rewards for her and for Len and for Melanie.

She'd made a settlement to him after the divorce. His lawyers said that he'd sacrificed his career for her, so that she could become rich and successful as she'd always wanted.

She'd paid up without too much argument. She could afford it, after all. Just as she could afford to be here, in the Sugar Loaf Lodge, and not care that they were having Christmas together without her. She wondered what they said when they unwrapped the expensive presents she always sent. She wondered if they thought about her and how she might be spending her day. She wondered if they thought she preferred being in the hotel to being at home with them.

She regretted not telling them the truth before. But she'd learned, through the years, that beating yourself up didn't actually help. And there was no point in wanting to change things that couldn't be changed. Only those that could.

She raised her glass slightly and smiled as she and Carmel wished each other a happy Christmas. Her smile broadened as their two friends joined them. She was lucky, she reminded herself. No matter what she would have liked to change, she'd still had a better life than her mother. Which was what she'd wanted most of all when she was eighteen years old.

Two Rock

The idea of going away for Christmas was enticing, but it was something that Jim and Laura couldn't really afford. Adding to their debt wasn't reasonable, Jim told himself as he read the ads on the back page of the newspaper, and he was usually a reasonable man. A few years earlier he wouldn't even have noticed the cost of a couple of days away, but times were tougher now and nobody was spending money on stuff they couldn't afford. Least of all people who had bought houses at the top of the market and were now firmly in negative-equity territory. Which was what they were.

Jim and Laura's commuter town house (the developer's claim that you could get into the city centre in forty-five minutes was still unrealistic, despite the fact that traffic had lessened during the recession) was worth about half of what they'd paid for it and was a millstone round their necks. They'd hoped to trade up eventually and move closer to the city, but that now seemed highly unlikely. Nobody wanted to buy houses in the commuter belt when there were plenty available nearer to town at knock-down prices. Every so often someone would bring out a report saying that property prices were on the up again, but Laura and Jim had a horrible feeling that they'd rise more in the areas they wanted to buy in rather than where they lived now. They felt stupid and cheated and angry with themselves, and with the bank too. But the way they looked at it, they had to keep going. There was no point in getting depressed.

Their bank manager had actually lost his job a few months previously, although Jim said it was through a redundancy programme and not because he'd lent them far more money than they could easily pay back. They wondered if he was struggling like them, but somehow they doubted it. They were living to the strictest budget they possibly could, in which every cent they spent was accounted for, which was why they should make a decision about spending Christmas with either Angela or Caroline and live with the consequences. The trouble was, thought Jim, that he wasn't sure that living with the consequences would ever be worth it.

Laura agreed with him. The whole thing about Christmas was totally doing her head in, and it seemed to her as though everything and everyone was getting out of control: her parents, his parents and, most scarily, her relationship with Jim. Neither the stress of how to spend Christmas nor his solution to it was doing them any good at all.

Yet it was all so silly and needless! What was the point in putting pressure on them to spend Christmas in one house or the other when it was just one day in the whole year, and when they visited both sets of parents over the festive season anyway? But this year was different, because it was Kirstie's first Christmas and both grandmothers seemed to think that it was a badge of honour to have the

143

baby spend it in their house. As if, Laura muttered darkly to Jim, Kirstie would know anything about it. She was only six months old, after all! The problem was that Laura's mother, Angela, and Jim's mother, Caroline, had morphed since Kirstie's birth from two apparently normal women into two of the most competitive grandmothers the world had ever known. The moment Laura had been allowed to have visitors in Holles Street hospital, both of them had turned up brimming with advice on the upbringing of their first grandchild.

'For heaven's sake!' Laura had snapped at her own mother after she'd listened to a litany of do's and don'ts. 'It's not an exam. I'll learn. You did, didn't you?'

'It was different in my day,' said Angela. 'We weren't expected to rush back to work. We had more help, too.'

'I'll be fine,' said Laura, although she wasn't entirely sure about that. She was feeling a bit sniffly and down but she didn't want Angela to know. Angela was never down. She'd see it as a sign of weakness and use it as an opportunity to lecture her even more.

Caroline, who came in later, put her arms around her and gave her a massive hug. Caroline had never hugged Laura before, and the experience was unnerving (Laura had always suspected that she was second choice as a daughter-in-law as far as Caroline was concerned; she was sure Jim's mother would have preferred it if he'd married his previous girlfriend, Samantha, a successful PR executive, instead).

'I'm so delighted for you!' cried Caroline. 'Here. Let me take photographs for my Facebook page.'

Laura didn't really want pictures of Kirstie on Facebook,

or indeed on any of the many other social networking sites that Caroline seemed to use. As far as Laura was concerned, she was the only one who should be putting up pictures of her daughter anywhere. But when she said this to Caroline, her mother-in-law looked mortally offended and said that only her closest friends would be able to see them, and that Kirstie was her grandchild as well as Laura's daughter . . . It had all got a bit heated, and Laura hadn't been able to stop herself bursting into floods of tears. When Jim walked into the room and found her blowing her nose, he'd told Caroline to leave, which had left Laura feeling guilty.

'You're the most important person in the world to me,' Jim had assured her when she eventually apologised for upsetting his mother. 'You and Kirstie. Don't worry about it.'

But she did worry about it. She worried about Caroline and she worried about Angela and she worried that she was caught between two women who'd lost the plot entirely. She worried that she was losing the plot herself. The grandmothers had taken to calling around to the house at unexpected times during the day to check on Laura and make sure that she was coping, which was driving her crazy. (Both of them felt – though they didn't say it to each other – that Laura was suffering a bit from the baby blues. Well, Angela called it the blues. Caroline had taken Jim to one side, mentioned post-natal depression and given him a number of websites to check out. Jim told his mother not to be stupid, that Laura was perfectly fine, but he did keep a closer eye on her afterwards, just in case she started exhibiting signs of not loving their wonderful daughter.)

Laura herself knew she wasn't depressed. She could cope perfectly well until Angela or Caroline arrived on the doorstep dispensing words of advice. Then she would get flustered and anxious and do stupid things; on one occasion she found herself changing Kirstie's nappy after already having just changed it five minutes earlier. (Caroline had been there at the time, and reported back to Jim that his wife was very frazzled, poor love, and that he should consider sending her for a consultation. Just in case.)

'I don't know what's got into her,' Jim told Laura later that evening. 'You're grand, aren't you?'

'Do you think there's something wrong with me?' demanded Laura. 'D'you think I'm losing my marbles?'

'Of course not,' Jim assured her. 'She's overreacting, I know she is. And I'm sorry for even listening to her. '

'Oh, I don't blame you,' Laura said. 'Both her and my mother are driving me bonkers these days, so I'm not surprised she makes remarks about it. Mum rang three times today because I told her that Kirstie had a bit of a cold. Every time I got the poor child to sleep, the bloody phone went off. I put it on silent eventually and then realised that I'd missed a call from my pal Bernie because of it!'

'They'll get things into perspective in a while.' Jim tried to sound philosophical. 'And I suppose it's good to know that they're both eager to help out.'

'If only they didn't give conflicting advice.' Laura looked hunted. 'I mentioned to Mum that because of her cold Kirstie was having trouble sleeping, which was why I was freaking out every time she rang up. She recommended vitamin C and taking her to the doctor for paracetamol or

146

its baby equivalent if it didn't clear up. Then your mother called and said it wasn't a cold at all and that she was teething. So she had different remedies for that. But in case it *was* a cold she suggested some homeopathic stuff which in a million years I'm not giving her!'

'Calm down.' Jim could hear that Laura was getting agitated. 'We both know she has a cold and it's getting better. So you do whatever you think is right for her.'

'Thank you.' Laura leaned her head on his shoulder. 'You're a pet, really. I don't know what I'd do without you.'

Despite the presence of the grandmothers, Laura was enjoying being a new mum at home with Kirstie. But because of their financial pressures she went back to work as soon as her paid maternity leave was finished. Both Angela and Caroline offered to look after Kirstie while she was out all day, which threw her into another bout of panic. The poor child would be totally confused by their conflicting views on how she should be reared. She'd probably end up with all sorts of issues afterwards and it would be all Laura's fault. If it had been an option she would have given up work and stayed at home, but that simply wasn't possible.

Caroline had made a few niggly comments about the disadvantage Kirstie would be at with Laura rushing back to the office, especially as it meant that her granddaughter would have to be bottle-fed, which Caroline insisted would lower her natural defences. She told Laura that babies did best with their mother's milk, and Laura said she knew that but there was nothing she could do about it, they needed her salary. Caroline said that it was fortunate she was around to help look after Kirstie.

Angela knew all about having to go out to work, because she'd done it when both Laura and her younger sister Celine were small, and she didn't think it had done them any harm. Made you independent if anything, she remarked, reminding Laura that her own grandmother had done a good job of looking after the two girls while Angela was working. Angela had resigned from her office job when she got pregnant with her third child, saying that it was too much effort to try to do everything. It'll be fun looking after Kirstie, though, she told Laura. I bet I'll be a lot better as a granny than a mammy.

With offers of help from both mothers, Laura was in a quandary. She didn't say to Jim that she'd prefer Angela to do the looking-after because, being totally honest with herself, she was more in tune with her mother's down-to-earth approach than with Caroline's yummy-grandmummy efforts, although she did agree that using natural products was best and she tried very hard to buy organic food whenever possible. (Angela said that organic produce was a waste of money; hadn't she reared four healthy girls on fertilised and sprayed food? Laura wasn't sure either way, but she wanted to do whatever was best for her baby.) She was also more confident about her mother's parenting abilities because she'd seen her looking after Celine, Deirdre and Janice and she knew that nothing panicked her. She thought that Caroline was much more likely to get into a fuss about things, although that was only based on the fact that her mother-in-law was always asking for updates about Jim's health and well-being.

Jim, however, was quite happy to think of his mother

148

looking after Kirstie. It would be very convenient, he said, since his parental home was only a fifteen-minute drive when you got on to the motorway, whereas even though Angela was closer, local traffic could cause horrendous delays sometimes. Besides, he said, Caroline wanted to help. He'd have thought, he added, that Laura would want that too, given that their relationship hadn't always been the easiest. It was good to think that Kirstie was bringing them closer.

'The thing is,' Laura admitted eventually, 'I'd really like my mum to do it.' She'd thought and thought about it and had finally come up with the perfect reason. 'After all, she's used to girls. Your mum had two boys.'

'I can't see that it makes any difference,' said Jim. 'A baby is a baby after all.'

'Still . . .' Laura used her most persuasive voice.

'My mum really wants to help out,' said Jim obstinately. 'I think she should have the chance. Kirstie's her grandchild too, you know.'

How could I ever forget, thought Laura. Caroline banged on and on about it often enough!

She took a deep breath. 'OK. How about my mother does three days and yours two?'

Caroline said that she was perfectly happy to divide it the other way round, but in the end Laura got what she wanted. Angela looked after Kirstie Mondays, Tuesdays and Wednesdays and Caroline had her Thursdays and Fridays. Both Laura and Jim agreed that they were actually very, very fortunate to have mothers who were prepared to mind their child at all. Most grandparents, Jim said, were silver surfers these days, wanting to be out and about having a good time and not worrying about things. Very few would commit themselves to looking after a baby. Laura agreed. Sandra Hannigan, her supervisor, was paying a fortune for a crèche for her two small children. She said that she was pretty much working to pay the crèche fees but that, in the end, they were a little bit better off if she kept her job. Though it was marginal at best, she muttered, and they were keeping the whole thing under constant review.

So even though balancing the desires of the grandmothers could occasionally be traumatic, and even though it some-times caused Laura and Jim to flare up with each other (which always reduced Laura to tears – she wished she didn't cry so much, but ever since Kirstie's birth she couldn't help herself), both of them were very grateful to their mothers for being so helpful and supportive.

At least, that was how it was until they started talking about Christmas.

It was Angela who brought the subject up first. Angela had always been very organised about Christmas, buying the children's presents every October and hiding them in the attic so they couldn't be accidentally discovered. She used her Credit Union account to save for the festive season every year, starting each January and putting aside a fixed amount, so that they always had enough money to buy what each child wanted. (And if any of them asked for an outrageous present, Angela somehow managed to persuade them that they didn't want it after all.) No matter what, every Christmas was magical and exciting in the McIntyre household, and Angela's careful budgeting meant that there was always plenty to go round.

She first spoke to Laura about it at the end of September.

'Oh for God's sake, Mam,' Laura said impatiently. 'It's months away.'

'Good to be organised, though,' said Angela. 'You and Jim will be having dinner with us as usual, I'm sure.'

'I haven't talked to him yet,' Laura said. 'On account of the fact that summer is only just over.'

'It'll be great,' said Angela. 'The girls will just love having Kirstie here.'

All three of Laura's sisters still lived at home. She supposed it would be a novelty for them to have a baby in the house. She didn't say anything to Jim. He would have freaked if she'd mentioned Christmas to him even before the clocks had gone back. He was already shouting at the TV over the Hallowe'en ads.

It was at the start of November when he told her that Caroline had asked them to Christmas dinner. Laura looked at him in dismay.

'But we never go to your mum's,' she said.

'We haven't until now,' he agreed. 'But she so wants to be part of Kirstie's first Christmas.' He smiled. 'She says she feels more like a second mother than a grandmother to her.'

Laura looked horrified.

'*I'm* Kirstie's mother,' she said firmly.

'I know. I know.' Jim hugged her. 'I was touched by what Mum said, that's all.'

'My mother assumed we were coming to her,' said Laura, deciding that she'd better come straight out with it. 'I didn't say no because I . . . well, I assumed so too.'

'Oh.' He frowned. 'But your mum won't mind, surely? After all, she has three other girls. My mother only has me and David.'

David was Jim's younger brother.

'And,' continued Jim, 'you've always said we should change it round a bit, go to my folks for Christmas day for a change.'

'I know, I know,' wailed Laura. 'It's just . . .'

'What?'

'My mum will be upset, that's all.'

'So will mine if I say no.'

'She'll get over it.'

'What makes you think that?' demanded Jim. 'Why should my mother get over it more quickly than yours? She has feelings too, you know.'

'I'm sorry!' cried Laura. 'I didn't mean . . .' She broke off as Kirstie began to whimper. 'We'll talk about this later.'

It was Caroline's turn to look after Kirstie the following day, and she arrived just after Jim had left for work. Laura was loading the dishwasher with dishes from dinner the night before; she'd fallen asleep in front of the TV after they'd eaten and couldn't be bothered to stack them when she'd woken up. She didn't tell Caroline this. Caroline thought that she and Jim had a proper breakfast every morning. She wouldn't have approved of the fact that Jim bought a takeaway coffee and muffin on his way into the office and that Laura bought Pop-Tarts to have with her cup of coffee when she arrived at the Revenue Commissioners. Caroline believed in healthy eating and insisted that a good breakfast was part of it. Laura agreed with her on a theoretical level. It was simply that, practically, it was never possible.

'What's this I hear about you not wanting to come to dinner with us on Christmas Day?' Caroline asked as she walked into the kitchen and draped her scarf over the back of a chair. 'You know you promised.'

'I did?' Laura was looking for her purse, which seemed to have disappeared into thin air.

'Last year,' said Caroline firmly. 'You said you'd definitely come to us.'

'I don't remember.' Laura finally found the purse on top of the chrome pedal bin. How on earth had it got there?

'You must remember,' said Caroline. 'It was when you called around on December the twenty-eighth. The first we'd seen of you.'

Laura put the purse safely in her bag. 'I'm sorry,' she said. 'I honestly don't remember. But if you say so . . .'

'Yes,' said Caroline. 'And I've got in loads of stuff.'

'You have?'

'Absolutely. So you have to come.'

'Um. Right.' To be fair, thought Laura, Caroline was entitled to think that her son and daughter-in-law would spend one Christmas with them. She'd just have to explain that to her own mother.

'But not Kirstie's first Christmas!' wailed Angela. 'I've so much planned already.'

'Mum, she's not even one yet. She won't notice.'

'*I* will,' said Angela. 'I wanted to do the same stuff with her as I did for you all on your first Christmases. The picture under the tree. The stocking on the fireplace. Unwrapping presents. You can't not come.'

Laura couldn't handle the guilt. 'I'll talk to Jim,' she promised.

'My mother has a whole schedule planned,' said Jim when Laura asked if it would be possible to compromise. 'She says it's dependent on us being there by lunchtime.'

'Oh for heaven's sake! It's not a military operation!' cried Laura.

'You think my mother's being military? What about yours? Frau General Obersturmführer of Organisation?'

Laura looked angrily at her husband.

'You're being hateful,' she said.

'You're being unreasonable. And so's your mother.'

'And so is yours,' cried Laura before she burst into tears.

After two days of tension, Jim broke the ice. He suggested that they stay at home for Christmas. They wouldn't visit either set of parents. They would set up their own traditions for Kirstie, which wouldn't include anyone else.

'I understand how you feel,' said Caroline, when Jim called round to break the news. 'It can be a stressful time, especially for a new mum who isn't coping. So I have a great suggestion. Me, your father and David will come to dinner with you. But you don't have to worry. We'll bring everything prepared. The turkey, the ham, the stuffing – everything. I'll have potatoes and vegetables ready to be cooked so Laura won't have to lift a finger. I know her oven and her microwave now anyway. I'll do everything to perfection.'

'That's very thoughtful.' But Jim wasn't entirely sure Laura would think that way. And he wouldn't tell her that Caroline thought she wasn't coping.

Laura looked at him blankly. 'I don't believe it.'

'It's a compromise,' said Jim. 'I know it's not us on our own, but at least we're not setting up a tradition of going to Mum's for Christmas, which is what bothered you.'

'That's not what I mean.' Laura sounded glum.

'What then?'

'While you were out, my mother rang and offered to do the exact same thing.'

'You're joking.'

'No,' said Laura. 'I'm not. Though obviously in our case it's Celine, Deirdre and Janice too.'

'Oh, for crying out loud!' Jim was exasperated. 'What is it about mothers that makes them so impossible?'

'I'm a mother too,' said Laura.

Jim said nothing.

'You think I'm impossible?'

He hesitated.

'You do.' Her lower lip trembled. 'I bet you're sorry you

ever married me.' She walked out of the room and slammed the door behind her. Even though she told herself she might have just proved his point.

They were walking on eggshells around each other. Jim didn't want to provoke another eruption of tears. Laura didn't want to annoy him any further. But the issue of Christmas Day continued to fester between them, and between their respective parents, and it was the only thing that anyone thought about.

Laura couldn't understand how it had got so out of control. When she told Angela that it was only one day and that she saw her half the week anyway, Angela burst into tears (obviously a family failing, Laura thought) and said that it was the most important day of the year. And that she'd always wanted to be there for her first grandchild's first Christmas.

Caroline said almost exactly the same thing to Jim.

At the beginning of December, he sat down in front of Laura and told her that the situation was ridiculous. And that he didn't want it to come between them. That he'd married her, not her mother. And that she hadn't married his mother either.

His words made Laura smile.

'Why don't we have both sets of parents for dinner this weekend,' he suggested. 'We can talk it through like adults. I'm sure your dad and mine will be sensible about it, even if our mothers aren't.'

Laura thought this was a good idea. On Friday evening,

after work, she nipped into Marks & Spencer and bought the food. She didn't normally do her shopping in the M&S Food Hall, which she found too expensive; her usual haunt was the local Aldi. But since this was an important night, she wasn't going to risk cooking something from scratch and having it all go horribly wrong. It was worth spending the extra money for M&S presentation.

The two grandmothers had dressed up for the occasion. Angela was wearing a red wool suit that Laura had last seen on her the previous year when she'd gone to the christening of a neighbour's child. Caroline had chosen a black and white dress that Laura had seen in the window of Brown Thomas two weeks previously when she'd been in Grafton Street. Angela's suit was warm and seasonal. Caroline's dress was coolly elegant.

'Thanks for having us.' Louis Devanney planted a kiss on his daughter-in-law's cheek. 'It's lovely to see you.'

'You too,' said Laura, who liked Louis more than his wife.

'Hiya, honey.' Her dad hugged her. 'Hope you haven't been slaving over a hot oven all day.'

Kirstie was sitting in her baby chair and gurgled at the newcomers. She was the sunniest, happiest baby in the world, Laura thought, as she watched her allow herself to be lifted up and cuddled. It was a pity that she was causing so much trouble!

The topic of Christmas wasn't raised until after they'd finished dessert (crème caramel, which Laura knew that Caroline liked) and Jim was pouring coffee.

'So,' Angela said briskly. 'Let's sort out this Christmas thing once and for all. I have a suggestion.'

'What?' Everyone looked at her.

'That Jim and Laura come to us as they always do. And that they go to you, Caroline, for New Year's. That way I get to see my granddaughter for Christmas but you get her for the beginning of the year.'

'They've always come to us for New Year's!' cried Caroline. 'Your suggestion is nothing new.'

'I didn't know they went to you for New Year's,' said Angela. 'Laura, you said you spent it at home last year.'

'New Year's Eve,' she explained patiently. 'Not New Year's Day.'

'Oh. Sorry. I got that wrong.'

'Did you?' asked Caroline. 'Or were you just being your usual disingenuous self?'

'What d'you mean by that?' demanded Angela.

'You do this kind of frazzled-mother thing,' replied Caroline. 'As though everything is last-minute. And unimportant. When deep down you know it's not.'

'Don't be silly.'

'It's true,' said Caroline. 'Jim says so.'

Everyone turned to Jim, who looked hunted.

'I just said that Angela isn't as disorganised as she seems,' he said feebly as Laura glared at him.

'I seem disorganised to you?' said Angela. 'Really?'

'Not exactly,' he said. 'Just . . . harried sometimes. But not . . . not disorganised, Angela. No. Absolutely not. After all, you start planning for Christmas months in advance.'

'Hmm.'

'Well, your suggestion is worthless. Louis and I have a better one,' said Caroline.

'Oh?'

'That they set up a new tradition and come to us. You've had them as a couple. We can have them as a family.'

'That's unfair,' said Angela. 'Besides, everyone knows that girls are closer to their mothers. I need my daughter and her daughter around me at this time. It's more natural.'

'Are you saying there's something wrong with my son?' asked Caroline.

'Oh for God's sake!' Laura looked at both of them. 'You're talking nonsense, the pair of you.'

'I'm just saying that it's important to have traditions,' said Angela.

'You're making them up as you go along,' retorted Caroline.

Laura looked pleadingly at her father, who shrugged help-lessly. Meanwhile Louis Devanney was pouring himself another glass of wine.

'Why don't you stay with them on Christmas Eve?' said Angela suddenly to Caroline.

'That's not the same.'

'I'm working on Christmas Eve,' protested Laura.

'Yes, but Caroline could cook you a nice organic chicken or something,' said Angela. 'It would be a wonderful present, because it takes the pressure off you.'

'The pressure *is* off her,' said Caroline. 'She doesn't have to cook on Christmas Day. At least she won't in my house, if we have them.'

'She won't in mine, either.'

'Would you both stop it!' cried Jim. 'We're not people

159

you can "have". We're not being passed around like a bloody parcel.'

'We don't want to pass you around,' said his mother.

'But is it Kirstie or is it me and Laura you actually want on Christmas Day?' he asked.

'We want you all,' said his mother. 'We want to be a family together.'

'We're all family,' said Laura's dad, Fred. 'We don't have to be together for that.'

Laura felt as though she was a spectator as the conversation whirled around her. Angela, adding to her suggestion about Christmas Eve, suddenly said that perhaps Caroline and Louis could stay overnight with Jim and Laura and so would be there on Christmas morning to see Kirstie with her presents. Louis said that this was quite a good idea, although Laura had caught her breath at the thought of it. But then Caroline reminded him that they did have another son and that David would be devastated at being left on his own at home, because obviously there wasn't enough room at Laura and Jim's for him too. Not that he'd been asked. Laura exhaled with relief.

'Nobody is being asked.' It was Jim who finally lost his temper.

'Maybe we could just call around,' murmured Caroline.

'And we could too,' said Angela.

'Quite honestly, I don't want either of you to do that,' said Jim. 'I've listened to more rubbish tonight than I could've believed possible. You're both being silly and selfish, and Laura and I will spend Christmas on our own.'

'There's no need to be rude,' said Angela.

'He's not being rude,' Caroline told her.

160

'I am,' roared Jim. 'I'm being so rude I'm telling you all to sod off home before I lose my rag completely.'

'You know they'll come anyway,' said Laura later that night when he told her that they would stay at home on Christmas Day, lock the door and not let anyone in. 'And then they'll probably have another row. And so will we, because I can't stand you being rude to my mother. Even if she deserves it.'

'I'm not having my marriage wrecked and our first Christmas with Kirstie ruined because of our families.' Jim's tone was forceful. 'No matter what it takes.'

He'd left it very late. Even though hotels were advertising on the back pages of the newspapers, many of them didn't have availability any more. Which made Jim think that the whole thing about recession was a con – it was only fools like him and Laura who were struggling; everyone else had plenty of money to splash out on expensive seasonal packages. Because even the cheapest of them wasn't really cheap.

The Sugar Loaf Lodge was a last-gasp attempt. They didn't have an ad in the paper but he remembered going to a friend's wedding there a couple of years earlier and it had stuck in his mind as a really nice place. Secluded but not isolated. Stylish but not stuffy. It would be lovely, he thought, to spend a peaceful, family-free Christmas there with his wife and baby. It would definitely take the pressure off Laura, who was looking pale and harried and even more tearful than usual. And although it could never become a tradition – his bank balance wouldn't stretch to it – it would be a wonderful first Christmas for Kirstie.

Laura was both relieved and horrified when he told her what he'd done. She was relieved that he'd decided something and that she simply had to go along with it. But she was horrified at the cost – Jim wouldn't tell her how much it was, but she looked up the website and nearly had a heart attack when she saw the rates; she was also a little concerned that Kirstie wouldn't wake in her own bed and have presents under her own tree and experience her first Christmas in her own home.

'My head has been done in so much with all this parental arguing that I don't care how much it bloody costs,' Jim told her. 'It's worth it. As for Kirstie's memories – there's no way she'll remember this Christmas, no matter what we do. So it doesn't matter about the bed and the tree and whatever. To tell you the truth, I only wish I'd thought about going away sooner. We could have gone somewhere hot. As it is, we were lucky with this booking. It's one of their annexe rooms that they don't normally use for visitors in the winter.'

'Are we going to freeze to death?' asked Laura.

'It's not that at all,' Jim told her. 'It's just that it's in a separate building a couple of minutes' walk from the house. The walkway isn't covered. All their other rooms were booked, and when I asked if there was any chance of a cancellation, because it was really important to us to get away, they suggested this.'

'It won't be awful, will it?' asked Laura. 'I'm not sure

about being away at all, but if it's awful . . . well, you don't want to have a bad experience at Christmas.'

'Bloody Christmas,' said Jim. 'Honestly, you'd swear it'd blight your life for ever if everything isn't perfect.'

'I know. I know.'

'It *will* be perfect,' Jim promised. 'Don't worry.'

Easy to say. Not entirely easy to do. Laura wondered how much they'd pay for Jim's decision in the future. And not just in monetary terms, either.

He was right about it, though. It was perfect. The room was warm and toasty and had a wonderful view over the rolling gardens. When they arrived on Christmas Eve, there were carol singers around the piano and a happy buzz of conversation in the bar. Because they'd had to wait until both of them finished work, it was late in the evening before they reached the hotel, but the charming woman behind the desk told them that the dining room was still open, or if they preferred, she could arrange for them to have dinner in their room. And she'd smiled at Kirstie and told her that she was the loveliest baby they'd ever had in the hotel, which, although Jim and Laura knew was just being polite, was still nice to hear.

They decided to have dinner in their room, and Laura nearly cried with delight when a waiter arrived with an extending table and proceeded to lay it perfectly. There was a half-bottle of wine 'on the house' and some puréed fruit to go with the jar that Laura had asked them to heat up for Kirstie.

163

'The thing is,' she said when they'd finished and were sitting on the enormous bed watching an Indiana Jones DVD on the flat-screen TV, 'I feel as though I should be doing this at home. But it's wonderful to be looked after.'

'I know,' he said. 'And we're away from the warring parents, so that has to be a good thing.'

'We haven't even had a row ourselves yet.'

Jim nodded. 'It's been stressful,' he said. 'Everything has over the past couple of years, but these last few weeks have taken the biscuit altogether. I'm sorry if I snapped at you.'

Laura smiled at him. 'I'm sorry too. Christmas is supposed to be a relaxing time. Why does it have to get so bloody complicated?'

'Relaxing?' Jim laughed. 'Everyone gets stressed out at Christmas. We're not the only ones, I promise you.'

'True,' said Laura as she stretched her feet out in front of her and closed her eyes. 'But nobody in the whole world is more relaxed than me right now.'

They stayed relaxed. On Christmas morning they opened the small gift boxes of chocolates that had been left in their room, then brought Kirstie for a walk through the grounds of the Sugar Loaf Lodge in her pram. They passed a couple on the frosted pathway pushing a top-of-the-range stroller in which an absolutely divine Asian baby was bundled up in a red woollen jacket and matching hat. Laura smiled in acknowledgement at the woman, who beamed back at her, sharing a connection that all mothers with babies had. When they came back to the hotel, they had hot chocolate with rum, which, according to Laura, made her feel as though she'd died and gone to heaven.

'I know we'll be broke after this,' she told Jim as they sat in the lounge together before they went to dinner that evening. 'And I know that our parents will be mad at us. But it's so, so worth it. Oh my God!'

'What?' For a moment he thought that either his mother or hers had turned up. It had been a possibility that had worried him ever since he'd told them both that he and Laura were going away for Christmas and that they'd been forced into the decision by their incessant bickering and pressure.

'I've just seen a guy who works in the Department of Finance,' she said. 'I know him because he often drops into the office and I've seen him at one or two of our nights out. He's quite senior there.'

'See, now you're hobnobbing with the high-ups.' Jim grinned.

'Maybe.' She grinned too. 'Meryl Chambers told me he was gay! But I so don't think so. Look at the woman sitting with him. She's gorgeous.'

Jim's eyes narrowed. 'She's vaguely familiar,' he said.

'Well, fair play to Liam, and now I'll be able to gossip about him.' Laura chuckled, then picked up her bag and took out her mobile phone.

'Are you taking a photo?' asked Jim. 'For evidence?'

'No.' She shook her head. 'I thought that maybe my mother would have phoned. It's Christmas, after all.'

'Well, it did all get a bit heated last time we spoke.'

Which hadn't been at the disastrous dinner they'd had at Jim and Laura's. In the weeks leading up to Christmas, both Angela and Caroline had begged Laura to reconsider, and as they were her child-minders and doing her a favour, she'd felt under an avalanche of pressure. Caroline had talked about being denied her rights as a grandmother. Angela had said that she was being shut out. And Laura had been forced to harden her heart and say that Jim had made up his mind and that was that. Angela had wanted to know where they were going and she'd refused to tell her, which had caused even more anguish.

The previous day, Christmas Eve, when she'd arrived home from work, her mother had barely spoken to her. She'd left presents under the tree, which had made Laura feel an absolute bitch (even though she'd had a bag of presents to give to Angela).

'The girls texted,' she said. 'They said that Mam and Dad were a bit subdued.'

'Don't worry about it,' said Jim. 'I haven't heard from my mother either.'

'I told Celine that we were having a wonderful time here, and she said "lucky you". I bet the atmosphere at home isn't great. Now I feel bad for wrecking their Christmas too.'

'You're not to feel bad,' commanded Jim. 'We're shelling out a fortune for us not to feel bad. We can argue with them again afterwards, but let's not think about it now.'

'OK.' But Laura couldn't help feeling a little bit guilty all the same.

It was after dinner before her phone vibrated with another text. This time it was from Angela.

166

'Hope you've had a lovely Christmas,' she said. 'All fine here.'

Laura felt a tear trickle down her cheek. 'We should've stayed home,' she said. 'We should've done something . . .'

'Would you stop!' Jim grabbed the phone from her and switched it off. He'd had a text from Caroline saying more or less the same thing, but he refused to allow himself to feel bad. It was right, he thought, to put his foot down over this. The two grandmothers had been interfering more and more in their lives since Kirstie's birth. He knew that they needed them to help with looking after her. He appreciated everything they'd done. But there had to be a line over which they didn't cross. There had to be boundaries. He wished they'd been able to afford to put Kirstie in a crèche. Then their parents wouldn't have felt such a degree of entitlement. But it was nice for Kirstie to have her grannies at home. He was exhausted thinking about it. Parenting was so bloody difficult, he said to himself. It really was. Especially when you ended up parenting your parents too.

After dinner they went to the lounge and took part in the charades. They teamed up with a pretty young girl who said that she was from Poland, and an attractive, though slightly tired-looking man, who they originally thought was her father. Laura had remarked that he was probably divorced and it was his year to have her for Christmas, and Jim had nodded in agreement. They'd been startled to find out they were wrong. But they'd had a good laugh with the couple, who said they were having a great time at the Sugar Loaf Lodge and that it had definitely been the right thing to do this year. A shadow had crossed the man's face even as he spoke, but it was fleeting and not mirrored in his companion's expression. And then they turned their attention to the charades again. They weren't doing that well at them. But they were having fun. Which was all that mattered in the end.

Laura and Jim agreed, as they went to reception to check out the following day, that it had been a fantastic break. Being looked after had been wonderful, and Kirstie had behaved beautifully for the entire time. They also agreed that it had been difficult to get over the guilty feelings, but that there were times when you had to do things that made you feel bad. At least we've made a stand, Jim said as the woman at reception, who he knew was also the owner, handed him the bill. It might have cost us a lot of money, but it was important to do it.

He scanned the bill, knowing that there was very little to add to the rate for their package as he and Laura hadn't ordered much from the bar, but wanting to make sure it was right anyway.

'That's all right, Mr Devanney,' said Claire as he took his credit card out of his wallet. 'It's been taken care of.'

'Sorry?' He looked at her in puzzlement.

'Your bill has been taken care of,' she said. 'And I was asked to give you this message.'

He opened the envelope she handed him and took out the Sugar Loaf Lodge Christmas card inside.

'We hope you have had a very special Christmas,' he read.

'We realise that you have to have your own time and your own traditions. We also want to say that we love you both, and Kirstie, very much, and if you want to call into either house on your way home we'd be delighted to see you. Love Angela, Caroline, Fred & Louis.'

Jim passed the card to Laura, who read it wordlessly.

'You both have lovely families,' said Claire as she looked at them. 'And I hope you have many more happy Christmases with them in the future.'

'I'm sure we will.' Jim cleared his throat. 'But we can't let them pay . . .'

'Mrs Devanney and Mrs McIntyre were very insistent.' Claire smiled at him. 'I spoke to both of them last night.'

'How the hell did they know we were here?' Jim wondered aloud. 'We were keeping it a secret. We were afraid they'd turn up.'

'It's probably my fault.' Laura looked apologetically at Jim. 'I told Celine. Just in case there was an emergency. I suppose my mother managed to worm it out of her.'

'Probably,' agreed Jim.

'But they didn't turn up,' said Laura. 'And they worked this out between them.'

'Christmas can be a stressful time,' said Claire. 'But you've all clearly come through it. And who knows what you'll do next year.'

'Who knows.' Jim smiled and put his arm around Laura. 'Maybe we'll all come here!'

'We'd love that,' Claire said.

'So would we,' said Jim. 'But I have a feeling that we'll be having it at home. And maybe, next year, that'll be just fine.'

Berleagh

Louisa hadn't wanted to come to Ireland at all. She didn't like travelling; the continuous jolting around in carriages and being told to sit still made her head ache. And it was far too hot to travel anyway. Her soft skin itched beneath her ivory cambric and she squirmed in the seat beside her mother throughout the journey (which caused Charlotte to continually -- and futilely – admonish her to sit still). Louisa hated the dress and wished she could wear pantaloons like George and Edward instead. But her mother always insisted on bundling her into fussy clothes and curling her hair and generally trying to make her look pretty and girlie like Emily. Emily was the favourite because she acted (so Charlotte said) like a proper lady. As you should do, she'd add crossly, whenever Louisa ran around the house shrieking and jumping about. Louisa couldn't see the point in acting like a proper lady. From her perspective, proper ladies didn't do much beyond sit around all day with their sewing, or play the piano, or read 'improving' books. Oh, and look silly whenever there was a man about, as Emily often did. Where was the fun in that? At least her father, the Earl, had fun. She knew that because he was always good-tempered and made jokes a lot of the time, even if her mother didn't think much of them. Louisa felt sorry for her father whenever he had to face her mother's disapproval. Charlotte's lips, already thin, would become even thinner, and her voice would remind Louisa of icicles dripping from the ceiling. She would tell Charles that he was a disgrace and that if he wasn't careful he would ruin them all. But her father would always reply that it would take a lot to ruin the Lachfort family, and then he'd wink at Charlotte and tell her he was going to his club for a rest from her constant nagging. Louisa wished she could go to her father's club too. It would surely be far more interesting than sitting around at home being ladylike!

It seemed like they'd been on the road for ever. Some of the journey had been in miserable drizzle, before the summer heat that was making her itch so much now. Louisa was fed up with it. She wanted to go home, although she knew now that going home would entail more unbearable hours in the carriage than continuing onwards. They'd passed the point of no return. They were actually in Ireland.

Her mother hadn't been too keen about coming either. A savage land, she'd called it, even though her father had told her not to be a silly woman. The land was good, he said, and not all the people were savages. And the house they'd been gifted, in an excellent position near the Sugar Loaf mountain, was perfect. Charlotte had sniffed at that in the special way she had of sniffing, which told Charles, without words, that he was a fool. Louisa sometimes practised that sniff herself. She used it most of all on her brother Edward, who was younger than her. Sometimes she managed to make her voice sound like Charlotte's too, which made him cry. She liked making Edward cry. It was fun.

Would they ever, ever get to this godforsaken house? she wondered. (She liked the phrase godforsaken, which she'd heard Charlotte use a number of times.) She wanted to get out of the damned carriage (she liked the word damned as well, though obviously only Charles could actually use it, and he was never supposed to in front of gentlewomen) and she wanted to run. Young ladies weren't supposed to run. But she wasn't quite a young lady yet. She was ten years old. So she could almost get away with it.

'Well,' said Charlotte when they finally drew up outside the house. 'Maybe this isn't a complete disaster, after all.'

'I told you it was nice.' The Earl smiled at his Countess. 'I told you you'd like it.'

'I haven't seen the inside yet,' she said sharply. 'It might be too dreadful for words.'

But it wasn't. White Hall was beautiful. Smaller, obviously, than the house they were accustomed to. But, said Charlotte, an acceptable summer house. Even if she still wasn't convinced that the land wasn't savage and that the natives wouldn't murder them all in their beds.

Louisa liked playing with her hoop in the grounds of the house. She would spin it along the pathways and across the grass, where it wobbled wildly. Charlotte, while not entirely approving of the hoop, felt that it was better than seeing

Louisa hitching up her skirts and running across the gardens. Which she did, frequently. Especially after the introduction of a beagle into the household. Charlotte had asked Charles what on earth they were going to do with the animal when they left, and Charles said that the staff would feed it.

'Eat it, I'll wager,' said Charlotte grimly.

Louisa, who'd heard the exchange, burst into tears and Charlotte spent a good hour comforting her and telling her that she'd been making a joke, and that nobody was going to eat JuJu, who was a prince among dogs and adored by everyone who knew him. (Except Charlotte.)

The accident was a silly one. Obviously, as an accident, it was nobody's fault. Just one of those things that happened. But Charlotte blamed herself, Charles blamed himself, and the children were all numb with shock. It had nothing to do with Juju or hoops or running around, or being in the wrong place at the wrong time. It was simply unfortunate. Louisa had been skipping across the lawn in an almost ladylike way, trailing a scarf behind her. She'd been singing her favourite song in her high, breathless voice, and the words had floated across the afternoon air: *Lavender's blue, dilly dilly, lavender's green. When you are king, dilly dilly, I will be queen.* And then they'd heard the shriek and a cry and then silence.

She'd tripped, they guessed, on the scarf. Louisa had tripped and fallen many, many times, and so seeing her flat on her face wasn't anything new. But this time, when she'd fallen, she'd hit her head on a stone, which had been half hidden by the grass. On a thousand other occasions, Charles

173

said later, it wouldn't have mattered. It would have been a glancing blow. Louisa would have done more damage to the stone than it had to her. But not this time. The stone had been a jagged one and had pierced Louisa's temple. She'd lain white-faced and immobile on the lawn while everyone gathered round her, not certain what to do.

They'd carried her up to her room and sent for a physician. She hadn't moved since the fall, and her breathing was shallow. Dr Bastable looked at the unconscious girl and her anxious mother and he wished he could be more positive. But he didn't like the look of things.

He told them to keep her warm and to sponge her face. Talk to her, he said. Tell her that you're here. Comfort her. They did all these things but it made no difference. Louisa's eyes stayed closed and her breathing grew even more laboured, while Charlotte cried bitter tears and wished that she hadn't always been so impatient with her joyous daughter.

Louisa could hear them. But she couldn't seem to make them hear her. Which was extremely annoying. Because she wanted to say that she was too warm and that she didn't need all these blankets around her. And that what she really wanted was to sit outside and smell the cut grass and run around singing 'Lavender's Blue'.

When she opened her eyes for the first time, it was dark. She blinked a few times and waited until she could make out the shapes in the bedroom. She was annoyed that her mother hadn't left a candle burning, because Charlotte knew Louisa didn't like the dark. And she didn't like the shutters being closed over the windows either. She shivered. She was cold now and the blankets didn't seem to be heating her up as they'd done before. She couldn't feel the weight of them on her shoulders. She wanted to pull them up to her chin and huddle beneath them. But moving was too hard. She seemed to be stuck to the bed. She whimpered softly. She didn't like being alone in the dark. She hated it. And she hated them for leaving her here.

It was dark when she opened her eyes the second time, too, but now she could see chinks of light coming through the cracks in the shutters. She was still completely alone.

She thought about crying, but she didn't. Crying was girlish and she wasn't going to be girlish, even though she was feeling very sorry for herself. She moved slightly in the bed. At least she didn't feel cold any more, or stuck to the bed, like she had before. She pushed the covers away and sat up. She felt strange, light-headed and floaty, but that was to be expected. She'd banged her head when she'd fallen. She'd heard them saying that. So it was normal to feel . . . not quite normal, she thought, as her feet touched the ground. She wouldn't have had to get out of bed at all if people had stayed to look after her. If it had been George, the eldest son and heir, who'd fallen and banged his head, she was sure that her parents would have mounted a round-the-clock vigil. It goes to show, she thought, that I'm not important in this family. The youngest daughter is never important. She's only a burden.

She walked across the floor in her bare feet and climbed up to open the shutters. They hadn't been fastened shut properly, because they opened before she had time to tug at them. And then she frowned. When she'd fallen the previous day, the sun had been high in the sky and the trees had been green. But now the light from the sun was weak and watery and the branches of the trees were bare. It didn't make any sense. Nor did the fact that despite being in nothing more than her nightdress, she didn't feel as cold as she knew she should. She shivered. But not because of the temperature. Only because she was suddenly frightened.

She walked out of the bedroom. The house was silent. And empty. She knew it was empty. She could feel it. She could also feel the panic rising in her throat.

'Mama!' She yelled as loud as she could, even though she knew that Charlotte would be furious with her for being so unladylike. But there was no response from her mother.

'Papa!' She began to run along the corridors. 'Emily! George! Edward!'

The house stayed silent. Louisa thought that maybe it would be OK to cry. But somehow she couldn't.

'Mama!'

She was at the top of the stairs. She looked down into the wide hallway below. And she stared at what she saw. Or what she couldn't see. Because the little tables that had been dotted around and covered with knick-knacks were now covered with sheets. Dust sheets. The paintings that hung on the walls were covered too. All of them. Including the one she'd laughed at when they'd first arrived, the one of her grandfather standing beside a chair, looking fat and pompous, his silver hair tied back from his round face.

She ran down the stairs and reached for the sheet to pull it off the painting. But she couldn't quite catch hold of it. She went through the open doors of the drawing room. The shutters were drawn here too, and like the shutters in her bedroom, they opened as she drew near. She couldn't understand that. Charlotte always closed them properly. Always. In the pale light that filtered into the drawing room, she could see that the furniture here was also covered in sheets. She started to tremble. She didn't like this one little bit. She really didn't.

She ran out of the drawing room and back up the stairs. She jumped into her bed and drew the covers over her head. She was having a bad dream; that was it. It just seemed so real because of the bang on her head. She would try to think of nice thoughts and push the dream out of her mind. And then tomorrow, when she woke up, she'd see that her mother was still there beside her, and that the rest of the family were there too, and that nobody had left her all alone in a cold, deserted house.

When next she opened her eyes, it was to the sun pouring into the room. She blinked a few times, struggling with the intensity of the light. She was having trouble remembering exactly what had happened to her. Recalling it was taking a huge amount of effort, searching her mind to try to get things in the right order. And then it came. Arriving at the house. Playing in the garden. Tripping and falling. And the horrible, horrible dream of the deserted house in winter.

She jumped out of the bed. The reason that the light was flooding the room was that the shutters were open. She remembered opening them herself. She hadn't closed them again which her mother would no doubt be cross about. But it was nice to know that the sun was shining, and good to see the trees covered in green leaves. She still couldn't quite rid herself of the dream that tugged at the edges of her consciousness.

She hurried out of the bedroom. She wanted to find everyone, to tell them that she was awake and feeling so much better. She didn't know what time it was, but from the position of the sun she guessed late morning. Her mother might be in the drawing room. Emily was probably practising her music. And the lucky boys were no doubt outside in the sun.

The dust covers of her dreams had been removed from the furniture and the paintings, which was a relief. There had been a part of her that had feared they'd still be there. But everything was as it should be in the hallway and the drawing room, although there was still no sign of any of the family. Louisa stamped her foot in annoyance. Now that she was feeling better again, she wanted to do things. And she wanted people to do them with.

The main door was ajar. She didn't realise that at first, but then she noticed the breath of air coming through the gap. She stepped outside into the sunlight. It hurt her eyes. At first she saw nobody. Then, from the far end of the gardens, a man approached. He was very tall, and was wearing a cut-away coat in gold fabric, which revealed a silver waistcoat beneath and well-fitting breeches. On his feet were low-heeled leather shoes. Their large silver buckles glinted in the sunlight. The clothes were similar, yet different to what she was used to. The man himself was familiar, but Louisa wasn't sure who he was. She felt that she should know, and yet she didn't. She was annoyed with herself. And then embarrassed, because she realised that she was standing outside the house in nothing more than her night-dress while a strange man was nearby.

Yet she couldn't move. In the same way as she remembered being stuck to the bed the night before, she was somehow stuck to the ground beneath her now. She told herself that she was a little girl and that it didn't matter that she wasn't properly attired, but she knew that her mother would be furious. Propriety mattered to Charlotte. Wherever she was.

The man walked across the garden and up the wide steps leading to the door. Louisa waited for him to introduce himself, but he ignored her, walking straight past her into the house.

'Well, really!' She was annoyed. There was no doubt that she shouldn't have been outside in her night clothes, but it didn't mean he could simply pretend she wasn't there at all. She followed him into the house. He was standing in the drawing room, looking up at a portrait. Louisa recognised it as one that had been done of her father a couple of years earlier. He was standing with his hand on the back of a chair, a serious expression on his face. When the artist had been painting it, she and Edward used to come into the room and make faces at Charles behind the artist's back. Their father had found it difficult to refrain from smiling.

And he'd eventually told them to leave the room or he'd box their ears.

'This was never an important place to you. Not after what happened here.' The man was speaking to the portrait on the wall, still apparently ignoring Louisa's presence. 'And it is not an important place to me. It could never be.'

Louisa stared at him. Who on earth was he, and what was he talking about? He had no claim on the house and no claim on her father. So why was he speaking to the portrait as though he knew him?

'I know that I have not always been the type of son you would have wished,' the man continued. 'I have not kept all our estates in good order. Certainly not this one. But I have maintained our wealth in other areas as much as I was able.'

This was ridiculous. Louisa walked up to him.

'Excuse me, sir,' she said. 'But who are you and why are you in my house?'

'It is funny how one thing can change a family for ever.' The man continued to look at the portrait. 'You were once a happy man.' A smile flickered at the corner of his lips. 'Despite my dear mama. We were a happy household. But after that summer, everything changed for us.'

'I asked who you were.' Louisa was angry now.

'It's strange how we all miss her so. With the passing of the years the pain has lessened. But not gone. It will never go. I understand that.'

'Why are you ignoring me?'

'Oh, Father . . .' The man sounded despairing. 'I never realised that being the head of a family was so hard.'

Father! Louisa looked at the man in astonishment. Why

was he calling her father his father? That was impossible. He was as old as Charles, surely. Maybe even older!

Then, suddenly, the man laughed. It was a laugh without humour.

'I must be going insane,' he said out loud. 'Talking to a portrait. People will be within their rights to say that George Lachfort is quite mad.'

Louisa took a step backwards. George Lachfort! But this man couldn't be George Lachfort. Her elder brother was but sixteen years old and a handsome fellow. This man looked old and tired and lined.

'How dare you claim to be George!' she cried. 'That's a monstrous lie, sir. When I find my father, you will be flogged.' She felt better after the outburst. Now he couldn't ignore her.

But he did. He turned and walked away.

'Come back.' She ran after him. 'Come back this instant. I have to talk to you.'

She caught up with him as he reached her father's study. She tried to grab him by the arm, but her fingers slid off the gold fabric of his jacket. And she realised that she hadn't been able to feel it at all.

She was back in her room. Back in her bed. Opening her eyes. It was the sound of the shutter banging that had woken her this time, clattering, she realised, against a window missing some panes of glass. She sat up and rubbed her head. All of the previous times she'd woken up were now etched in her mind. She could remember them clearly.

Especially the last time. Seeing the man who couldn't see her. The man who'd called himself George Lachfort. She shivered even though she didn't feel cold, even though she couldn't feel the wind that had blown the shutter open.

It was dusk. She was still alone. And she was very frightened. She didn't understand what had happened to her; what was still happening to her. She wanted to believe that it was all to do with the bang on her head, but how, she wondered, how could she keep thinking and dreaming, and how could everything be so real and vivid, if she was still unconscious? She closed her eyes again and tried to visualise her mother beside her. If she concentrated hard enough, she thought she would be able to hear Charlotte's voice. She could hear someone, for sure. Saying that she was a silly, silly little girl. And she thought that perhaps she could hear crying (well, she wasn't surprised at that; they would surely be worried about her if she was still unconscious). Was it Emily she could hear? Emily telling her to come back? Back to where? Back from where?

Louisa opened her eyes again. She got out of bed. The half-light made it difficult to see the room, but she couldn't help thinking that everything looked faded. Neglected. She looked at the shutter, which was still banging against the window. It was hanging from its hinges.

There was something terribly, terribly wrong. She'd thought so the first time she'd woken, when she was all alone. And the other times too. But most especially the last time. And now she was sure.

She got up. The bedroom door swung open as she neared it. She jumped back, frightened, before walking through.

Except for the creaking of the house in the wind, everything was silent. Like before, White Hall was empty. But this time the emptiness was more unsettling. This time it seemed permanent.

She went downstairs. There were no dust covers. The furniture and portraits were gone. She thought she could see faint marks on the walls where the portraits had hung, but it was hard to tell, because the walls themselves were marked with damp. And mould. She went through to the drawing room. The portrait of her father was gone too. The music room was empty. And every other room in the house. She was shaking. They had left her here. Left her to rot! And they didn't care.

She ran up the stairs again and into her mother's room. Then into her father's. Edward's. And Emily's. They were all empty too. And then she went into George's room. There was something lying on the window casement. It looked like a miniature portrait. She rushed over and tried to pick it up. But she couldn't. It was as though her hand couldn't grasp it properly. She cried out loud. What had happened to everything? What had happened to everybody? What had happened to her?

When she opened her eyes for the sixth time, she knew. She was here, but they weren't. She was here because somehow she hadn't been able to leave. But they had. A long, long time ago. It was all very clear to her now, as though someone had explained it to her while she was sleeping. Her spirit was still in this house, but her family – they had long since gone.

Their children had gone too. And their children's children. Time had passed by and life had gone on without her, but somehow her spirit was connected to this house and it wouldn't leave. Couldn't leave.

When she realised this, she felt older. As though she'd grown up in the time she'd been asleep. She didn't know how that had worked. What had happened to her in those years when she wasn't conscious. What she did know was that while she was unaware of what was going on, time was passing. People were living and dying. Including the people who had been closest to her, the people she'd loved the most. Including Louisa herself.

She wondered why nobody came to the house any more. Surely George's own family would want to be here? Or perhaps not, she thought. After all, Mama hadn't wanted to come that summer. So maybe George's family didn't either. And maybe he was a softer father than their own papa had been. She frowned as she recalled seeing George alone in the house, talking to her father's portrait. What if he hadn't had a family at all? But that was impossible. George Lachfort would have been a catch. Girls were always being silly about him. She remembered that. Some woman would have managed to marry a daughter off to him, surely?

What about the others? She wanted to know, she really did. She wandered through the house, trying desperately to find information. But there was nothing. And even when there was, like the miniature in George's room, she couldn't pick it up. She could move around, because every time she approached

184

a door, it would swing open, but she couldn't actually touch the doors. Or the windows. And she couldn't pick things up.

She could feel the house dying around her. She could see the outside beginning to creep in. Ivy twisted its way through the gaps in the windows. Spiders spun webs around the rooms. Mice set up homes in darkened corners. She thought there were bats too, but she couldn't be certain. She'd never seen a bat before. She didn't really want to see one now.

It was a bit silly, she told herself as she glided through the cobwebbed rooms, that she was a ghost and yet she didn't want to see bats. And that she didn't like the look of the cobwebs. And that she jumped every time she heard an unexplained noise. Ghosts were meant to scare people, not be scared themselves. But nobody came to the crumbling building for her to scare. And the truth was that she wasn't really scared any more. Just lonely.

She was getting used to waking up in bed and knowing that she was alone. She realised that out of all the rooms in the house, hers was the only one in which the furniture had been left behind. Though it was beginning to look rotten now. Woodworm had eaten into the chest of drawers, and everything else reeked of damp. (Or would have, she knew, if only she could smell.) Other animals besides the spiders and the bats and the mice had made shelters for themselves within the walls. Goats. Sheep. And birds, lots of them, who now nested in the rooftops. She was getting used to them all. They didn't scare her any more.

It was the people who eventually started coming to the

house who scared her. She didn't think they were part of her family. She didn't recognise any of them. Their clothes changed every time she saw them. Men had stopped wearing breeches and now wore other garments instead. Strange fabrics and not nearly as beautifully woven or embroidered . . . not embroidered at all, in fact. And the women! Louisa was embarrassed at first as their dresses grew looser and lighter and ever shorter. The first day a woman walked through the almost ruined house showing her ankles and her stockings, she shrieked so loudly that she felt sure she had been heard. The woman actually seemed to have had sensed something, because she turned to the man beside her and told him that she didn't want to stay, that the place was giving her the creeps. And that she was certain it was haunted. Louisa had giggled at that. She wasn't haunting the house. She was just stuck there.

The clothes changed more and more. One day – a beautiful summer's day, when Louisa had been quite pleased to wake up in her crumbling bedroom – a group of people tramped through the grass and stood in front of the house. At first Louisa hadn't realised that there were women among them as well as men. They were all wearing short trousers, and over them, types of undergarments with writing on them. Louisa thought it was quite shocking, although quite interesting too. If she'd been able to wear those clothes when she'd been little, then maybe she wouldn't have tripped and fallen. But it was odd, all the same, to see men and women laughing and joking together and showing so much naked flesh. Louisa knew that her poor mama would have died of shame if she'd thought that men would see so much of her legs. And if her legs had been as brown as the legs of the women who were sitting on what used to be the pillars at the top of the steps to the house and eating food out of their hands.

'It's supposed to be haunted.' One of the girls laughed. 'But then I suppose every falling-down house in the country is supposed to be haunted.'

'What sort of ghost?' asked the man sitting beside her.

'Dunno.' The girl bit into an apple. 'Probably some poor woman who was wronged.'

'According to this . . .' another man took a book out of the bag he had been carrying on his back, 'tragedy struck when Louisa Lachfort broke her neck in a fall. She was only nine or ten at the time. The family left the house and never returned.'

Louisa was startled. She moved her head from side to side. She didn't think she'd broken her neck. Just banged her head. In fact she was certain that was all that had happened. The book was wrong.

'Poor little Louisa,' said the girl.

'Broke the Earl's heart, apparently.' The man was still reading. 'He died shortly afterwards.'

This time Louisa was shocked. She couldn't believe her father would have been so upset by her death that he'd died too. Her father didn't love her that much. Emily was the favourite. And George was his heir. If either of them had died she could've understood her father's grief. But not over her.

'And the mother contracted pneumonia a few years later and that was the end of her.'

Oh, Mama, thought Louisa. How terrible for you.

'Any more information?' asked the girl.

The man shook his head. 'After the Earl died, the house passed to the eldest son, who had no interest in it. It was left to various family members but nobody seems to have wanted it. And then it was taken over by the state.'

'Well, hardly taken over,' said the girl. 'It's a mess, isn't it?'

'Would've been nice to see it how it was,' said the man.

The girl nodded. Louisa glided down the steps and looked up at the house. She could still see it the way it was, with its beautiful white-stone façade and its gleaming windows. She wished it was like that now.

'C'mon.' The girl crumpled up the paper from which she'd been eating her food and pushed it into her bag. 'We'd better get going.'

She ran down the steps more quickly than Louisa, who was still standing at the bottom, had expected. She gasped as the girl ran straight through her. And the girl gasped too, then cried out.

'What?' The man looked at her. 'What's wrong, Georgie?'

'I don't know.' Georgie looked confused. 'I just felt . . .'

'What?' he asked again.

'As though someone had walked over my grave.'

'Don't be silly,' he said. 'You're fine.'

'Yes . . .' But as she walked away from the house, Georgie looked back again.

Louisa waved at her.

'Oh my God!' Georgie shrieked.

'What?'

188

'I saw someone.' She stared at the house. 'I can still see someone. There's a girl on the step, Aengus. Surely you can see her too?'

'Get a grip, Georgie.' Aengus laughed. 'There's nobody there.'

'The beer has gone to your head,' said another man.

'Seriously.' Georgie was shaking. 'Can you see her, Honor?'

The other girl shook her head. 'You're imagining things.'

'I'm not.'

Louisa was listening to them with interest. She found it hard to follow their conversation, because their English was strange. But she was still in Ireland. So maybe that was why. She waved again.

'We've got to go,' said Georgie. 'I'm getting seriously freaked out here.'

'All right, all right.' Aengus laughed. 'We'll go.'

They hurried through the gardens. Louisa watched them go. She was sorry she'd frightened the girl named Georgie. And she wondered how it was that Georgie was the first person who'd been able to see her in more than a hundred and fifty years.

She was waking up more frequently now. She thought it was because there was more activity at the house. People had come to study it. Strange people who lit candles and prayed and seemed to be trying to contact the dead. One time a large group set up in the ruined drawing room. A woman dressed entirely in purple urged them all to hold hands while she tried to get in contact with the sorrowing spirits.

'We are here to help you,' the woman said. 'We are here to help you pass on.'

Louisa listened intently. The woman was stout (as Mama would have said) and she had ample bosoms that quivered as she spoke.

'Talk to us,' she intoned. 'Speak to those who would speak to you.'

Was it possible, wondered Louisa, that this woman could speak to her? Was it possible that she could help her to go somewhere else? To be with her mama and papa and the rest of her family? Suddenly Louisa wanted that very badly.

'Hello,' she said timidly.

'Be not afraid,' said the woman loudly.

'Hello!' This time Louisa shouted. 'I'm not afraid.'

'I feel a presence.'

Louisa was excited. Could it be that she was finally going to communicate with somebody at last?

'It is a spirit guide,' said the woman. 'An eagle.'

An eagle! Louisa was surprised. And confused. There had never been any eagles around the house. Could she have meant beagle? They'd had a beagle named Juju. She was excited again. What if the woman had contacted the spirit of their dog?

'Fly, fly, great eagle,' cried the woman. 'Bear us on your wings.'

For shame, thought Louisa. There was no eagle. This woman was a charlatan!

'Do not believe her!' she cried. 'There is no eagle. Only me. I'm a girl. And I want to go home!'

*

190

More people came and more people tried to contact the spirits, but even though Louisa tried to talk to them too, she couldn't. And eventually they stopped coming. There was a lull, then other people came. They talked about rebuilding the house, restoring it to its former glory. Louisa liked these conversations. It would be lovely to have the house rebuilt, although she didn't know what that would mean for her. If everything changed, would she be forced away? And if that happened, would she be able to be with her family again? She missed them all so much.

One day big yellow machines roared into the gardens and woke her. She cried out in fear as she saw the mechanical beasts advance on the house and begin to dig holes around it. She screamed loudly and told them to leave, but they kept on and on, digging and drilling and making terrible noise. For the first time since her death, she wanted to be a proper ghost. She wanted to scare them away.

When the men left for the night, she glided towards the machinery. She could hardly believe that these things could be so powerful. She wafted into the seat of one of them and stared at the control panel in front of her. She frowned as she looked at the buttons. And then suddenly the beast roared into life again and she was so frightened she fainted.

She realised that she hadn't actually fainted. What had happened was that she had gone into the unconscious state again. She wished she knew what happened when she was in that state. She'd always thought that when she died she would go to heaven and meet up with her family there.

Clearly she had died. And clearly they were also now dead. But she couldn't remember any time in heaven. Nor any time with them. She was certain that if she'd been allowed into heaven she wouldn't have been allowed out again. She wondered what she'd done wrong all those years ago. And if she would ever be able to put it right and finally be reunited with the people she'd loved.

The next time she woke up, there were two people standing at the foot of her bed. Naturally it was no longer a proper bed. It seemed to her that she was still in it, but she knew that wasn't really the case. Just as she probably still wasn't wearing her nightdress. Although she still saw it whenever she looked at herself.

'It's wonderful.' The man looked at the woman. 'We can make a go of this, Claire.'

'I know,' the woman said. 'And I have a name for it. The Sugar Loaf Lodge.'

'Perfect,' he said.

They hugged each other. And then they kissed. And then, there in the half-built house (because while she'd been unconscious, the yellow beast machinery had obviously done some work), the man and the woman began to do things to each other that shocked Louisa to her core.

She didn't fall asleep again. She stayed awake all through the renovation of the house. She was too excited to speak. She watched as it was transformed from a dead building into a living, breathing place. As it was turned into a hotel.

She was enthralled by the new things that the man, Neil, and the woman, Claire, were putting into it. The amazing plumbing with the hot water that gushed forth as soon as a tap was turned. The machines that meant that people from far away could speak and they would be heard in the hotel. The shining tablet that contained pictures and words and that Claire called 'that bloody computer'. For a long time Louisa thought that the name for the tablet was 'bloody computer', and she wondered why. There was no blood. No gore. Just words and pictures. But eventually she realised that the magic tablet was just 'computer' and that 'bloody' was used as a swear word (of which both Claire and Neil seemed to know quite a few).

She liked them. She liked the way they laughed and joked with each other and the way they worked together. She liked their clothes and their hair and the way that they lived their lives. Although, she thought, it was very hard work. Claire was the mistress of the house and there were servants, but they didn't tend to her. They tended to the guests.

But oh, thought Louisa, if only we had had all this luxury when we were travelling to Ireland. If only we could have stayed in an inn such as this, with comfortable beds and hot water and all the things that made the Sugar Loaf Lodge so very beautiful.

She wished her parents could see the house now. She wished they could learn about this new world. She liked the fact that she had learned so much. She liked seeing all the people who came to the hotel. But she was still very lonely.

*

Neil and Claire were worried about Christmas. Louisa knew that it was something to do with the economy and people not having enough money to spend. She understood that. Her father had spoken about the economy too, and problems with trade. It seemed that despite all the changes that had happened in the world over more than two centuries, some things had not changed at all. She hoped that they would get the guests they needed. She didn't want things to go wrong for them. They were her family now, even though they didn't know it. Every time someone new arrived, she whispered 'welcome' into their ears. Occasionally someone would hesitate for a moment after she spoke and then continue on their way. She wasn't sure if it was because they heard her. She hoped so. It made her feel good to think that she was welcoming people to her family home. And so did gliding through the house, watching the guests and making sure they were happy. Because if they weren't . . . well, she'd worked out a plan for that. She talked to the bloody computer.

She'd discovered that she could do this quite by chance.

One day, when Claire had left the little office (which had been where the scullery was in the old house), Louisa had sat in the chair in front of the computer and stared at it. She could see writing with the names of the guests and the rooms they were staying in. Over the years she had seen lots of written words. It had taken her a long time to learn the new way of writing and spelling and saying things. But she understood it now, most of the time.

It was while she'd been staring at the name of one guest that the picture in front of her changed and she realised that the computer was showing information about that guest and the room in which he was staying. There were little boxes beside words like 'soap' and 'towels', and Louisa worked out that this was telling Claire what the guest needed. There was also a comment box in which the computer said 'No flowers in room. Allergic.' Louisa concentrated on another name and saw different information. She wondered how Claire knew this. So she watched and learned that the guests wrote their comments on cards in their rooms. Or that when they made their reservation to stay in the hotel they told Claire things that they needed. Louisa understood that listening to the guests and serving their needs was what made the Sugar Loaf Lodge so successful.

So she listened too, when they were alone in their rooms or sitting at the bar chatting. And when Claire wasn't there, she made comments in the computer for her. Which meant that Claire was able to leave extra hot chocolate in the room called Mullacor before the two elderly ladies staying there asked for it, and turned up the heat in Longduff even though the weather was mild because the couple there felt the cold.

Claire had thought that Neil was leaving the comments and remarked on it to him one day. But he'd looked confused and said that it was nothing to do with him, which had made her frown.

'Someone typed in that Grumpy Old Man Humphries in Scarr wanted an extra blanket,' she remarked.

'Bernadette?'

Bernadette was the chambermaid who looked after that room.

'No,' said Claire. 'None of the chambermaids use the

computer. They leave the comment cards in the office, that's all.'

'You must have put it in yourself,' said Neil. 'That's the only way.'

'I didn't.'

'You're working too hard. You're forgetting.'

'Maybe.'

But Claire wasn't convinced.

Nevertheless, she stopped worrying about it. Although Bernadette, Petra and the other staff all denied inputting stuff on to the computer, she felt sure that one of them must have. Or that Neil had, even though he'd denied it too. It didn't matter. The comments were always up to date and always useful. And there was no point stressing about it, because the thing was that anticipating her guests' needs gave the Sugar Loaf Lodge the edge it needed. Their website was full of complimentary remarks by satisfied guests who said that being there was like being looked after by a guardian angel.

And as the comments continued to appear on the computer, Claire sometimes thought she had a guardian angel of her very own.

Louisa couldn't see her own reflection. She'd realised that a long time ago. More than two hundred years ago, she told herself as she sat in the hallway (now some kind of living area with a bar) and watched the guests playing charades. Her mama had enjoyed charades, although the game had been played somewhat differently in her time.

Louisa was amused by the actions of the guests now, even though she had no idea of the books, the plays and the movies they were trying to act out. (She was fascinated by the movies. The first time she'd seen television, she'd cried out in terror, but now she loved it. She learned a lot from it.) Her mind wandered back to her lack of reflection. She wondered what she looked like. If one day someone could see her, what exactly would they see? Did she still look like a little girl in a nightdress? Or had she changed at all?

She felt as though she'd changed. Each time she woke up, it was as though she'd grown older. She didn't feel like a ten-year-old child any more. Well, how could she? She was now more than two hundred and twenty-five! She'd adapted to the changing world around her. She'd become a modern person. Although, obviously, a modern dead person, which was hard to accept. She'd also learned that she wasn't a very good ghost. Because, except for that girl years ago who'd claimed to have seen her, and excluding the people who had from time to time wandered around the ruins of the house and said that it gave them the creeps, nobody had noticed her presence.

Except, in a casual way, Claire, who would sometimes look at the computer and wonder aloud how it was that it was updating itself with information about their clients.

Louisa sat in the reception area on Christmas Eve and thought about these things while she waited to whisper her welcome to the next set of guests. They were the last to arrive that day; she'd already whispered into the ears of the guests in all of the other rooms. She'd tried to make them feel relaxed and happy, although the truth was that some of the guests this year were not relaxed at all. Some of them, quite frankly, were extremely tense. But hopefully, thought Louisa, that would have changed by the time they left. And they'd thank the Sugar Loaf Lodge for helping them.

The front doors opened and a tall, bony woman with grey hair strode across the floor to the walnut desk where the receptionist, Sarah, was sitting. The woman looked familiar to Louisa, although she couldn't understand why. It wasn't as though there was anybody left alive that she knew. And she had never met anyone outside the confines of the house and gardens. She'd attempted one day to leave the garden, but she simply hadn't been able to. Each time she'd reached the boundary, an invisible force had seemed to trap her inside. She'd tried over and over to step through it, but she couldn't, and eventually she'd had to accept that there were limitations on where she could go. That was probably why ghosts got such a bad press, she thought, using an expression she'd once heard Neil say. We're stuck in a certain place and we get bored. That's why we're so cranky. But I'm lucky, because ever since Neil and Claire came here, I've never been bored.

The woman at the desk turned around and looked towards the door. A younger woman had followed her, although how much younger Louisa couldn't tell. She found it diffi-cult to guess at the ages of people in these times. They all lived a lot longer. And the women, especially, did amazing things to keep themselves looking young and beautiful. There was so much maquillage they could use, so many tricks they had – Louisa knew her mama would have loved all the jars of cream and paints and powders.

'Do you have the reservation email, Emily?' asked the older woman.

Emily opened her bag and began to search inside.

'I don't need it,' said Sarah pleasantly. 'What name is the booking under?'

'Georgina Forde and Emily Hennessy,' said the older woman. 'We're sharing a room.'

'A twin,' added Emily helpfully. 'This is my mum.'

The receptionist smiled at them.

'You're both very, very welcome. Claire asked me to let her know as soon as you arrived. Do you want to wait here or go straight to your room?'

'We'll go to the room,' said Georgina. 'Don't want to distract her if she's busy. Which she must be.'

The two women checked in and were given the key to their room. Louisa stood behind them and whispered, 'Welcome, Merry Christmas.' A puzzled expression flitted across the face of the older woman, but she kept walking. Her daughter didn't appear to have noticed anything. Louisa followed them. They were staying in Berleagh, the room that had been her bedroom. It was decorated in the same duck-egg blue that it had been back then, and in some ways looked very similar, except, of course, that there were electric lights, the beds were bigger and more comfortable and there was a deep-pile carpet on the floor. And there was the new stuff too. The television and the computer and the warmed marble floor in the bathroom. (Louisa loved the bathroom. She loved the flush toilet. She loved the ever-present hot water. She longed to be able to stand beneath the shower and allow it to cascade over her as she'd watched various guests do.)

'It's lovely, isn't it?' said Emily. 'So gracious and elegant.'

'And forty years ago it was a wreck,' said Georgina. 'Claire has done a brilliant job, hasn't she?'

It was then that Louisa suddenly remembered. Like an instant photograph. Georgina. Georgie. The woman who'd come to the house with her friends. The woman who'd seen her. Who'd been frightened by her. She couldn't understand how she hadn't recognised her before.

Louisa stood in front of her and waved. The older woman frowned slightly. Louisa waved again.

'D'you have any paracetamol with you, Emmylou?' asked Georgina.

'Yes.' Emily turned to her. 'Headache?'

'A bit,' said Georgina. 'Tiredness, I think.'

'Here you are.' Emily handed her some tablets.

Georgina swallowed them quickly. Louisa kept waving her hands in front of her. But Georgina didn't seem to notice.

Ten minutes later there was a knock on the door and Claire walked in. The three women embraced and Emily told her that everything was wonderful, that she'd done a fabulous job and that it was great to be here and to see her again for the first time in so long.

'I think I was ten,' said Claire. 'You guys came over from England to visit us, remember? We went to Galway.'

Emily nodded. 'I was so excited at the idea of seeing my Irish cousins at last.'

'And we were looking forward to seeing your English glamour,' said Claire.

'We had great fun,' Emily said. 'It's such a pity we lost touch.'

'But fantastic that you found out about the hotel. And really, really wonderful to have you here.'

'I hope you're not doing yourself out of decent income because of us,' said Georgina. 'You're not charging half enough.'

'You're family,' said Claire warmly. 'I'd prefer it if you didn't pay at all.'

'We know times are tough,' Georgina told her. 'Family or no family, you've got to earn a living.'

'We're doing OK,' said Claire. 'It's been a difficult year but we've kept our heads above water.'

'Well, we were delighted to come,' Emily said. 'Otherwise we were facing a bit of a gloomy Christmas.'

'A solitary Christmas,' Georgina corrected her. 'I'm not sorry your father left, Emily. I'm just sorry he didn't do it sooner.'

Louisa, listening to them, felt a sudden chill in the room that had nothing to do with her ghostly presence. She didn't do chills. She didn't know how. The atmosphere was due to Georgina's remark, which had caused Emily's face to darken and Claire to look uncomfortable.

'All right, all right!' Georgina sounded impatient. 'I was impossible to live with. I know.'

'Not impossible, Mum,' said Emily gently. 'Just . . . difficult for him sometimes.'

'I'm an artistic person,' her mother said. 'I'm attuned to different things. He never really understood that.'

Louisa followed Emily and Georgina everywhere they went. She sat near them in the lounge when they had pre-dinner drinks and she perched on the ice bucket beside their table when they went into the restaurant. She realised that this was the first time the two of them had spent Christmas alone together and that neither of them was entirely sure that it would end up being a good thing. She listened to their conversation, interested in how much they talked about their feelings. Feelings had never been very much discussed when she was a girl. Behaviour had been far more important.

Emily asked Georgina about the time she'd visited the house. Louisa was eager to hear her reply.

'We came out on our bikes,' Georgina remembered. 'It was a glorious day. The house was falling apart – it was really just a ruin. Aengus was interested in old houses and he was the one who suggested it. It had a different name then. White Hall. And you could see that it probably had been. A lot of the masonry was grimy with age, but it would have been white when it was built.'

'Like it is now,' said Emily.

Georgina nodded. 'Anyway, we visited it and it made a real impression on me. There was a sad story about a little girl who'd died.'

Louisa remembered one of the boys reading out the story. Which hadn't been accurate, because she very definitely hadn't broken her neck.

Georgina frowned. 'It affected me a lot, that story. I kept on thinking about the little girl.'

You did? wondered Louisa. Really? You thought about me? Why didn't you come back?

'Yes,' said Georgina. 'I couldn't help it.'

Emily looked at her curiously.

'I thought I saw her,' said Georgina blankly. 'I thought she waved at me. I know it was nonsense and I was imagining it, because nobody else saw her, but it freaked me out at the time.'

Louisa was overcome with excitement. She stood in front of Georgina and waved again as vigorously as she could. But the older woman gave no sign of having seen her. Louisa felt very frustrated.

'So . . . the paintings?' Emily asked in sudden wonderment. 'All those paintings?'

'Of the little girl,' said Georgina. 'Her name was Louisa.'

Paintings, thought Louisa. What paintings?

'You never said.' Emily sounded accusing. 'All that time and you never said. Even in the interviews. Even to us. To Dad. You never told us.'

'I know,' Georgina said. 'I can't explain it, Emmylou. She got into my head. I had to paint her.'

I got into your head? wondered Louisa. You kept thinking about me? So much that you painted me? But why then can't you see me now?

'When I eventually learned that Claire and Neil had bought this place, I simply couldn't believe it,' said Georgina. 'I wanted to come sooner, but I was afraid.'

'Of what?'

'That seeing it restored would sever the connection.'

'With the little girl?'

Georgina nodded. 'She's been with me my whole life. She's with me now.'

Louisa fell off the ice bucket. Georgina could see her! She waved again.

'Now? Literally?' Emily looked around the room. 'Where?'

'Spiritually,' said Georgina. 'I know she's here. But I can't see her.'

Louisa wanted to cry with disappointment. She wanted to be seen. She wanted someone to know that she still existed. And she wanted to let them know that she cared.

On Christmas Day, Georgina and Emily joined Neil and Claire for Irish coffees and mince pies in their private rooms. They came mid-afternoon, when the guests were either lounging in the bar or out walking in the magnificent grounds, and when the demands on the staff were at their lowest.

'Happy Christmas,' said Georgina as she handed Claire an oblong gift-wrapped parcel.

'Thank you, Aunt Georgie.' Claire smiled at her. 'You didn't have to.'

'Of course I did.'

Claire slid her finger beneath the Sellotape of the wrapping and took out the small painting. She gasped with pleasure.

'An original Georgie Forde! How marvellous. And how lovely, too!'

Louisa, who had stuck with Georgina and Emily all day,

looked at it. And her mouth fell open in the way that used to make Charlotte tell her to close it before she caught a fly.

The painting was of her. Standing on the steps of White Hall as it had once been. Her arms were stretched out, reaching upwards towards the sky. Her hair was flowing in the wind. Her eyes were bright blue and excited. She looked as she remembered herself looking. Except for her eyes. Because her eyes had been green. Charlotte used to call them emerald eyes, which made her laugh. But all the same, the girl in the portrait was her. Carefree and happy and alive. She missed that feeling. She missed being alive.

'It's wonderful,' said Neil. 'Who is she?'

Georgina explained about the ghost, and Neil laughed.

'We read about her. It was such a sad story.'

'Did you know that Mum saw her?' asked Emily.

'What?' Both Neil and Claire turned to Georgina at the same time.

Georgina looked at Emily in annoyance.

'It was probably my imagination,' she said dismissively.

'Maybe,' Emily said. 'You have a very vivid imagination. But maybe it was real.'

'She's supposed to haunt the house,' Claire said. 'According to the legend, she walks through the corridors, weeping. Though we've never had reports of anyone seeing her.'

I'm not surprised, thought Louisa. I never walked the corridors weeping. I was too brave for that. I never cried. Not once.

'A real ghost!' Emily laughed. 'That's brilliant. So, Mum, maybe you're the only person who's actually seen her.'

'There are no such things as ghosts,' said Georgina firmly.

Yes there are! cried Louisa. There are and I'm here and I want you to know that.

'I believe they used to have séances here years ago, but nothing came of them,' said Neil.

'Maybe you're on her wavelength, though, Georgina,' said Claire.

'Well, actually . . .' Georgina hesitated.

'What?' demanded Emily.

'Maybe we all are indirectly.'

'How?'

'When I did the research on the house, I tried to trace the family. The Lachforts. It seems that a branch of them changed their name slightly. From Lachfort to Forde.'

'You've got to be kidding me.' Claire's eyes widened. 'You don't think our ancestors actually lived here, do you? That we're part of the family? That's too much to believe.'

'The branch I'm talking about wasn't exactly a legitimate one,' Georgina told her. 'Seems that the eldest son had what you'd call a bit of a dalliance with a local girl. There were rumours of a son. He was supported by George for a time. Called himself Edward Forde. Went to England. Did well in business. Had a huge family, and some of them settled back here.'

'When did you discover all this?' asked Claire.

'Bits and pieces over the years,' said Georgina. 'The records aren't very good, and to be honest, a lot of it is educated guesswork. But I couldn't help feeling a pull to the place.'

'Like us,' said Claire to Neil in astonishment. 'When we saw it, we just knew.'

'You've never seen the ghost of Louisa, though, have you?' Emily grinned at them.

'Well, no . . .' but Claire went on to explain about her feeling of a guardian angel watching over them.

Louisa was enthralled. She was looking at them all differently now, suddenly seeing in the way Claire was holding her head an echo of the way Charlotte would sometimes look at her; seeing her brother George's eyes in Georgina's; and – how could she have missed this? she asked herself – realising that Emily had the Lachfort nose, a little too long and a little too pointed, something her own sister Emily regularly bemoaned. She would say that she'd never get a husband with a nose like hers, and Charlotte would laugh and say that of course she would and then, when Emily had left the room, would murmur that it would be wonderful, though, if people could change their noses, because it did detract from her eldest daughter's beauty. And prospects.

Louisa didn't know if Emily had ever found someone to marry. Despite the nose.

'It's such a sad story.' Claire was holding up the painting of Louisa. 'And she's such a pretty girl. I wonder what she was like as a person.'

Suddenly the tears welled up in Louisa's eyes. These were all lovely people. And they were her family. Still here, hundreds of years later. Still part of her life. Or her death. Whichever. Nevertheless, they cared about her. And she cared about them too. But the truth was that no matter how much she cared, she would always be apart from them. They could never see her or talk to her. She could never be part of their lives. They would grow older and eventually

207

pass on, and even if their own children came here, they'd never see her either. It seemed as though she was doomed to linger on for ever, always having to find new people, but always being alone.

She'd never cried. Not since she'd woken. She'd felt fear and anxiety, and sometimes she'd wanted to cry. But she never had. Eddie and George used to tease her when she was little, and when they'd reduced her to tears, they'd called her a cry-baby. Which had at first made her cry even more. But later it had made her determined never to cry in front of them. In front of anyone.

'Mum?' Emily looked at Georgina. 'Are you all right?'

Georgina was staring across the room. She could see the figure of the girl. Taller than she'd remembered. Her hair loose around her face. Wearing what seemed to be a nightdress.

'What is it?' asked Emily.

Georgina shook her head. 'Too much ghost talk.'

'No,' said Claire slowly. 'Not at all.' She was looking across the room too.

'Oh my God,' said Emily slowly.

'I don't believe it,' said Neil.

They all looked. They could all see her. They could see the tear slowly falling down her almost-transparent cheek.

'Louisa?' said Georgina. 'Is that you?'

It was like hearing her mother's voice. Like hearing Charlotte. The words seemed to come from a million miles away, yet suddenly it was Charlotte she could hear. Calling her name. Faint but clear.

'It's me,' she said shakily. 'You can see me. Can you hear me?'

'Yes.' Emily spoke first. 'I can hear you. I really can.'

'You're real,' said Claire in wonderment. 'I can't believe you're real. Are you the one who's helped? Are you the guardian angel?'

'I don't know anything about angels,' said Louisa shakily. 'I only know about ghosts.'

'Are you there, Louisa?' Charlotte's voice was stronger now, and Louisa could feel her presence even more keenly than the presence of the people in the room. 'We need you. Come on. Come now.'

'You've been here for us,' said Claire. 'You've helped. All the time. Thank you.'

'Come on, Louisa,' said Charlotte. 'You've got to come with me. Please.'

Louisa could hear the despair in her mother's voice, and suddenly she began to sob, heavy, choking tears that streamed down her face. All of them – Georgina, Emily, Claire and Neil – made an involuntary move to get up and go to her. But as they watched, her filmy, insubstantial shape wavered in front of them like a swirling mist.

'Louisa!' cried Georgina.

But Louisa didn't hear her. Because as the tears streamed down her face, she felt another presence move towards her, a familiar warmth as her mother's arms enfolded her.

'You silly, silly, girl,' said Charlotte. 'You should have cried before. Then I could have reached you.'

'Mama.' Louisa had never felt like this before. Never felt so peaceful and so right.

'Yes,' said Charlotte. 'It's me. You've come to us at last.'

*

The spirit, the presence, the ghost – none of them quite knew what to call it – had gone. They stared at the spot where they'd seen Louisa, but nothing of the translucent figure remained. They sat in silence, waiting and wondering if she would ever return.

'Was she real?' asked Emily eventually. 'Or did we imagine her?'

'She seemed real to me,' said Claire. 'But maybe you put too much whiskey in those Irish coffees, Neil? Could we be having a mass hallucination brought on by too much drink?'

Neil shook his head.

'Maybe she'll be back,' said Claire.

'Or maybe she's gone for good.' Georgina picked up the portrait of the young Louisa and stared at it. 'It's strange, but I don't . . . I don't feel her here any more. For the first time in years, I don't think she's with me.'

The face that looked back at her was still vibrant and smiling. Still full of the joy of living. Still the face she knew so well. And then Georgina frowned. Because Louisa's bright, excited eyes were no longer the azure blue she'd painted them. They now shone with a pure emerald green.

Conavalla

Alex had spent the previous Christmas in exactly the same way as the preceding twenty Christmases: at home with Dorothy, his wife. Ever since they'd married at the ridiculously young age of twenty-one in her case and twenty-five in his (it hadn't seemed young to them then), they'd been rock-solid. The sort of irritatingly loved-up couple that didn't really need other people in their lives. They had friends, of course, and socialised regularly, but most people were of the opinion that Alex and Dorothy Lennon would be perfectly happy if they were the only two people left in the whole world.

Both of them were absolutely content in each other's company. They liked spending time alone together, not needing to talk, perfectly in tune with each other's moods. They were happy to be alone at Christmas, too, when Dorothy would cook up a traditional storm for the two of them, after which they would flop on the big sofa and watch whatever movie was on TV before falling asleep, her head resting on his shoulder. Dorothy's mother had invited them for Christmas dinner the first year they were married, but Dorothy said that she wanted to have a crack at it at home

211

with Alex. She insisted on cooking a turkey and a ham (far too much food for two people; neither of them could even think about eating turkey or ham for months afterwards), and they sat down to a quiet dinner followed by the TV movie and snooze. Even though it wasn't exciting, it ended up becoming what they always did on Christmas Day. It was their tradition, they decided, and lots of their friends, caught up in family-from-hell-type Christmases, envied them fiercely.

New Year was different. They liked to go out for New Year. They would book a restaurant in town and then hook up with family or friends to do the countdown and wish everyone health, happiness and prosperity. But Christmas was theirs alone.

It had been theirs alone last year, too, although not the way it used to be. Alex had cooked dinner under Dorothy's instruction because she'd been too weak to do it herself. And she hadn't been able to eat much of the ready-to-roast turkey breast or small smoked ham joint that he'd bought. She'd moved everything around the plate, as she'd been doing for so many weeks, but eating was too much of an effort. Alex had watched her, his heart breaking, but he'd said nothing. They'd both made an agreement not to say anything at all.

But as they'd gone to bed that night, Dorothy had allowed an exhausted sigh to escape from her and said, 'Well, that's got Christmas out of the way,' and Alex had known what she meant. Dorothy was dying and her time was numbered in days, not weeks. She'd been utterly, utterly determined not to die on Christmas Day. It would ruin it for ever for him, she'd said breathlessly, and she didn't want to do that. So she'd managed to hang on until the second of January. She'd woken that morning and smiled wearily at him and he'd gone down to make her a cup of tea, even though he knew she probably wouldn't drink it. When he'd come back to the bedroom ten minutes later, she'd slipped away.

He still felt a terrible rage at not having been with her for her last moments. He'd wanted to be there, holding her hand, reminding her that wherever she was going, he would always be thinking of her, and that one day he'd be there too. He wanted to tell her to wait for him. But instead she'd made the journey alone while he was pouring boiling water into a teacup. It seemed wrong to Alex. Trivial. And unfair.

But then everything about Dorothy's illness had been unfair. They both agreed on that. Life *was* unfair, as Dorothy frequently reminded him, when they ran into a bump on the way. Although this was more than a bump. This was devastating. Nevertheless, she insisted it was better that it was she who was going to die at forty-two rather than a woman who had a young family to look after. Alex had snorted at that and said that he needed looking after and that she'd always done that, but she'd smiled and said that he allowed her to look after him but he was perfectly capable of taking care of himself.

He hadn't done a very good job of that in the first weeks after her death. It was the only time in his life that he wished they'd had children, because he'd thought that perhaps children would've given him a reason for living. You couldn't go to pieces if you had other people depending on you, he thought, but he was completely alone and was perfectly able

213

to go to pieces every night without anybody knowing. Of course people did know – his sister, Antoinette, rang him regularly to check that he was OK and panicked every time he didn't pick up the phone after a couple of rings; and his brother-in-law, Conal, called to the house a few times to make sure everything was all right. But when they realised that he was getting by, they stopped calling, because Alex was short and impatient with them, not wanting to talk, only interested in sitting in front of the TV on the big sofa as he'd done with Dorothy and allowing tears to trickle down his face.

He needed to do this in the evenings because he had to be strong during the day. He worked in a multinational financial company, and having a career in finance meant that you didn't let your emotions show even if your beloved wife had died. Besides, the industry was going through a particularly difficult period and nobody had time to be emotional about anything other than profitability. 'Blood on the streets' was the expression that the insiders used when the markets were dangerous, and this was a particularly gory time. In some ways he was glad of it. It meant that he didn't have much time to harbour dark thoughts about Dorothy and the injustice of it all.

Dorothy had worked in finance too, but she'd always been a sceptic about what they did. 'Not a real job for a grown-up,' she used to say. 'It's only gambling when all's said and done.' He'd try to point out that they were helping businesses to grow and companies to raise vital cash, thus keeping the wheels of commerce oiled and moving, but she'd laugh at him then and say that it was all a pretence but it paid the bills and, very fortunately, paid for the luxuries they'd acquired a taste for too.

She'd been right about that, he thought, in the way that she was right about so many things. Which was why he'd loved her so much. From the moment he'd first met her, sitting in St Stephen's Green during her lunchtime, to that awful, awful day when the doctors had told her that there really wasn't much more they could do, she'd been the only woman in the world for him.

And now she was gone.

And this year Christmas was going to be very, very different.

He went for a walk in the grounds of the Sugar Loaf Lodge shortly after arriving on Christmas Eve. He'd started walking a lot after Dorothy's death; it had helped him to get rid of the anger and frustration and sorrow he felt about being left behind. Because that was how he thought about it. She'd gone and left him behind, and it was a new and uncomfortable feeling. He hadn't wanted to sit on his own watching TV after that. He'd needed to be out and about. But not in the pub. He was afraid that if he went into a pub on his own, he wouldn't be able to leave. He craved the solace of oblivion that a skinful of pints would give him, but he knew it wasn't the answer. Dorothy had always been one for facing up to things. She'd faced up to her illness without flinching. (Well, not quite. But pretty much. Everyone had been awestruck by her bravery and dignity.) The least he could do, Alex thought, was face up to life without her with the same level of courage. Which meant not getting pissed every day, even though that was what he wanted to do. Walking was a substitute. Once he got into the habit, he simply couldn't stop.

When he got back from the walk he went straight to his room. He could hear music playing as he opened the door. He recognised the band instantly – Riverside, a Polish band that reminded him a little of Dire Straits. He was a fan of Dire Straits. But neither they nor Riverside could really be considered as providing seasonal music.

Kassia was in the middle of the room, playing air guitar. She was totally engrossed in the music, shaking and rotating her head so that her long blond hair whipped from side to side. Alex could almost see the guitar in her hand. She'd once gone to the World Air Guitar Championships, she'd told him. She was thinking about giving it a go herself one day. Her idol, she said, was Suzi Quatro, a woman who'd stopped playing a real guitar long before Kassia was even born.

He turned down the music on the iPod dock and her air-guitar playing stuttered to a halt. She looked at him and smiled. He smiled in return.

Kassia Kaminska was one of the most beautiful girls he'd ever seen in his life. Even now, without make-up, her hair tangled, and wearing nothing but the white Sugar Loaf Lodge towelling robe, she was stunning. She was tall and slender, with flawless skin and enormous blue eyes. Her skin was lightly tanned (she'd been to Tenerife with some friends

216

the previous month and had retained a dusting of colour), and her face shone with happiness.

'This is such a cool place,' she told him as she brushed golden strands from her eyes. 'They have everything!'

'I know,' said Alex. 'That's why we've come here.'

'I get a good feeling from it too.'

'Hey, so do I.' He grinned at her.

'Oh, Alex.' She wrapped her arms around his neck and kissed him on the lips. 'I do so love you.'

He hadn't been looking for someone to love him. Twenty-one happy years with Dorothy had meant that he didn't notice other women. Well, that wasn't strictly true; he noticed them all right, but they didn't register as anything more than attractive eye-candy. And even if he saw a woman who was more beautiful than Dorothy, the fact that he was in love with his wife meant that nobody could ever equal her. Gorgeous women populated the financial company where he worked, but they meant nothing to him. Even after Dorothy died, he didn't really notice them. They were work colleagues, nothing more. When Jennifer Cassidy asked him if he'd like to go to the theatre with her one night, he hadn't even considered the fact that she might be interested in him and asking him on a date. He'd simply replied that he couldn't. It wasn't until he was talking to Antoinette a few weeks later that he realised the significance of Jennifer's request. And then he felt bad about it, because Jennifer was an attractive woman in her late thirties whom he liked. Who could, quite possibly, be a suitable date for him. If only he was in the mood for meeting people who could be suitable dates.

Antoinette told him that it would take time for him to recover. It had been a tough year for him. She understood that he needed space to grieve. But she begged him not to turn into a recluse just because he'd lost Dorothy. It's a pity, she added, that the two of you were so damn close.

Alex had almost got annoyed with Antoinette over her comments, but in the end he didn't bother. He didn't have the energy to get annoyed. And he knew what his sister was saying, even if he didn't agree with her. Because he wouldn't have traded his life with Dorothy for anything.

He first spoke to Kassia on the phone. He'd called the television company when he'd suddenly lost the signal from the digital box. He'd been in a rage about it because he'd been getting ready to settle down and watch *The Abyss*. It was the first movie he and Dorothy had gone to together and he always watched it when it was on TV, even though they actually had the special-edition DVD. But somehow it was different when you had to plan to watch it. An unexpected viewing on TV was far more interesting. Alex arranged his evening around the start time of the movie, but with five minutes to go, the 'lost signal' message appeared on the screen in front of him. Although when it came to financial products there was nobody more clued in than Alex Lennon, he was utterly useless with technology. Dorothy had always been the one to look after their computer and the television – he didn't even know if they had Sky or NTL or some other provider altogether. He did know that switching off and on again worked quite well with both the computer and the TV, so he did that, but the 'lost signal' message remained. He could feel himself panicking. He couldn't miss *The Abyss*. He simply couldn't. It was important for him to watch it. If Dorothy had been with him, the two of them would've sat down beside each other and watched it together. He couldn't let her down by missing it now. He scrabbled around in the sideboard beneath the TV and eventually found a brochure on which Dorothy had written, in big black letters, 'Technical Support Line'. He dialled the number, thinking that if they put him on hold for hours he'd actually drive there and punch someone. Deep down, he knew that he wouldn't; as well as being useless with technology, he hated violence, but he liked thinking about punching someone anyhow.

'Technical support, Kassia speaking, how can I help you?' The voice was soft and gentle and took Alex by surprise.

He explained his problem, adding that he was paying for a service and that he wanted to watch this movie now.

'I've already missed the start of it,' he added unnecessarily.

'Have you switched it off and on again?' asked Kassia calmly.

'For heaven's sake! D'you take me for a fool?'

'Have you checked the leads going into the back of the box?'

'Umm . . . not exactly.'

'Do that now,' she told him. 'Make sure that they're all tight.'

Alex did as she said. A message about his viewing card appeared on the screen.

'Have you taken out your viewing card and re-inserted it?'

'I don't know what that is.' Alex looked at the digital box in front of him. 'Or even where it might be.'

'It's like a credit card, in the slot on the right-hand side of the box. Press the button beside it to eject it.'

On a certain level Alex had known about the viewing card. But on another he'd completely forgotten about it. If this works, he thought as he slid it out of the slot, I'll feel like a right plonker.

'When you've removed it, perhaps blow gently on it and then put it back,' said Kassia.

'Blow on it?'

'Just in case there's dust on it,' said Kassia.

Alex looked at the card in his hand, blew on it, and re-inserted it. The programme recommenced almost immediately.

'Oh,' he said. 'It worked. I was confused by the message on the screen. It's not very helpful.'

'I understand.'

'Well . . . thank you.'

'You're welcome,' said Kassia.

'I'm sorry for bothering you.'

'It's my job.'

'Yes, but it was such a stupid thing . . . the leads . . . the card . . . I should've guessed . . .'

'That's all right.' Her tone wasn't in the slightest bit patronising. 'It's nearly always something minor. But not

220

really stupid, because with all this stuff, things can go wrong. They might be small things, but that's no consolation to someone who can't watch one of the best movies of all time.'

'You like *The Abyss*?' He was surprised.

'Love it,' said Kassia. 'It's one of my favourites.'

'Really?'

Most people had never heard of it. It wasn't an A-grade movie, after all, even though it had been directed by the great James Cameron. No truly major names. Although, as Alex sometimes said, a good solid lead in Ed Harris as well as Mary Elizabeth Mastrantonio, who was very, very like Dorothy in appearance. He'd wanted to watch it for Mary Elizabeth. To remind him.

'Really,' said Kassia. 'So sit down and enjoy.'

'Yes,' said Alex. 'I will.'

He hung up and sat down in front of the TV. But he didn't see much of the movie, because he cried through most of it.

Ten minutes after the film ended, the phone rang.

'Mr Lennon?'

'Yes.'

'Kassia Kaminska. I'm just ringing to check that your TV is functioning normally.'

Goodness, he thought, what great service.

'Perfectly,' he told her. 'Thank you so much for asking.'

'And you enjoyed your movie?'

'Absolutely.' His voice cracked.

'Are you all right?' asked Kassia.

'No,' he said. 'Not really.'

'I'm sorry,' she said, and hung up.

Two minutes later, his phone rang again.

'I couldn't talk to you on the other phone,' said Kassia as soon as he answered. 'It's recorded. For quality and training purposes. I am ringing you on my mobile.'

'Why?' asked Alex.

'Because you sounded so sad,' she told him.

'I'm sure you often get calls from people who are sad,' he said. 'You're technical support, after all. They're probably sad that they can't fix whatever it is themselves.'

Kassia laughed. Her laugh was gentle and sweet, just like her voice, and it seemed to wash over him.

'Mostly they are angry when they phone us,' she said. 'Because they believe it is all our fault.'

'Even if it's a loose connection and the viewing card,' said Alex.

'Even if.'

'I'm not sad.' As he uttered the words he started to cry again. He was angry at himself for the tears.

'I'm sorry,' said Kassia. 'I know I shouldn't have called you. But I couldn't help it. I feel things, you know. Like sadness. And I interfere. I shouldn't. Sorry.'

'That's OK,' he said. 'It was nice of you. I'm sure you don't have much time in technical support for making phone calls to customers who sound a bit sad.'

'Not usually,' she agreed. 'But it is a quiet night tonight and . . . anyway, I will let you get back to your viewing, and I'm glad that we were of service.'

'Thanks again,' said Alex. 'Good night.'

He hung up. But he couldn't get her voice out of his head. He wondered what she was like, Kassia Kaminska, who was still at work in technical support services at eleven o'clock at night so that she could tell morons like him to take out the viewing card and put it back in again. He looked at the caller list on the phone and saw her mobile number. He hit dial.

'Hello?'

'It's me again,' said Alex.

'Nice to hear from you,' Kassia said. 'I hope everything is working all right? There are no more technical problems?'

'What time do you finish work?' he asked.

'Midnight,' replied Kassia. 'Why, are you expecting a problem before then?'

'Would you like to meet for a coffee?' He blurted out the words.

Kassia hesitated.

'Somewhere very public,' said Alex, realising how odd his request must sound to her. 'I'm not a stalker or anything. Please don't worry.'

'Our technical support is in Ballsbridge,' she said. 'There's an all-night coffee place nearby.'

'Sounds good,' said Alex, who lived in Rathgar and so wasn't that far away. 'In the café, then?'

'OK.' She gave him directions.

'See you soon,' he said and ended the call.

*

He arrived at the café at a quarter to twelve and settled into one of the comfortable chairs with a newspaper. Reading the papers was an important part of his job, but he found it hard these days to care very much. So although he had theoretically gone through that day's *Irish Times* already, almost every story seemed new to him as he looked at it now.

Occasionally the door to the café would open and he'd glance up expectantly, but the customers were generally getting takeaway coffees and didn't even glance in his direction. So when she pushed open the glass door and stepped inside, he didn't, at first, realise it was her. It was her gentle voice that had attracted him to her, but he wasn't expecting her to be so beautiful. Yet she was; standing there in a black leather jacket, white wool skirt and black boots, her gleaming hair falling softly around her face. She was the kind of girl who immediately attracted attention. He knew, because he'd lived with a woman for twenty-one years, that she was wearing make-up, but it was a subtle enhancement of her high cheekbones, wide blue eyes and generous mouth, not war-paint. She was a girl who, when Dorothy was alive, they would both agree was a real stunner and then turn their attention to something else. But this time Alex's attention was focused entirely on her.

She looked straight at him because he was the only other customer in the café. Her forehead creased slightly, matching his own enquiring frown.

'You are Alex?' she said.

'You're Kassia?'

She sat down opposite him. Which surprised him in a way. He'd thought that she might just walk out without speaking to him. Because clearly Kassia Kaminska was young enough to be his daughter. Alex told himself he should have thought of that before suggesting that they meet for coffee. Women working in technical support centres were bound to be young girls. It just hadn't occurred to him before.

'Hello,' she said and extended her hand. 'It's nice to meet you.'

'It's nice to meet you too,' said Alex. 'What sort of coffee would you like?'

They were both Americano drinkers, although Kassia confessed to liking lattes in the morning. They both liked rock music (when he met her on another occasion he said he'd give her a Dire Straits CD and she said that she didn't have a CD player; all her music was on an iPod). They both liked adventure movies, especially *The Abyss*, but also *Independence Day* and *The Bourne Identity*. Their favourite holiday destinations were all sun locations. They had a lot in common. Except for the fact that Kassia was twenty and Alex was forty-six. That Kassia was young, free and single and that Alex was still a grieving middle-aged widower.

'Are you out of your mind?' demanded Antoinette a few weeks later when he told her about his new girlfriend. 'It's not that I don't think you should get out and enjoy your-self again – the last couple of years have been horrendous for you – but what are you thinking of, dating a Russian teenager?'

'She's Polish, not Russian.' Alex corrected her. 'And she's not a teenager.'

'Might as well be,' Antoinette said. 'For heaven's sake, Alex, get real. I don't know what this girl wants, but it's not your good company.'

'Why?' asked Alex. 'Why shouldn't she want my company?'

'Because you're too old for her,' replied Antoinette brutally. 'You're a different generation. And actually I do know what she wants – your money.'

Alex laughed. It was the first time he'd laughed in front of Antoinette since Dorothy's illness.

'She's not after my money,' he said. 'I'm not rich enough.'

'To her you probably are,' said Antoinette.

His eyes darkened. 'That's incredibly racist of you,' he said. 'You can't assume that just because she's Polish she needs money or is looking to pick up someone with money.'

'I'm not thinking of it because she's Polish, you moron!' cried Antoinette. 'It's because she's just a kid. You're a father figure with cash, that's all.'

'You don't know what you're talking about,' said Alex. 'But then, you never did.'

Alex wasn't rich enough for a proper gold-digger to target. He had a reasonably good job, the mortgage on his house was low, and he drove a two-year-old BMW, but he wasn't a trophy husband. Nor was he an extravagant man with extravagant tastes. But Kassia wasn't extravagant either. She cycled to work most of the time, and once, when he'd offered to pick her up afterwards, she'd said that it was fine, she preferred the bike.

He asked her why she'd come to Ireland and she'd told him that it was because everyone said it was a nice place with friendly people. She hadn't intended to stay for more than a couple of months, but she was enjoying her time in Dublin and had started dating a guy from the cable company. John Storey had found her the job in technical support, and even though they weren't going out any more, they were still friends. Alex had been a bit concerned about the still-friends part of it, but then he'd learned that John was now going out with a girl from Mullaghmore and so he stopped worrying.

Anyway, the thing was that Alex – to his unutterable surprise – looked forward to meeting Kassia whenever he could, and she looked forward to meeting him too. There had been quite a lot of conversations at the start between them about the age gap, but as they told each other solemnly, they were good friends who shared a lot of interests. There were times when they were out together, when Alex felt the eyes of other people upon them, making judgements. It wasn't that he thought he was decrepit and ancient-looking, and forty-six was probably the new twenty-six, but sometimes he could see people mentally calculating the difference in their ages and wondering (until Kassia kissed him publicly on the cheek, as she often did; she was a warm, kissing sort of girl) what the connection was between them. It annoyed him beyond measure to think that some people would regard her in the same light as Antoinette did simply because she was young and beautiful and not Irish. And it annoyed him even more when people spoke about her as though she was nothing more than a sexual plaything.

'Great for the morale,' Jimmy Shine in New Accounts said to him one afternoon.

'You randy old dog,' Martin Halpenny told him.

'How on earth did you manage to grab that?' asked Brendan Lawless enviously.

Alex supposed that he would've reacted the same way if any of his friends had turned up at the company's autumn fair with a woman as gorgeous as Kassia on their arm. He probably would have made the same assumptions. That for her it was all about nabbing a well-off man. That for him it was all about sex with a hot, young woman. That they were both getting something out of the relationship. But that there was no way they could possibly be in love.

Kassia unbuttoned his cotton shirt. The tips of her fingers grazed his chest as each button opened. Her movements were slow and unhurried. She was, Alex admitted, a very sensual woman. Dorothy, too, had been sensual. But it was hard to remember that part of Dorothy when it had been impossible for them to do anything remotely sensual for the last year of her life. (Not because she didn't try. Not because he didn't want to. But because neither of them could help thinking that there was no future in what they were doing any more.)

'I love you,' said Kassia again.

He loved her accent. That was even more sensual than her long legs, long hair and more-than-a-handful breasts.

'I love this part of you.' She kissed the base of his throat. 'And this.' She kissed him on his stomach. 'And most of all . . .' She moved lower and he twined his fingers in her spun-gold hair.

The first time he'd made love to Kassia was three months after he met her. They'd gone to the cinema together and she'd asked him back to her studio apartment.

'It's very small,' she said. 'But I like being by myself.'

He nodded. 'Compact,' he agreed. 'But nice.'

It was neat, tidy and well maintained. The furniture was modern. The walls were off-white and covered in framed photographs.

'Poland,' she said. 'This one is my parents.' She pointed to a couple standing outside an anonymous house. The woman was slight and pretty. The man was stocky. Both were smiling.

'This one is my brothers.' She showed him another photo, of three young men, all bundled up in heavy coats and wearing wool hats. 'Last winter. Very cold.' She grinned at him.

'Are all your family except you still in Poland?' he asked.

'No, no. Danek now is in England. Iwan in the Netherlands. Jerzy still home.' She smiled. 'We travel a lot. But in the end, home is very important.'

Alex nodded. 'Do you miss home?'

'Sometimes,' she confessed. 'But not everything about Poland is perfect.'

'Did you have a boyfriend there?' As soon as he asked the question, Alex knew it was stupid. She was a gorgeous young girl. She must have had plenty of boyfriends. And how pathetic a question was it to ask in the first place?

'Lots and lots.' She grinned mischievously at him. 'Luiz and Mirco and Slawek and Wictor . . .'

'OK, OK.' He held up his hands. 'I shouldn't have asked.'

'Nice boys,' she said. 'Not as nice as you, though.'

He smiled. 'Thank you, Kassia. But I guess I'm not a boy. In fact . . .'

'Don't say.' She put her finger over his lips. 'Don't say.'

She was looking into his eyes. He was looking into hers. And suddenly, for the first time since Dorothy's death, he felt alive inside.

He cried afterwards. He didn't know why but he couldn't help it. Kassia lay beside him and let him sob. She didn't say a word. Eventually she rolled on to him and kissed him again. He held her tightly and they made love for a second time. After that, he didn't cry.

Antoinette nearly flipped altogether when he told her his plans for Christmas.

'Now I know for sure you've lost your mind,' she told him. 'You're spending all that money on her to go to a luxury hotel? You and Dorothy never went to luxury hotels for Christmas.'

'That's because we liked being at home,' said Alex. 'Dorothy was traditional like that.'

'Dorothy was right,' said Antoinette. 'Christmas is a time for families. Not for . . . for . . .'

'For what?' asked Alex dangerously.

'Oh for God's sake! For some kind of sordid love-nest thing.'

'It's not sordid.'

'Even so. It shouldn't be about . . . whatever it's about for you now.'

'Why not?' he asked.

'Come on, Alex.' Antoinette tried to sound understanding. 'Nobody knows more than me how difficult this Christmas will be for you. That's why I wanted you to spend it with me and Conal and the boys. With family who love you and care about you and understand you.'

'You're right,' said Alex. 'It will be hard. Very hard. And that's why I don't want to do something that reminds me . . .' He shrugged. 'I want it to be different.'

'It would be different with us,' Antoinette pointed out. 'You've never spent Christmas with us. We have such a good time. Conal does a fantastic dinner, and—'

'And that's your Christmas, not mine,' interrupted Alex. 'You have your traditions. Dorothy and I had ours. Now I want to do something different and not at all traditional. I don't want to get stuck into someone else's tradition.'

'So why doesn't this Kassia girl want to go home to her family?' demanded Antoinette. 'Don't they have a Christmas tradition of their own?'

'She's working until Christmas Eve lunchtime,' said Alex. 'She's back to work on St Stephen's Day lunchtime. She's going home for New Year instead.'

'The whole thing is crazy,' said Antoinette. 'You're crazy.' She looked at her brother and her eyes softened. 'I want

231

you to be happy, Alex. You know I do. But taking up with this girl isn't the way.'

'I like her,' said Alex obstinately. 'I want to be with her. We're going to the Sugar Loaf Lodge for Christmas and that's an end to it.'

Kassia had been very surprised when he told her what he had planned.

'You want us to be away together?' She looked at him from her brown eyes. 'For Christmas?'

'Yes,' he said.

'To stay in this hotel overnight?'

'Yes,' he repeated.

'You and me only?'

'Yes,' he said for a third time.

'Are you sure?'

'Absolutely.'

She smiled. When Kassia Kaminska smiled, her entire face lit up.

'I look forward to it very much,' she told him.

'So do I,' he said.

They ordered room service for lunch, then watched *Mission: Impossible* on TV, so dusk was already drawing in by the time they got dressed and went downstairs. The big lobby of the hotel was full of people.

It wasn't odd to be away from home at all, thought Alex, as he steered Kassia to the bar. Plenty of people had made the same choice as him. The group of women laughing together, for example. Older women, some with clusters of rings on their fingers, so he guessed they were widowed. Antoinette would probably like him to hook up with a sensible widow, he thought. Even though these women were older than him by ten or fifteen years. He wondered how she would feel about that!

His eyes turned to a couple sitting together – two people older than him – and his heart constricted at the sight of them. He'd hoped that he and Dorothy would grow old together, but life, the bitch, had other plans. There was a young girl too, who was clearly waiting for someone, because she kept glancing at her watch and checking her phone. Even though she looked anxious, there was a maturity and self-possession about her that Kassia had yet to find. There was a guy on his own too, sitting at the bar, gazing moodily into space. Alex wondered about him. Was he also waiting for someone? It didn't seem likely, because unlike the girl, he wasn't checking the time every few minutes and he didn't keep looking anxiously at the doors. It might be nice, Alex thought, to do Christmas totally by yourself. Away from all the pressure to have a good time. Away from all the people who wanted to shoe-horn you into their idea of what your perfect Christmas should be. Perhaps, he thought, that's what I should have done this year. Perhaps it would have been better.

'Are you OK?' Kassia whispered gently into his ear.

'Yes, absolutely,' he told her.

'Thank you for bringing me here.'

'Thank you for coming.'

*

He'd bought her a necklace for Christmas. A Newbridge silver-plated necklace, which was neither too expensive nor too cheap and looked stunning on her. She'd bought him a jumper in indigo blue.

'It matches your eyes,' she told him on Christmas morning as they sat in their room, once again wrapped up in their robes.

'You think so?' He held it up to his face.

'Definitely,' she said.

He liked the way she said 'definitely', with a strong Dublin accent. He liked her Polish accent too, but hearing her say 'def'ntly' made him smile.

'You are happy?'

'Yes,' he told her. 'Very happy.'

'So am I.' She kissed him on the cheek. 'I am very happy with you, Alex.'

His mobile phone rang. It was Antoinette.

'I called to wish you a happy Christmas,' she said.

'Thank you. Same to you too.'

'Are you having a good time?'

'Yes.'

'You're not . . . not lonely or anything, are you?'

'Not a bit.'

'You don't have to pretend, Alex.'

'I'm not.'

'We all understand how hard last year was. We understand you need a fling. We do. Really.'

He listened to Antoinette while he watched Kassia. She was neatly folding the wrapping paper from their gifts to each other.

'It's just that we don't want you to get too caught up in something,' said Antoinette. 'On the rebound, so to speak.'

'I'm not . . .' He broke off, not wanting to use words like 'on the rebound' in front of Kassia. 'I'm not caught up,' he said eventually.

'Oh come on!' exclaimed Antoinette. 'You're obsessed with that girl. You're with her all the time.'

'I was with Dorothy all the time too,' said Alex. 'It's the way I am. I can't help it.'

Kassia glanced at him at the mention of Dorothy's name.

'I've got to go,' he told Antoinette. 'I'm having a lovely Christmas and I hope you are too.'

'Is your sister OK?' asked Kassia.

He nodded. 'She's fine. Everything's fine.'

Later that night they played charades with a group of other guests. It was a game Dorothy had been good at. She'd always been able to guess the answers quickly, even with incomprehensible mimes and obscure books or movies.

'I'm a good guesser,' she used to say. 'And I remember titles. I'm good at titles.'

Kassia was hopeless, though. They'd teamed up with a young couple who made some inspired guesses, but they still came last in the competition. However, they laughed a lot and enjoyed chatting to Jim and Laura, who explained that they'd come to the Sugar Loaf Lodge to escape their families.

'They can be horrific this time of year,' Alex agreed.

'Although it is nice to be with people you love.' Kassia moved closer to him and put her hand on his arm.

'You two are great.' Laura smiled at them. 'At first we thought – well, we weren't sure how you were connected. But you're lovely together. Absolutely perfect.'

'You will embarrass him,' said Kassia, who knew exactly what they'd been thinking. 'He hates that he is so much older than me. He is always reminding me that I am a young girl who needs to get out and have friends and enjoy life. He forgets that I am doing this with him.'

'We all think we know what's best for other people,' said Laura. 'But we can only do what's best for ourselves.'

She was very wise, that Laura girl, Alex thought later that night. She was right about doing what was best for yourself. But what was best for him might not be best for Kassia. He'd always known that. Because there was no question about it: she had a life ahead of her that would surely be better if she was with someone closer to her in age. Even though he didn't feel as old now as he'd done a few months earlier. When Dorothy had slipped away from him, he'd felt about eighty. But things were different now. Thanks to Kassia, he'd got his mojo back. He felt good. And it was all down to her.

But he couldn't depend on her for ever. It was certainly true that young, pretty girls could be attracted to older, wealthy men. (Though surely someone older and richer than him, with heart and prostate trouble, would be better fodder for fortune-hunters, he thought.)

But that wasn't the case with Kassia Kaminska.

Antoinette had certainly been wrong in thinking that

Kassia cared about him for his money. She wasn't an impoverished immigrant. Her family wasn't poor and depending on her to send back cash. Her father was a director of an oil and gas exploration company. Her mother a qualified chemist. Kassia had been brought up in a loving home with a good standard of living. She'd come to Ireland to improve her English and to spend some time away from home, not because she was an economic migrant looking for work.

She'd be going back to Poland one day. He knew that. She knew that. When she said that she loved him, she meant in the here and now and not for ever. But that was OK. He could live with that. He *was* living with that.

And for Alex, the joy of living was the best present that he could possibly have got that Christmas.

'Hey, Alex!' She was smiling at him, her iPod in her hand. 'Wanna do some Christmas air guitar with me?'

'Absolutely.' He got to his feet.

She hit play.

And the two of them laughed out loud as they rocked in the bedroom together while Suzi Quatro belted it out from the speakers.

War Hill

For the past ten years, Michelle had done Christmas at home. Or, as she sometimes put it, Christmas had done her. Done her in, she would mutter darkly, recalling the cooking and the cleaning and the decorating and the present-wrapping, which started at the beginning of December. (And the shopping, naturally, which started even earlier.) So many things to do for just one bloody day! It was a nonsense, really it was. And yet if she didn't do it, she felt guilty. As though she'd let everyone down. As though she'd burst the Christmas bubble.

Three years ago, she hadn't bothered to ice the Christmas cake because nobody actually liked the icing and they always left it on the side of their plates, but there'd been uproar. Christmas wasn't Christmas, apparently, unless the cake had its smooth white coating, red ribbon and little white snowman on top. Christmas also wasn't Christmas without the real pine tree laden with the glass balls that they'd built up over the years. To make it a proper Christmas, the house had to smell of cinnamon and spices. And finally, the whole family had to turn up at Michelle's, even though there were twelve of them now, which turned cooking dinner into a major production. The diners were Michelle herself, her husband Derek, their eldest daughter, Kimberley (and, since the previous year, her son, Luka), their other children, Paul, Jessica, Samantha and Davey, Michelle's parents, Arthur and Dolores, and Derek's mother, Pammie.

Michelle wasn't the only one who could have taken Arthur and Dolores or Pammie for Christmas Day, but that was how things had turned out. In the early years she and Derek had actually alternated between going to his parents and hers. But when his father died, the system changed. Derek had thought that it would be nice to ask Pammie to their house. And it was Michelle who'd suggested that Arthur and Dolores should come too. It was only meant to be for one year. Yet somehow it had become a regular arrangement. Michelle often wondered how she'd allowed herself to be the lynchpin of a tradition that meant that neither Derek's brothers and sisters (Lou, Brian and Kevin) or her own (Margaret, Patricia, Catherine and Peter) ever had to worry about a turkey and ham dinner with all the trimmings followed by plum pudding with brandy sauce for a dozen people. (Eleven really, she supposed. She herself never ate anything. She was too stressed to bother.)

Catherine had once said that she envied Michelle's Christmas dinners. Proper family Christmases, she had said. Everyone around the table together, just like it was meant to be. Michelle had suggested that Catherine should try it out herself, but Catherine had quickly pointed out that she didn't have room in her apartment for such a big crowd. And besides, she and Laurence, her husband, always went to his parents. It was their tradition.

239

In fact, Michelle realised, the rest of her family's tradition was based around going out to dinner. She was the only fool who'd got landed with being the place that everyone came to. She told herself that she enjoyed it really. And there was definitely a part of her that felt very proud as everyone sat down at a table which truly did groan with the weight of the food she'd cooked. But just for once, she thought every year, just for once it would be nice not to have to bother. It would be nice to be the one who was looked after, rather than the one who was doing the looking after. And it would be nice to be able to sleep during December instead of lying in bed going through checklists over and over again.

Derek had first mentioned this year's Christmas in August. They'd been lying out in their postage-stamp back garden enjoying an unexpectedly hot day given that the summer had, for the most part, been cloudy and cool. An unexpectedly quiet day too, because Kimberley had taken Luka for a walk (she was on another diet, and pushing the pram around the estate was part of her weight-loss plan); Paul and Jessica were out with their respective girlfriend and boyfriend; Samantha had gone to Portmarnock with her best friend Nicola and her family; and Davey (their youngest, the drunken mistake, who they loved madly) was at a summer football camp. Adding to the unaccustomed serenity of number 18 Palmer's Park was the fact that their neighbours on both sides of their terraced house were on holidays and so there was no music blaring from number 16 as would usually be the case, nor was Dommo Harrison from number 20 disturbing the peace with the noisy motor-mower and hedge-trimmers that were taken out every weekend from May to September.

Michelle had been almost asleep on the plastic sunlounger when Derek spoke.

'Not long now till Christmas.'

His words penetrated her mind and her eyes snapped open.

'Would you shut up about Christmas,' she told him sharply. 'I'm trying to enjoy the fact that summer's finally arrived, for God's sake.'

'I was just thinking,' Derek said defensively, 'that I need to paint the dining room before then. It's looking a bit tatty.'

The dining room (not a separate room; just a part of the kitchen really) always looked tatty. That was because it was the place where everyone congregated.

'We could really do with a new table,' Derek added. 'When Luka gets a bit bigger there won't be room for him. Not with everyone else too.'

'I'd love to do something different this year,' said Michelle dreamily. 'I wish we could go away. Susan Cassidy's going to the Canaries.'

'We can't afford it.'

'I know.'

'You wouldn't like the Canaries anyway,' said Derek. 'Not at Christmas.'

'Yes I would.'

'Sure, she's only going because she doesn't have anyone to spend Christmas with,' said Derek dismissively. 'Ever since she split up with Con, she's been at a loose end.'

'No.' Michelle disagreed with him. 'She's having a great time. Wasn't she in France earlier this year? And didn't she go for a city break to Madrid?'

'On his bloody money.'

'She has her own job,' Michelle reminded her husband.

'So who's she going with to the Canaries?'

'Her sister-in-law.'

'Not Natasha? Con's own sister?'

'They were always great friends.'

'You women never cease to amaze me. I thought Natasha would've supported him and not stayed pally with Susan.'

'Nat was friends with Sue long before she and Con got married,' Michelle reminded him.

'Huh.' Derek, who had also been lying on a sunlounger, got up. 'I'm getting a tinnie from the fridge. Want one?'

Michelle shook her head. She closed her eyes again. And dreamed of Christmas in the Canaries.

But when the opportunity came along, she decided not to go for the Canaries after all. She thought it would be too much hassle, rounding everyone up, keeping them together at the airport, making sure that Davey didn't disappear somewhere before the flight was called and cause them to miss it altogether. (Davey had an uncanny ability to vanish into thin air. One minute he'd be standing beside her; the next he was gone. It drove her demented.)

The idea of the Sugar Loaf Lodge came to her while she was working the evening shift at the checkout in the shopping-centre supermarket. The two customers unpacking the trolley were talking about it, saying that someone called Grace had booked it for Christmas and that it would be fun for the four of them to be there this year. They said that Grace always picked the best spots and that she was fantastic really, wasn't she, looking after them year after year, arranging everything so that nobody else had to worry. Michelle had heard of the Sugar Loaf Lodge. It had been featured in the in-store magazine earlier in the year as a luxurious place to stay.

When she got home she looked it up on the family computer. They had Christmas packages. She phoned them straight away.

She didn't say anything to anybody. She let them think that everyone would gather as usual at Palmer's Park on Christmas Day for her traditional dinner. She knew that she'd have to tell them sooner or later, but she kept the secret tight to her chest, enjoying the fact that she was the only one who knew it. When, at the beginning of November, Derek asked her whether she'd baked the Christmas cake yet, she said that she'd get around to it shortly. When Pammie phoned a couple of weeks later and asked if she needed any early Christmas shopping done, she told her that everything was under control. She hugged herself every time anyone said anything about Christmas. It was like a tonic to her, knowing that twelve people wouldn't be squashed around the dining room table that year.

She allowed Derek to do the painting, though. He'd been right about the dining room. It was very tatty.

*

243

Samantha and Davey helped her with the decorations. Davey talked about the Nintendo games he wanted for Christmas, making sure that she knew exactly which ones to get. And what accessories he wanted too. Samantha said that gift vouchers would do her just fine. It was better to be able to buy something she really liked rather than something Michelle thought she liked. The older children didn't ask for anything. They knew that money was tight that year. Which was why they said nothing when they noticed that she hadn't bought tins of biscuits, large bottles of lemonade and the trays of lager that were usually stacked in a corner of the kitchen.

She kept her plans secret until the day before Christmas Eve, when the whole family (except, of course, her parents and Pammie) were lounging in front of the TV.

'I have something to tell you,' she said into a lull in both conversation among the children and the programme on TV. Kimberley looked up from tickling Luka under the arms, but the rest of them ignored her.

She cleared her throat. 'Something important to tell you,' she said more loudly.

Derek, who'd been reading the *Evening Herald*, lowered the paper and looked at her. The others turned towards her too.

'There's a change of plan this Christmas,' she said.

'What sort of change?' It was Derek who asked the question. He closed the newspaper and put it to one side. 'I thought you said you'd got everything under control?'

'I have,' said Michelle.

'But you haven't bought the lager yet,' Derek said. 'I asked you about it. Don't tell me you're expecting us to have a dry Christmas!' His voice was suddenly anxious.

'Oh, don't be silly,' said Michelle.

'What's the change of plan, Mam?' asked Samantha.

'We're not spending it at home,' Michelle told her.

The children, and Derek, looked at her in astonishment.

'What d'you mean?' he asked eventually.

'I thought it would be fun to go away. Just for a day or two,' she added.

'Too right it would be fun,' Derek agreed. 'But (a) we can't afford it, (b) it's a bit late to try and organise something now anyway, and (c) we have fun here. Don't we?'

'Yes,' said Michelle. 'We do. And I like having you all around. But it's exhausting for me, and just one year I'd like a rest from it.'

'We help out,' said Kimberley. 'You know we do.'

Michelle nodded. Her family's notions of helping out were very different from her own. Whenever they helped out, things took twice as long. But she knew that they did their best.

'I wanted to give myself a Christmas present this year,' she told them. 'I thought about what the best one would be, and going to a hotel is it.'

'A hotel!' Paul looked astonished. 'All of us? For Christmas Day?'

'For three days,' said Michelle.

'Listen, love, I know you might want to do this,' said Derek urgently, 'but we really can't afford it. Even the most basic hotels jack up their prices for Christmas. The cost of dinner alone . . .' His eyes widened as he calculated dinner for twelve in his head and he felt a little sick jolt in the pit of his stomach.

'I wasn't thinking of a basic hotel,' Michelle said. 'I've booked the Sugar Loaf Lodge.'

The entire family stared at her as though she'd lost her mind. Derek started to laugh.

'This is a joke, isn't it?' he asked. 'It's your way of making us appreciate you more. I understand that. I know you feel put-upon sometimes. I know Christmas is hard work for you. I'm sorry that we don't pitch in as much as we should. But this year we will. I promise you. We'll help with the veg and with setting the table and anything else you need. So you'll get a break. As much as the rest of us.'

'I know I'll get a break,' said Michelle smugly. 'The Sugar Loaf Lodge does welcoming drinks and Christmas dinner in its world-famous restaurant. You get a full breakfast and a buffet lunch . . . and it has a magnificent spa. I've booked us into the spa, by the way,' she told Kimberley, Jessica and Samantha. 'I thought we could do with some girlie time.'

'Michelle . . .'

'It has a games room too,' she added. 'Snooker and pool, that sort of thing. Enough to keep the boys happy, I'm sure.'

'Michelle, sweetheart, it's a lovely idea but it's just not possible. You can't have borrowed the money for this, the bank would never give it to us.' Derek looked worried. 'And if you've gone to one of those money-lenders . . .'

'I didn't borrow the money,' she said. 'What d'you take me for? I never borrow money for things like holidays. Only for cars and stuff. But we don't really need a new car. The people carrier's still in great nick.'

'Michelle . . .' Derek was concerned about her now. She was living in some fantasy world. He wondered if she'd been under massive strain at the supermarket. It was always manic in December. It would send anyone round the twist. 'Stop talking like this. It's nonsense. Look, maybe after Christmas you and I could go away for a few days. To Galway, perhaps. Remember that lovely little B and B we stayed in the year before last? That'd be nice, wouldn't it?'

'Well, maybe,' she said. 'But that'd be a completely separate trip.'

'What's going on?' Derek asked finally. 'What's this all about?'

'I won some money.'

Her secret was out. Finally she'd told them. Part of the reason she hadn't said anything before was because she'd been afraid. Afraid that if she said it out loud it would all turn out to be a terrible mistake. Even after she'd got the money and lodged it carefully in her account, she'd still be worried it might disappear. She'd logged on to the bank every single day to check that it was still there and that nobody had robbed it. And when she'd decided to blow a chunk of it on the Sugar Loaf Lodge, she'd waited with bated breath until her booking deposit cheque had cleared.

'You what?' Derek stared at her.

'Won some money,' she told them.

'On what?' asked Samantha.

'The lotto,' she said. 'Not the main prize,' she added hastily. 'Not millions or anything like that.'

'How much?' asked Paul.

'A nice little bit,' she told him. 'Enough to bring us all

to the Sugar Loaf Lodge for Christmas. Enough to give myself a Christmas present.'

Derek didn't know what to say.

'Jeez, Ma, couldn't you have used it for something else?' asked Kimberley. 'Like getting the house done up or something? Or buying new clothes. Or going on holiday. Or . . . well, stuff. You're always giving out about not having stuff. And now you have a bit of money and you're spending it on a few nights in a hotel instead?'

'Yes, I am,' said Michelle.

'I don't fucking believe this,' said Derek.

'What don't you believe? That I won it? I did.'

'You won money and you never said a word? When did this happen? And you didn't think to consult me about how to spend it?'

'It was my Quick Pick and my money,' she said firmly. 'It was a little while ago. And I know what you would've wanted to do. Have a party for the neighbours. Buy a new bike. Go on holiday. Build an extension. You wouldn't have let me spend it on going away at Christmas.'

'No – because you're being ripped off,' said Derek.

'Not if I'm getting what I want,' said Michelle.

'But what about us?' asked Derek. 'And what we want?'

'Every year you say you all want to be together,' she reminded him. 'Every single year. And we will all be together. Just not in this house.'

Kimberley giggled suddenly. 'It's very posh, though, isn't it? The Sugar Loaf Lodge. We'll stick out like sore thumbs.'

'No we won't,' said Michelle. 'We'll get some new clothes to wear. We'll look great.'

'How much did you win?' asked Paul again. 'Ten grand? Twenty grand? Fifty grand?'

Michelle shook her head.

'More than that?'

'You don't need to know,' she said. 'All you need to know is what I'm doing with it.'

'Do the parents know?' asked Derek.

'Not yet.'

'They might not want to go,' he said.

'Anyone who doesn't want to go doesn't have to,' said Michelle. 'But I'm going. And that's final.'

They stood in the foyer of the hotel, their eyes wide with amazement. Arthur, Dolores and Pammie were sipping the complimentary mulled wine while Michelle dealt with the check-in. Derek watched her, surprised with the ease with which she was chatting to the woman behind the walnut reception desk. He was feeling a little overwhelmed himself, not sure if he fitted in with the style and the glamour of the people who were sitting at one end of the long room. There was a tall girl in a tight pink dress texting on her mobile phone, flicking her glossy curled hair out of her face with a casual gesture. The dress should have looked tarty, Derek thought, but on this girl it looked stunning. There were men in rugby shirts over jeans and men in suits and ties. They were accompanied by elegant women, all well dressed, all perfectly groomed. Everyone looked rich, thought Derek. And he didn't feel comfortable with that. He didn't care that he wasn't rich. But he didn't want to feel poor. These people were making him feel poor despite the fact that he was wearing a suit himself. Michelle had made him come into town with her, even though she knew he hated it at Christmas. Then she'd walked determinedly into Brown Thomas and made him buy the suit. It was the most expensive suit he'd ever owned and he was horrified by the price of it.

'I need to know,' he'd said to her. 'How much bloody money did you win?'

'You don't need to know,' she said. 'I told you it wasn't the jackpot, so that gives you a ballpark.'

'Why won't you tell me? I'm your husband. I deserve to know.'

Michelle frowned. 'If I tell you, you'll make plans. And I'm the one making plans.'

She appreciated that she was being controlling. But she'd never been in control of money before and she was liking every minute of it. She had to work hard not to appear totally controlling, though. Which was why she'd given the children money to buy their own clothes. She wasn't sure what they'd end up with, but she wasn't going to stress out about them. However, she would've stressed out over Derek if she'd allowed him to go out by himself. He hadn't bought a shirt or suit ever since they'd got married. He hadn't a clue about clothes. Left to his own devices he'd wear an Ireland football shirt or a Dublin GAA jersey over jeans every day. Maybe occasionally he'd swap the sporting tops for T-shirts. But that would be it.

'We might make a show of you yet,' he muttered as they followed a porter to the rooms. 'You could regret ever doing this, you know.'

*

Michelle didn't regret a single moment. It was her best Christmas ever. Dinner in the award-winning restaurant was great (being really honest, she thought her own tasted just as good, but not having to jump up and down every five minutes made all the difference – and not having to load and unload the dishwasher was bliss); the entire family had fun playing charades – and winning – instead of slouching in front of the TV or disappearing to log on to the internet; she and Derek danced in the lounge to music from the old-fashioned band, which had been sort of romantic (romantic enough to make him hold her close to him and whisper that he loved her); and the final joy was the spa treatments with the rest of the girls, which were the last word in pampering and luxury and allowed them to gossip happily among themselves about clothes and make-up and girlie things that Michelle normally didn't have time for.

'Are you going to be able to leave?' asked Derek as they lay side by side in the huge bed with its plump duvet and cool pillows.

'Sure I am.' She grinned. 'But this was great.'

'Why didn't you tell me?' There was a hardness in his voice.

'I told you why. You'd have wanted to spend it on something else.'

'Don't you think that if you'd told me I would've done what you wanted?'

'Maybe,' she said. 'But I'd've felt guilty about it because I'm sure you'd have come up with loads of other things you wanted to spend it on instead. And the way I looked

251

at it was, if you didn't know and couldn't think about it, then I could do what I wanted.'

'It's an awful lot of money to shell out on a couple of days,' he said. 'We could've done so much more with it.'

'I know,' she told him. 'I do really. But the thing is – I didn't want to do more things. I wanted to do one thing.'

'I suppose I understand that,' he said. 'I still wish . . . I wish you'd felt you could have told me.'

'I should have, yes.'

'I feel as though you don't trust me,' he said.

'Now you're being silly.'

'I don't think so. I want to think that you could tell me everything.'

'Do you tell me everything?' she asked.

He hesitated.

'I don't expect you to,' she said while he tried to think of a reply. 'I really don't. This isn't about you, Derek. It's about me. About me feeling . . . feeling that I'm making the important decisions for once in my life.'

'You always make the important decisions,' said Derek.

'I ask for things,' she said. 'You make them happen. That's the way it usually works.'

'I couldn't have done this.' He sat up and waved his arm around the room. 'I could never have afforded to bring you here.'

'That doesn't matter.'

'I felt a bit of an eejit,' he said. 'When you made your announcement.'

'I was afraid you might. But I couldn't say anything

252

beforehand. I thought it would break the spell. I thought it might all go wrong.'

He smiled suddenly and looked down at her. 'I understand that. I suppose I should say thank you. Because it was great fun. But you're right. I wouldn't have let us come here. I would have made you spend it on more drink and a bigger turkey and extra stuff for the house, and you're right, it wouldn't have been for you.'

She smiled at him too. 'D'you know what? You understanding that is the best present I could ever have.'

He laughed and lay down again. He pulled the duvet around his shoulders and snuggled up to her. 'C'mere, Mrs Murphy. Let me give you another present. A present you're never going to forget.'

'Oh!' She giggled as his hand found her breast. And began working its way lower.

'I love you,' he said.

'I love you too.'

'Happy Christmas.'

'Happy Christmas.'

He was snoring. He always snored after sex. And alcohol. But not otherwise. She slid carefully out of the bed and tiptoed into the bathroom. The marble tiles were warm beneath her feet. She loved the underfloor heating. She thought it would be great in their own bathroom, which was north-facing and never truly seemed warm enough, even when the radiator was on full blast. She wondered how much it would cost. She wanted to get it done. She knew she did.

She stared at her face in the mirrored wall behind the sink. Her skin still glowed from the beauty treatment (or maybe, she told herself, it was glowing from the sex. But the beauty treatment had definitely made a difference). It must be fantastic, she thought, to be able to afford that sort of thing all the time. To be able to take for granted the sort of life they'd led over the last few days. Not to have to juggle everything. Not to have to worry all the time. That was what made you tired. That was what ground you down. The constant worrying.

She allowed her breath to escape slowly. She'd always be a worrier, she knew that. She worried about Kimberley and Luka. No matter how much support she gave them, it was hard to be a one-parent family. She worried about Paul, who was lazy at heart. And Jessica who was too clever for her own good sometimes. She worried about Samantha's obsession with her looks and with copying tarty-looking celebrities. And she worried about Davey, who was loud and boisterous because he was the youngest in the family and wanted to make himself heard. She worried about them all, and about Derek too. He'd been made redundant twice, and that took a toll on a person. And even though his job seemed secure at the moment, you never really knew when the day would come that the men in suits walked in and told you you were no longer needed. It was important for Derek to have a job. And for him to feel as though he was the provider in the family. She knew that he hadn't enjoyed the last few days as much as she had, simply because he wasn't the one who'd paid for it.

So she had to keep the rest of the money a secret from

him. From all of them really. She would try to find ways to help them when they needed it without them knowing that there was a stash of cash salted away in her newly opened deposit account. She'd never had a deposit account before. There'd never been enough money to deposit. The lottery win had changed all that. She hadn't lied to them. She hadn't won the jackpot. But she'd won the Monday lottery prize. One million euros. It was a breathtaking sum of money. She couldn't tell them about it. They'd squabble and fight and Derek would want to stop working, but she knew, she just knew, he'd lose it if he stopped. So she had to manage things carefully. It would be a different sort of managing to the sort she'd had to do up until now. But she knew she could do it. She'd been managing carefully all of her life.

People were wrong about money not buying happiness, she thought, as she climbed back into bed. Right now she was very happy. Happier than she'd ever been.

The happiest resident of the Sugar Lodge Hotel. Who'd had the happiest Christmas.

She closed her eyes.

And not even Derek's contented snores kept her awake.

Slievemaan

Sorcha rang him on 25 November and asked him straight out what his Christmas plans were.

'For God's sake,' said Patrick irritably. 'I'm up to my neck in work. I haven't even thought about Christmas yet.'

'It's nearly December, Patrick. It'll be on us before we know where we are.'

'So what?'

'I wanted to know whether you were thinking of coming to ours this year,' she said bluntly.

'No,' he replied. 'Why would you think that I might?'

'Because I thought it would be nice for you,' said his younger sister. 'I thought that maybe this year you . . .'

'Look, thanks for asking,' he said quickly. 'I do appreciate your thinking about me. But I'll be fine whatever I decide to do.'

'It's just that you don't do anything!' cried Sorcha. 'You sit at home and you grumble and mope and . . . and we're all worried about you.'

'I don't mope!' He laughed. 'I do exactly what I want to do. Why in God's name should you be worried about me?'

'It's Christmas,' she said doggedly. 'It's good to be with family at Christmas.'

'I'm really touched that you care,' he said. 'Honestly I am. But I don't need to be with anyone.'

'You do,' said Sorcha insistently. 'You should be with us and the kids – or even with Tana and Jonathan . . .'

'Give me a break.' He groaned. 'It's supposed to be a time of peace and goodwill, and I'd find precious little of that with the two of them.'

'Hum, maybe,' Sorcha admitted, tacitly acknowledging that time spent with their elder sister and her erudite husband wasn't ever restful. Tana and Jonathan were both university lecturers who believed that knowledge was more important than wealth and that it was everybody's duty in life to learn as much as they could about the world around them. They also believed that they were best equipped to impart that knowledge to everyone they met.

'You know what it'd be like,' said Patrick. 'Two minutes in and they'd have the Trivial Pursuit DVD up and running and making me look like a total slacker because I don't know who succeeded Tutankhamun as Pharaoh of Egypt, or something equally useless.'

Sorcha chuckled. 'They do go out of their way to make you feel thick, don't they?'

'Yup,' said Patrick. 'And since they don't have very far to go in my case, I'm reluctant to give them an easy ride.'

'All the same,' said Sorcha persuasively, 'it is Christmas, Patrick, and you should think about what you really want to do.'

'I know exactly what I want to do,' he said. 'I want to do

exactly the same as I've done for the last three years. It may not be your idea of a good time, Sorcha, but I enjoy it.'

His sister sighed deeply but she didn't try to persuade him any further. And that, thought Patrick, was a result, because every year around this time she attempted to make him visit her or Tana for a few days of what, as far as he was concerned, would be absolute and utter torture, and every year he managed to get out of it.

He'd never been much of a Christmas fan. He'd liked it, obviously, when he was younger and he'd believed in Santa Claus. (How was it, he wondered, that children actually did believe in a fat man coming down a chimney? They were so damn sceptical about so many other things. It was probably the presents part that swung it for them. Anything less than a large bribe wouldn't have cut it.) But ever since he'd stopped believing (not until he was nine; he was very gullible), it just hadn't been the same. Christmas had then been a bit of a disappointment, because in a post-Santa world you never got the cool presents and your parents always gave you stuff they thought you wanted rather than things you actually did. However, there'd been a substantial period of time in his twenties when the lead-in had been a great excuse to get totally wasted and try it on with a variety of girls in the office; then the Christmas holiday period itself became a necessary few days to allow him to recover – but that was before he'd met and married the gorgeous Verity, who had an entirely different view altogether. Verity had done Christmas in a way that nobody else he knew did it; she was a complete Martha Stewart of baking and home decorating and turning the house into a seasonal showpiece that could easily have been featured in one of Stewart's own magazines.

'It's Christmas,' she used to say when he told her that co-ordinating the entire place in a single colour theme for the festive period (soft purple and silver that year) was surely taking things a bit far. 'You have to make an effort at Christmas.'

And indeed, Patrick did agree that their home was wonderful at that time of year, smelling as it did of cinnamon and ginger and other baking spices, and decked out in suitably festive style. (He wouldn't have minded just a little bit of it being left un-Christmassed – even the bathroom had a sprig of mistletoe above the mirror and cinnamon-scented candles lining the shelf around the bath.) To be fair to Verity, it wasn't just Christmas with her. She was a born home-maker regardless of the season, but it was at Christmas that she truly came into her own.

The three Christmases before Amber had been born had been quietly sophisticated. They'd invited their circle of friends around for Verity's legendary seasonal buffet, accompanied by Patrick's equally legendary heavy-on-the-alcohol cocktails. But after their daughter came along, the buffet and the cocktails were replaced by family get-togethers (mainly Verity's family; she wasn't crazy about either Tana or Sorcha and their kids); while unbreakable wooden ornaments and tubby Santa Claus models made an appearance instead of the ethereal Murano glass angels that she'd bought in New York years before he'd met her. Christmas had become a bit more boisterous, but was still a time of traditional cooking, carefully wrapped presents and the transformation of the house. It also became the time when Charles and Antonia, Verity's parents, came to stay with them for a couple of days. Which, as far as Patrick was concerned, was the fly in Verity's seasonally scented ointment, because he couldn't stand either of them, and his reserves of peace and goodwill began to fly out the window as soon as his parents-in-law walked in the front door.

Charles was a businessman who'd co-founded a travel company and had the good judgement (or maybe the good fortune) to sell it just before people started to put their own holidays together on the internet. He'd made a lot of money out of it over the years, enough to keep Verity in true Martha Stewart style, and to wonder constantly about Patrick's own wealth-generation prospects.

Patrick was an engineer. He worked for a company that was primarily involved in laying pipes, which sometimes necessitated him spending time overseas to supervise various projects. These overseas postings rarely lasted more than a few months, but Verity didn't ever come with him because the pipe-laying usually took place in remote outposts rather than major capital cities, and she wasn't good at being cut off from civilisation. (She'd thought his being sent to places like Minsk was cool when they were going out together, but changed her mind after he brought her on a Siberian visit. There was, she told him, cool and bloody freezing, and she didn't do the latter.)

The issue of Patrick's job had become a stumbling block between them, but as far as he was concerned it wasn't an insurmountable problem. It was just a question of deciding how best to deal with change.

Charles also felt that it was time for Patrick to rethink his career prospects, and he wasn't shy about saying so.

'You have a family now,' he told Patrick on Amber's first Christmas. 'It's not just yourself you have to think about.'

Patrick was annoyed at the older man for the tacit implication that he'd been a selfish sod until then. He thought that going abroad was often a bit of a hardship, certainly from his point of view. He enjoyed his work and he liked going to new places, but he always ended up feeling homesick after the first week. He missed Amber and he missed Verity. He thought that Verity missed him too.

Wrong, wrong, wrong.

Even now, when he obsessed about it, as he often still did, he got a stabbing pain in his stomach and he could feel himself gasping for air. He wondered whether other men felt the same way whenever they considered their wrecked marriages. Or was he the only stupid sod who still wanted to cry when he remembered the day that his wife had left him for another man?

He hadn't had the slightest idea. He'd been getting on with his life, working hard, earning money, proud of his family. He hadn't realised how becoming a father would make him feel; he hadn't been prepared for the sense of responsibility that had engulfed him the moment he'd picked up his daughter and looked into her dark blue eyes.

'I'd do anything for you,' he'd said. But that had been a lie, because in the end he hadn't.

He hadn't changed jobs. He'd been offered a promotion in the engineering company and he'd taken it because he'd thought it would be good for him (less long-term overseas travel and more money) and because he'd thought that Verity would be happy. But she'd actually been annoyed, because he'd just come home and told her about it instead of discussing it with her first. What he hadn't known then was that Charles was trying to arrange an interview for him in a company managed by one of his business acquaintances. Patrick had been annoyed too – he didn't like the idea of his wife and her father trying to organise his life. The job wasn't an engineering job. It was in administration, which filled Patrick with horror. He told Charles, who'd come to talk to him about it, that he wasn't a pen-pusher and that he never would be. Job satisfaction, he said, was far more important than the undoubtedly higher salary that the administration position would have given him. Charles had retorted that the time had come for Patrick to grow up and stop getting his hands dirty like a kid, and to be a bit more strategic about his life. Patrick's response was that he was happy with his life and so was Verity, and that Charles should just butt out.

He hadn't expected to fight with Verity about it. He thought she understood how he felt. He assumed she was on his side. But she wasn't.

'This is a great opportunity,' she protested. 'You could be in management.'

Patrick had snorted at that and told her that he wasn't a management person and never would be. And that he liked what he did. He'd never for a second imagined that it would lead to the end of his marriage.

It didn't, not directly. But Verity had been peeved by his dismissive attitude and Charles had been annoyed with him too, and the following Christmas, when they were all gathered around the dinner table, there had been an undercurrent of tension that had never been there before. And then Patrick had been asked to go to Abu Dhabi for three months to be part of a pipe installation team there, and he'd accepted the job even though Verity didn't really want him to. But he'd thought that it would be a good idea to show her and Charles who was in charge in his family.

It hadn't been a good idea at all, though, because while he was away Verity had met Steven, a chef with his own restaurant, and somehow Steven had become the love of her life.

So she said, anyway, when Patrick came home.

'But what about us?' he'd asked in bewilderment.

'I'm sorry,' she said, and he thought she sounded sincere. 'I just don't love you any more.'

'What about our family?' he demanded. 'What about Amber? What about your future? How can it possibly include a bloody chef, for God's sake! I thought your father wanted you to marry someone who didn't get his hands dirty!'

'Daddy doesn't run my life,' she told him. 'Steven and I love each other. He's there for me so much more than you ever were. Besides,' she had the grace to look shamefaced, 'Dad likes him. He thinks he has great potential. He thinks he could be a real force in the gourmet world.'

Patrick felt as though he had been whacked by a monkey wrench. Did she really believe what she was saying? Was she truly in love with this jerk? Did she really think he'd be around more than him, when everyone knew because of all those celebrity-chef TV programmes that running a restaurant was demanding and difficult and time-consuming – and just because the person was in the country it didn't mean that they were more available than someone in bloody Abu Dhabi anyway. Besides, there'd surely be massive tension in the kitchen because Verity herself, in her Martha Stewart mode, loved to cook, and how would that possibly work with a prima donna chef in the wings? Patrick pointed all this out to her, but she dismissed it as the jealous ranting it actually was. Meanwhile he gave the whole thing a few months, telling himself that she'd been feeling lonely and neglected and berating himself for not having realised how difficult it was for her when he was away. He'd forgive her, he decided, when she came running back to him. He couldn't help loving her. And he missed Amber dreadfully. But somehow, incredibly, Verity's relationship with Steven had lasted. And then the chef had suddenly become a celebrity himself, thanks to his own TV programme, which, to Patrick's rage, was an instant success. Patrick raged even more when Steven invited the cameras into his home for a Christmas special and he recognised Verity's handiwork in the wreaths and the place settings and the candles and the decorations in the home that she now shared with the chef in the rolling Wicklow hills.

'He understands me,' she'd said to him when he was trying to save his marriage. 'He doesn't make jokes about the way I like things to be nice.'

Which was a low blow, because Patrick had always joked about the cinnamon and the wreaths and everything else even though he didn't mind it really and had actually said so on a number of occasions.

But the real blow, as far as he was concerned, the one

that left him reeling, had been losing Amber. The law, he decided, was an utter joke when it came to fathers' rights, because he couldn't help feeling like a bit player in the new Steven-Verity-Amber unit. He was given access to his daughter and holiday times were split between Verity and him, but it was as though he should consider himself lucky to be able to have a relationship with his own child. Even if she always seemed very happy to see him. Especially at Christmas.

The break-up of his marriage had soured his already ambivalent feelings towards the whole Christmas carnival. And too much festive fun made him think of the times when he'd been surrounded by holly and mistletoe but had also thought that he was surrounded by love.

So for the last few years he'd junked Christmas altogether. He'd steered clear of the decorations and the trees and all that palaver and he hadn't bothered with the turkey and ham extravaganza dinner thing at all. He would go to Tesco and buy one of their Finest range of ready-meals (last year it had been chicken with chorizo and manchego cheese) and he'd eat it sitting on the sofa in front of the TV, while watching the kind of movies that Verity had never let him watch, like spaghetti Westerns or the entire *Star Wars* movie franchise. (He was aware that he might have been edging into nerdy anorak territory by indulging in *Star Wars*, but he'd always enjoyed the movies and it had been years since he'd seen any of them.) He would drink beer with his dinner – not truly because he preferred beer to wine when eating, but mainly because he knew that the idea of beer and food would piss off his ex-wife and the chef. On 26 December

265

he would go to the horse racing at Leopardstown, where sometimes he won and sometimes he lost, but at no time did it matter very much to him either way. And on the twenty-seventh he was usually back to work, where he cleared away any cards that were still lurking around the place and generally got everything ready for the year ahead.

'You're like Scrooge, Uncle Patrick,' his youngest nephew, Sorcha's son, had once said to him, and he'd replied that he wasn't a bit like Scrooge because he usually got people presents, but if the children wanted to think of him as Scrooge, that was perfectly fine and he'd keep the gifts for himself. At which Rory looked horrified and assured him that he wasn't Scrooge-like at all and could he please have his Christmas present as usual.

Patrick quite liked to be thought of as grumpy Uncle Scrooge. It was how he felt. Scrooge, he thought, had a lot to recommend him. He was very much misunderstood.

The day after Sorcha called him, it was Tana who phoned.

'We are totally concerned about you, Patrick,' she said in the brisk tone she always used when talking to him. 'We accepted that the first year after Verity left you, you might not have felt like having a good time, but it's been a few years now and you really can't go to seed every single December. It's not like she died, you know.'

Patrick felt his grip on the receiver tighten. As far as he was concerned it was actually worse, although he knew that not a lot of people would understand that. But the fact was that Verity was out there having fun with someone else, doing all the Christmas stuff with someone else, allowing his daughter to be given presents by someone else – and

266

that someone else was the tosser chef whose *How to Make Christmas Simple* cookbook had been a best-seller since September. If Verity had died (and he did feel bad about allowing the thought to filter into his brain, but still), if she'd died, then everyone would have been hugely sympathetic and caring and they wouldn't try to tell him to get over it with such impunity – they'd be sensitive to his loss. Plus, if she'd died, Amber would still be his. So actually he would have been much better off.

Whenever he thought like this, Patrick was sure that he was the most horrible man in the world. But he couldn't help it.

'Patrick?' Tana's voice jolted him back to the present.

'I've got plans this year,' he said.

'Oh? What sort of plans?'

He hadn't got plans. But he sure as hell knew that he didn't want to stay with his over-achieving sister and her Mensa-member husband.

'I'm thinking of going to a hotel.'

'Really?' She sounded astonished. 'You? A hotel?'

'Why not?' he asked. 'I spend a lot of time in them one way or another.'

Which was perfectly fine. When he travelled, he was usually put up in a hotel. Though not always a very good one.

'What hotel?' Tana asked.

'Somewhere nice,' he replied.

'Where?'

'I'll tell you when it's confirmed.'

Which meant that he then had to go online and search for

hotels that had rooms over Christmas, which wasn't actually as easy as he'd imagined because most of the packages were priced for two people and the cost of the single supplement was utterly outrageous. You'd imagine, he thought savagely as he scrolled through the screens, that hotels would realise that some people were choosing to go away *because* they were on their own. It was really rubbing salt into the wound to charge them even more for the privilege.

The first hotel he found that wasn't crucifying the single traveller was the Sugar Loaf Lodge in Wicklow. He remembered taking Verity there for a meal in its much talked about restaurant on the night of her thirty-first birthday. He'd been astonished that she wanted to go to what he thought was probably a pretentious place in the mountains, but she'd said that she'd heard a lot about it and it was meant to be lovely and it would be such fun. (He should've known, he thought grimly, that nothing good could've come from her flirtation with great food.) Somewhat to his surprise, he'd liked the hotel, and the food hadn't been at all bad, even though he'd had to ask them to substitute a plain salad for the quail that had been part of the set dinner menu. Which they'd done, no problem, and without making him feel like a food philistine for not wanting quail.

The hotel itself had been truly lovely, nestling as it did between the mountains and with spectacular views across the valley, and they'd talked a bit about coming back for a few nights, but they'd never got around to it.

According to the website, there was only one room available. He filled in the online booking form and sent it straight away. The confirmation email came back almost at once.

He sighed in satisfaction. He would be somewhere different for Christmas after all, and people wouldn't be able to point to him and say that he was a saddo for eating Tesco's Finest in front of the telly this year. Even if, deep down, that was what he would have preferred to do.

He arrived in the late afternoon on Christmas Eve, just as the weak winter sun began to slide beneath the horizon in a pale orange glow.

'Mr Ballantyne, you're very welcome.' The receptionist's voice crackled through the intercom as the gates swung open. 'Please drive up to the Lodge and the porter will meet you.'

He remembered that about the hotel. Everyone called it 'the Lodge' as though that was what it was, when they knew perfectly well it wasn't. He suddenly thought that he had made a mistake in having changed the routine that had served him perfectly well for the past three years.

The concierge greeted him and arranged for his car parking, and then carried Patrick's case into the reception lobby.

Patrick felt a bit of a dork having his case carried for him – he was only here for two nights, after all, and there wasn't much in the case. But he knew that this was the way these so-called exclusive hideaways liked to do things.

'It's lovely to see you, Mr Ballantyne,' said Sarah, the receptionist, who, Patrick noticed, wore her caramel-blond hair in the same chignon that Verity used to wear and which he'd always enjoyed undoing. 'Please accept a complimentary glass of mulled wine, and we hope you have a very happy Christmas at the Sugar Loaf Lodge.'

'I'm sure I will,' he said automatically, as another hotel employee handed him a glass of wine. And he would, he thought, if he could get the receptionist in a clinch behind the real Christmas tree, which was filling the air with its heavy pine scent. That took him back. Not to Christmases with Verity (because she always used an artificial tree, although it looked stunning), but to Christmases as a kid when his father used to bring him and Tana and Sorcha to buy the tree together. Tana would want a tall, angular tree while Sorcha preferred small stubby ones. He and his dad used to listen to them arguing about it and they would laugh at 'women', and then his dad would somehow always manage to select the perfect tree for them all. And then they'd go home and decorate it, and they didn't use colour co-ordination and Murano glass angels but old baubles that had been handed down through the family for years. None of them matched but it didn't matter, because their Christmas tree was always a kaleidoscope of colour and magic.

I wish I still believed in Santa, thought Patrick. I wish magic existed. I wish my marriage hadn't gone down the tubes. And I wish I was at home in front of the telly.

'You're in Slievemaan,' Sarah told him as she handed him an electronic key. 'All of our rooms are named after mountain peaks.'

Patrick knew that already. It was on their website. And they were hardly mountains, he thought to himself. Nobody who'd ever seen a real mountain range would call anything with a highest peak of 925 metres a mountain.

He stopped the porter from carrying his case to the room. It really wasn't necessary, he told him. He could manage.

270

He knew that exclusive boutique hotels weren't about managing; they were about being pampered and looked after, but there was only so much looking-after a grown man could take. He picked up his bag and told the scrumptious receptionist that he could find the room himself, and he walked off down the glass passageway that led to the residential area. The hotel was warm, which he appreciated, because according to the display in his car, the outside temperature had been hovering just above 1 degree Centigrade. Patrick was used to working in cold conditions, but he didn't like feeling cold when he was inside.

He reached the end of the passageway and saw a sign pointing to the left for a number of rooms, including Slievemaan. He followed another corridor until he arrived at the oak-wood door, which he opened by swiping his card. The hotel was a mixture of old and new, he realised, as he pushed the door inwards. The décor was traditional but the amenities were modern. Excellent, in fact, he decided as he peeked inside the bathroom and saw a TV monitor integrated into the enormous mirror behind the contemporary-designed washbasins.

He dumped his bag at the end of the very inviting king-sized bed with its huge soft duvet and array of pillows and thought that maybe staying here would be OK after all. Certainly more luxurious than the small town house he'd been renting ever since the break-up of his marriage. Perhaps it was time for a bit of luxury in his life.

He slid out of his shoes and lay down on the bed. It was beyond comfortable. He closed his eyes and fell asleep.

*

It was his mobile phone that woke him with the insistent shrilling of the old-fashioned telephone ring that he used. He looked at the caller ID and saw that it was Sorcha.

'So, how's things?' she asked. 'What's the hotel like?'

'Lovely,' he told her. 'I was asleep when you rang.'

'Sorry.' She laughed. 'Will you be all right there, d'you think?'

'For heaven's sake,' he said. 'I'm an adult. Why wouldn't I be all right?'

'It's just that it's so emotional at Christmas,' said Sorcha. 'Everyone has family around them, and you're on your own and . . .'

'Please don't start all that again,' said Patrick. 'It's people who make it so emotional. At this stage in my life it's just another day, and the truth is, dearest sister, I'm only spending it here so that you lot will leave me alone.'

Sorcha was silent.

'OK, that didn't exactly come out the way I meant,' said Patrick apologetically. 'It's not that I want you to leave me alone; it's just . . .'

'It's fine,' said Sorcha. 'You're a miserable git and you want to stay that way.'

'Ah, come on,' he said plaintively, 'you're misrepresenting me.'

'All we want is for you to enjoy yourself.'

'I do. And I will.'

'I hate that bitch.' Sorcha's tone was suddenly venomous.

'Sorry?'

'Miss Butter-Wouldn't-Melt-In-My-Pretty-Rosebud-Mouth Verity.'

'Sorcha!'

'Ah, Paddy, she's a right cow,' said Sorcha. 'She always was.'

'I thought you liked her.'

'She made me feel bloody inadequate, what with all of her cooking and stuff,' said Sorcha. 'And she was very critical of my mince pies one year.'

'Pie Wars,' said Patrick in amusement.

'And she was a bitch to you, and I hate her for that.'

'You never said any of that before.'

'Because there was a chance that she'd come to her senses, ditch the chef and come home,' said Sorcha. 'It's usually a mistake to diss someone's ex. Just in case.'

'Diss away,' said Patrick.

'She's made you a grumpy old man,' said Sorcha. 'And you're not really.'

'I always was,' Patrick assured her. 'I just didn't let it show before.'

The package he'd bought included dinner in the restaurant that night and an afternoon buffet in the Grand Ballroom the following day. He decided to have a pre-dinner drink in the Djouce bar (the bar, like the rooms, was named after one of the mountain peaks, but fortunately it didn't live up to its name and did, in fact, serve alcohol). Patrick ordered a bottle of Miller and drank it sitting in a deep armchair, which was placed beside one of the long picture windows looking out over the now dark valley.

There were a lot of people in the bar and the adjoining

lobby, both of which were alive with the buzz of conversation and laughter. Patrick wondered if everyone was as happy as they sounded – if the family group laughing uproariously in the bar (he assumed they were a family group, grandparents, parents and children) truly was a happy family or whether they were all there on sufferance; if the middle-aged couple by themselves (anxious-looking woman, determinedly cheerful man) would have preferred to spend Christmas with their children rather than alone in a hotel, or if they were thrilled not to be part of the whole big family thing; if the four older women, chattering animatedly as they knocked back their own pre-dinner drinks, had come away together because their children couldn't be bothered to invite them or if they were delighted not to have to sit through yet another interminable family dinner.

He sipped his beer and thought about other people, which he normally didn't do at all. These days he didn't do much thinking about anyone. Not even about himself. When he'd finished the beer, he walked across the lobby and into the restaurant. It too had views over the valley, and there was a terrace directly outside, where Patrick remembered sitting with Verity after their meal. She'd told him that it was one of the best birthdays ever.

The maître d' led him to a table set for one, tucked away in a corner. Patrick supposed that they wouldn't really want him in full view, a single person at a table on his own, wrecking the notion that everyone was having a good time with family and friends. People didn't usually spend Christmas Eve on their own. It looked odd. Perhaps, he thought, he should have spared their blushes and ordered room service. Maybe it was his Scrooge-like nature that had prevented him from doing that when the five-star meal was already paid for.

He'd been smart, though. He'd brought his iPad with him. Patrick liked gadgets. He had an iPhone and an iPod (for which he'd bought the coolest of Bose speakers); he had a digital radio and the most expensive laptop he could afford. He'd bought the iPad as soon as it was available and had loaded it up with as many books as he could. He brought it with him whenever he was eating out alone, because it was much easier to manage at the table than a normal book.

'Would you like to see the wine list?' The wine waiter hovered by the table, and Patrick nodded. He looked at the menu for the evening and noticed that quail was on offer again. Was there a plague of the damn birds in Wicklow? he wondered. Did the chef shoot them personally? The main course offered a choice of beef or sea bass. Though they both sounded good, Patrick remembered that the portions offered were suitably designer in size, and he decided he'd order both roast and garlic potatoes to go with his choice. He also elected to have a half-bottle of red wine.

When he'd given his order (telling the waiter not to bother with the quail and accepting the offer of vegetable tart instead), he switched on his iPad and continued with the psychological thriller he'd started the previous day.

He was halfway through chapter four and had just finished his vegetable tart when the glass doors to the restaurant swung open and Santa Claus walked in. The children in the dining room, initially shy, beamed at him when he wished them all a merry Christmas and told them that he hoped they'd be good. A boy of about seven looked at him sternly and asked if he didn't think that he should be out starting to deliver presents already, because there was a lot to do. At which Santa waved theatrically towards the windows. Outside lights came on and highlighted a large sleigh in the gardens beyond.

'I just took some time out,' said Santa. 'I'm well on the way. Got here early, so I'm letting Rudolf and the lads have a bit of a rest. That's why you can't see them.'

The children nodded.

'We've got cookies in our room for you,' said the boy graciously.

'And when I'm leaving your presents I'll be sure to have them. Thank you very much,' said Santa.

Patrick couldn't help grinning at their belief and enthusiasm. Meanwhile Santa went to every table, handing out individual Belgian chocolates to the diners.

'You on your own?' Santa's benevolent tone dropped when he reached Patrick's table.

'Afraid so.'

'Well, look, have a great Christmas.' He gave Patrick an extra chocolate. 'I hope that you get whatever you want.'

'Thanks.' Patrick was surprised to feel a lump in his throat. He couldn't believe that he was feeling emotional just because a guy he didn't know who was dressed up in a Santa outfit had done his job and been nice to him.

'That the iPad?' asked Santa.

Patrick nodded.

'A lot of them on the list this year.' Santa chuckled.

'Lighter than real books,' said Patrick.

'Ah, I'm a bit old-fashioned myself.' Santa's eyes twinkled over his white beard. 'I like the real thing.' He offloaded a few more chocolates on to Patrick's table. 'All the best, mate.'

'Thanks,' said Patrick again. 'Happy Christmas.'

Santa left the restaurant in a flurry of ho-ho-hos and a chorus of goodbyes from the children.

Patrick returned to his iPad. He didn't know how he was going to eat all the chocolates.

Normally when he sat in a bar on his own there were people to talk to. But not tonight, because they were all with someone else. The Sugar Loaf Lodge wasn't the kind of place a lone person strolled into for a quick pint and a bit of chat. He'd made a mistake in coming here if he'd thought that he would be more sociable than at home. There was no one for him to be sociable with.

Unless the girl in the pink dress was on her own.

He'd noticed her earlier, as he'd been checking in. His attention had mainly been fixed on the sexy receptionist, but he'd caught sight of the other girl walking by in her short dress and high heels while at the same time texting on her mobile. He'd supposed she was telling her boyfriend or husband to get his arse in gear. It was usually men who were doing that as they waited for women, he reckoned, but there would always be the exception to prove the rule.

He hadn't thought much more about her other than that

she was attractive in a very different way to Verity. Verity had a sweet and wholesome look about her. Her hair was soft brown and her eyes a muted blue. Everything about her was understated (or, amended Patrick, it had been, because the last time he'd been to pick up Amber, Verity and Steven had been going to some TV awards show, and he'd hardly recognised her beneath the crust of make-up. She'd said it was because of the TV cameras. He'd snorted). But anyway, most of the time she was apple-cheeked and pretty. The girl in the pink dress was not.

She was glamorous. She was perfectly made up; even Patrick could see that. He knew that the dewy glow on her skin wasn't just down to nature. He could tell that the perfect colour of her cheeks was courtesy of a pot. And even at this distance he was certain that the long, sweeping lashes framing her kohled eyes weren't her own. He wouldn't have been able to see her natural eyelashes. Nobody with hair that particular shade of honey blond would ever have lashes as dark as the night.

Her fuchsia-pink dress stood out among the winter colours of black, red and gold that so many other people were wearing. It was a short dress, probably too short to be suitable for the surroundings. It looked even shorter when she got up and walked to the bar, because the girl had very long legs. And she was wearing very, very high heels.

He wondered how she could walk in them. Verity had once bought shoes with a higher than usual heel and she'd complained that every move brought her one step closer to breaking her ankle. But the girl in the lobby, now at the bar, didn't seem to have any problems wearing the shoes.

She'd stridden confidently across the marble floor, not hesitating even once.

She ordered a cosmopolitan. She waited while the bartender mixed the drink and then she walked back to the seat she'd been sitting in, near the grand piano. She looked angry.

Patrick decided that he wouldn't like to be in the husband or boyfriend's shoes when he finally made an appearance. He doubted that there was much festive cheer in the girl, cosmopolitan cocktail or not.

The four older ladies were now sitting around one of the tables chatting animatedly. They all wore lots of jewellery and their diamond rings glinted beneath the lights of the chandeliers. Probably all rich widows, he decided. Maybe from the same family? It was hard to tell. He watched them idly for a while, and then one of them, the tallest, dressed in a gold trouser suit and wearing gold sandals, walked over to him.

'Do you play bridge?' she asked.

'No.' He was startled.

'Pity.' She clucked in irritation. 'We hoped you might. Gillian doesn't, you see. Very annoying. We need a fourth.'

'Sorry,' he said. 'I'm not your man.'

'Are you on your own?' demanded the woman in gold.

'Yes.'

'At Christmas?'

'Yes.'

'Join us anyway,' she said. 'We can't play bridge. We might as well talk to someone new.'

He wanted to say no, but the force of her personality prevented it. So he walked over to their table.

'Patrick,' he said.

'Grace,' said the woman. 'This is Gillian, Philomena and Carmel. We're the Golden Girls.'

'Pleased to meet you,' he said.

'Gill and Phil are sisters,' Grace said. 'Carmel and I are friends.'

'Any husbands among you?' Patrick wasn't sure he should ask, but he couldn't help himself.

'Not any more.' Grace gave him a rueful smile. 'I got rid of mine a long time ago. Phil had better things to do with her life than spend it chained to the kitchen sink. Carmel's Ralph passed away over ten years ago, Gill's Iggy just this summer.' Her voice softened at the last words and she shot a sympathetic glance at her friend.

'A blessing,' said Gill firmly. 'Motor neurone. He's better off.'

'Gill took good care of him,' said Phil. 'He had a full life. How about you, Patrick? Why are you here all by yourself?'

'Divorced,' he said.

'Oh dear.' Carmel was sympathetic. 'It's such a shame. Ever since that law was passed, you hear of more and more divorces.'

'It wasn't originally my idea.' Patrick didn't want them thinking he was a heartless sod who'd walked out on his wife and child. 'She had an affair.'

'No!' Gill's eyes opened wide.

'It does happen,' Grace said cuttingly. 'Remember Constance Molloy?'

The four ladies nodded in unison.

Patrick wanted to hear all about Constance Molloy, but Phil said they shouldn't speak ill of the dead. Patrick wondered whether at this time in their lives they knew more of the dead than of the living. They weren't that old, though. Sixties probably. Which wasn't supposed to be old any more.

'Do you come here every year?' he asked.

Grace explained that they always spent Christmas together although not always at the Sugar Loaf Lodge. Although, she added, it was by far the best place they'd ever come to.

'This is my first year with the girls,' Gill clarified. 'I was at home with Iggy the other times.'

'I'm sorry for your loss.' Patrick knew that people often said that when someone had died. They'd said it at his own mother's funeral.

'Thank you.' Gill smiled at him. 'You're very kind.'

She was nice, he thought. Nice and sweet and just as a mother should be. She reminded him, with her carefully styled grey hair, very slightly of his own. Not of Verity's. Antonia was a hard-hearted old bitch. Maybe a bit more like Grace than Gillian, although that was making a very general assumption about Grace just because she was forceful. That was what people did, though. All the time. They made assumptions.

'So why are you here?' asked Carmel.

'I didn't want to visit either of my sisters and I thought this was a good bet,' replied Patrick.

Phil nodded. 'You're right. But you were looking a bit left out.'

'Not really,' he assured her.

'Is this your first Christmas since the divorce?' asked Gill.

281

'No.' Patrick told them about the Christmases in front of the TV with the Tesco dinners, and they all nodded as he spoke.

'That's the trouble,' said Grace. 'There's such a fuss made about doing certain things. Especially at Christmas. Everyone wants you to do what they expect. And most times they're things you don't want to do anyway.'

'I'm very fond of my sisters,' Patrick said. 'But they have kids of their own, and quite honestly I'd just feel like a spare part if I descended on either of them.'

'Even though they keep asking you?'

'Especially because they keep asking me,' said Patrick. 'I don't want them feeling sorry for me!'

The ladies nodded again.

'I know exactly how you feel,' said Gillian. 'After Iggy died, my sons kept asking me to stay with them for a while. But I just wanted to be left alone.'

'Still, alone isn't really a good Christmas option, is it?' remarked Phil. 'That's why we're all here.'

'Huh. I'm here to have a good time,' said Carmel robustly. 'I can't wait for the dancing later.'

'There's dancing?' Patrick looked aghast.

'Like you wouldn't believe,' Grace assured him.

He danced with all of them. They insisted on teaching him how to dance properly, and he almost got the hang of it. They were good fun and they didn't ask him any more questions about his broken marriage. There wasn't time. They were laughing too much.

The girl in the short pink dress wasn't dancing. She was drinking yet another cosmopolitan. Patrick reckoned that she was going to have an almighty hangover on Christmas morning.

He woke at nine-thirty, which he thought was quite early given that he'd stayed up till nearly two in the morning with the Golden Girls. He'd wanted to go to bed as soon as the dancing finished, claiming that he was absolutely whacked, but they insisted on him staying up and chatting a little longer, and they kept him so amused with anecdotes about their lives that he didn't realise how late it had become.

They were already at breakfast when he arrived; in fact they'd almost finished and were, according to Gill, heading off for a walk. It was such a glorious morning, she told him, there was no way they could possibly stay indoors.

She was right. The gardens of the Sugar Loaf Lodge looked as though they had been specially decorated for the residents. The sky was a washed blue and the ground was covered with a hard white frost. The bare branches of the trees were dusted with frost too, so that it was almost possible to believe that it had snowed. Very traditional, thought Patrick as he tucked into bacon and sausage. Verity would have approved.

He'd phoned the house as soon as he'd woken up and talked to Amber, who could hardly speak with the excitement of having got the doll she wanted and the latest Wii games, as well as a new dress and shoes and matching ribbons. The Wii games were from Santa, and Patrick had given them to Verity the last time he'd called to the house. He'd also given her another doll and a board game that

Amber had wanted, though from what his daughter had told him it was the Wii games that were the biggest hit.

'So how's it going in the hotel?' asked Verity when she'd taken the phone from their daughter.

'Great,' he said.

'Having fun?' She said it as though she didn't expect him to.

'It's a blast,' he told her. 'Buckets of fun.'

It wouldn't have been any fun without the company of the Golden Girls. Until he'd met them he'd planned to head back to his room and watch TV. He'd actually been wondering if it would be totally tacky to select one of the adult movies. There was a seasonal one called *The Twelve Lays of Christmas.* Which could have been fun too.

Tana and Sorcha both called him and he assured them that the hotel was fine and that he was having a good time and that he didn't feel lonely and that it was more exciting than being at home with his Tesco dinner. Which was partly true.

He went for a walk himself, because it was too beautiful to stay inside. Lots of other residents had the same idea, and he was getting quite tired of saying hello to people. But it was only when he saw the couple with the young baby, who'd been sitting near him in the restaurant the previous night, that he felt an ache in his heart. He remembered pushing Amber in her buggy with Verity beside him. Back then he'd thought that he had it made. He smiled at the couple and walked on past them. Eventually he left the grounds of the hotel and trudged along the narrow twisting road that led deeper into the mountains. Hills, he reminded himself, even though the backs of his legs were beginning to ache from the incline. It was refreshing, though. And mind-cleaning. And definitely better than being in front of the TV watching *The Twelve Lays of Christmas*.

The girl in the pink dress was sitting in the lounge when he returned. She wasn't wearing the pink dress today, though. She was wearing a pair of black trousers and a red polo-neck jumper. She looked younger than the night before, with her hair tousled around her face and without the carefully applied make-up. Prettier, Patrick would have said, if less alluring. He caught her glance as he stood hesitantly, undecided about what he was going to do next. He rather thought that a hot whiskey after his bracing walk would be nice, but it was a bit early for hot whiskies. So maybe a coffee would do for now.

'Hi,' he said, feeling that it would be rude to stay silent, It was Christmas after all, and people talked to each other at Christmas. 'Have you been outside yet?'

She shook her head.

'Cold, but worth it,' he assured her.

'That's nice.'

Her voice was husky.

'You OK?' he asked.

'Absolutely,' she said.

She couldn't be on her own, he thought. He knew he'd

285

seen her by herself the previous night, but he was also certain he'd spotted her chatting to one of the couples. So perhaps she was their daughter, pissed off at having to spend Christmas with them at the hotel. He nodded to himself. That was probably it.

'I'm just going to get myself a coffee,' he said.

'Enjoy.'

He hesitated, almost asking her to join him. But then he simply wished her a merry Christmas and walked to the bar.

He looked back after he'd been served.

She wasn't there any more.

There were games organised for the afternoon. Not Wii games or PlayStation games but old-fashioned board games. Patrick didn't get involved, though he did stay in the lounge with his iPad while the others set up the boards and got stuck in. The Golden Girls were in their element, beating everyone at Scrabble and having a pretty good run at Trivial Pursuit too, although they eventually succumbed to the man called Andrew and his quiet wife, who seemed to know everything about everything and who, Patrick had thought, were the parents of the girl in the pink dress (or, today, the black trousers and red polo neck). Who was nowhere to be seen.

'There's charades later,' said Phil. 'We're good at that.'

'You're good at everything,' Patrick told her.

'Not quite.' But she laughed.

*

He was hungry by the time the buffet was served. He went to the Grand Ballroom (which might have been a ballroom but wasn't really grand, although that actually made the setting more intimate than it might otherwise have been), where a carvery had been set up and the residents were jostling for position, apparently fearful that they would be left without food, despite the enormous joints of meat being presided over by the chefs.

It hadn't occurred to Patrick to reserve a table, mainly because, once again, he'd been thinking of eating alone in his room in front of the TV and thus preserving his personal traditional Christmas. It seemed odd, however, to sit on his own, and when he'd finally finished piling his plate with food, he stood indecisively at the edge of the buffet and scanned the room.

Would it be totally inappropriate to barge in on someone else's table? he wondered. Even though it was Christmas?

'Excuse me.'

It was the girl in the black trousers and the red polo neck.

'Hi.' He smiled at her. He was doing a lot of smiling, he realised, which was very unlike him these days.

'I was wondering . . .' She looked at him hesitantly. 'Would you mind awfully if I joined you for dinner? It's just that you seem to be on your own and I am too, and I didn't think . . . Well, it's just not right, is it, being on your own?'

'No, it's not,' he agreed. 'And I'm very grateful for you sitting with me because otherwise I might have been labelled the saddo single bloke again.'

'Surely not a saddo?' There was the faintest hint of dry

humour in her voice. 'I thought I saw you salsaing with the old girls last night.'

'Yeah, well, not usually my thing.'

'Impressive, though.'

'You thought so?'

She nodded.

They both walked over to one of the round tables and sat down.

'Would you like to share a bottle of wine with me?' asked Patrick.

'I'd love to,' said the red polo neck girl.

'Red or white?'

'Red,' she said. 'I need the belt of something red.'

He looked at her, startled.

'White is crisp and lovely and summery,' she explained, 'and I know you can get pissed on it, but red is better.'

'D'you want to get hammered?' he asked.

'Pretty much,' she replied.

'Um, right.'

'We're just sharing the table and the wine,' she told him. 'We're not friends or anything. And it's none of your business whether I get hammered or not.'

'Sure. Absolutely.'

She was the polar opposite of Verity, he thought, as she filled her glass with the wine he ordered. Verity never got hammered. And certainly not on purpose.

She was funny, polo neck girl. He asked her her name and she said that he could call her Mrs Scrooge, because that

288

was how she was feeling about this particular Christmas, very bah-humbuggy about it all.

'Because,' she said, her voice slightly slurred from the glass and a half of Sangre de Toro she'd knocked back quickly, 'it's all so false, isn't it? People pretending that they give a shit and thinking that they should be warm and loving and wanting that really but not being in a position to deliver . . . Don't you think. . .' her voice rose slightly, 'that love is a crock of shit when it comes down to it? I mean, you probably don't know enough about it because you're a man and therefore you go round breaking people's hearts, but generally speaking girls are brought up to believe in it, and even when we're really smart and clever and use our brains to think instead of just emoting about everything, we still allow ourselves to get turned over by some guy who promises us the earth and delivers sod all.'

Break-up girl, he decided then. Someone who'd been dumped just before Christmas and who'd taken herself off to the hotel to get away from it all but was now finding herself surrounded by couples and families and everything she most wanted to avoid.

'And you can't trust men,' she said peevishly. 'I mean, they say one thing and do the other. Why is that? You're a man. Explain it to me. Explain why you say you'll call when you don't.'

'I'm sorry,' he said. 'I can't.'

'And it's like – don't give too much away, don't tell her that you care in case she thinks it's serious when it isn't, it's only sex because you've had a bet with your mates or something.' She topped up her glass and took a defiant mouthful of the ruby-red liquid.

'I've never had a bet with my mates about a girl,' said Patrick. 'And if I had, I'd probably lose it.'

'I suppose it would depend on the bet.' She slumped back in her chair. 'I hate men. I do really.'

'All men?' he asked.

'Oh, pretty much,' she said confidently, sitting up straight again. 'I'm thinking that maybe I won't do men any more. They're more trouble than they're worth.'

'I could say the same about women.'

She shook her head. 'No. We're more reliable.'

He was going to make a riposte, but he realised that he didn't want to argue with her. She was drunk and miserable, which didn't make a good combination and would probably lead to things being said that both of them would rather not. Honestly, he thought, the guy should've waited until Christmas was over before giving her the bullet. It wouldn't have been that hard. Now Christmas would be tainted for her for ever in the same way that it had been tainted for him. Because much as he wanted to, he couldn't really disentangle Christmas and Verity and the whole disintegration of his marriage.

Her eyes were closed. She was attractive, he thought, in a way that had more to do with character than with prettiness. The polo neck suited her more than the pink dress had done. She wasn't, he reckoned, a pink dress sort of person. Not at heart. She didn't really seem to be the sort of person who would fall for the love and kisses and happy-ever-after routine. She seemed stronger than that. Which perhaps went to show what a poor judge of character he was, because obviously she *had* fallen for it and it was cracking her up and he felt sorry for her.

And he wanted to sleep with her.

He shuddered. He didn't know where that line of thought, of desire, had suddenly come from. He didn't want to sleep with her. It was a terrible idea.

Although . . . he looked at the curve of her breasts beneath the red polo neck and followed the contours of her slim body with his eyes . . . she might be a good package to unwrap. He liked slender girls with big boobs and she fitted the bill exactly. Verity – with a smaller chest and wider hips – had been a bit of an aberration on his part, a departure from his normal tastes. A wonderful departure though. He'd enjoyed making love to her. But he preferred big boobs. Which probably made him the same as millions of other men on the planet! He defended himself against his own argument that big-chested girls were every man's fantasy. So what if they were! Didn't every woman want George Clooney? Or someone like him?

She hadn't eaten any of her food, which was probably why the glass and a half of wine had gone straight to her head. She was still sitting upright in her chair, with her eyes closed.

Oh well, he thought. At least she's here at the table. Making me seem normal. If normal is sitting opposite a girl with big boobs and closed eyes.

He worked his way silently through his plate of roast beef, potatoes and veg. He was hungry, probably from the walk earlier. And possibly from the cold as well. Not that the Sugar Loaf Lodge was cold – far from it, what with its log fires and toasty central heating – but the Grand Ballroom overlooked the gardens, and in the fading light of the day, he could see the film of frost on the grass again. So it was Christmas-cold outside.

It was romantic, he thought. If you believed in romance. Which meant it was wasted utterly on him and Mrs Scrooge.

Mrs Scrooge. Did that mean she was married? Was the real case not that she had been dumped by a casual boyfriend, but that Christmas had made her realise that her marriage was over too? They said that the festive season put an extraordinary strain on families. Perhaps she and her husband hadn't even been able to make it through Christmas day.

He glanced at her hands. She wore a Claddagh ring on her engagement finger and a small hoop of coloured stones on the third finger of her right hand. Very restrained jewellery. Her earrings were plain gold studs, and on a long chain around her neck, glinting against the red wool of her jumper, was a gold cross. Mystery girl, he thought.

I still want to sleep with you.

She hadn't opened her eyes by the time he'd finished his food. He didn't like to leave her so that he could raid the dessert buffet. He was becoming slightly concerned about her apparent ability to sit motionless and silent. He wondered whether she was sleeping or if she had passed out (though managing to pass out and not fall over was a neat trick). He didn't quite know what to do with her.

A waiter came and asked if they wanted coffee, and he

ordered two espressos. The waiter put one in front of each of them, but Mrs Scrooge didn't open her eyes.

Patrick drank both coffees and then moved around the table so that he was right beside her.

'Hey,' he said softly. 'It's time to wake up.'

She said nothing.

'Please,' he said. 'We can't stay here all day, and I don't want to leave you on your own.'

She didn't move.

'I can bring you back to your room if you like,' he offered. 'Just to make sure you're OK.'

'Oh, sod off,' she said without opening her eyes.

He liked her and he still wanted to sleep with her, but she was damn hard work.

'C'mon, Mrs Scrooge,' he said. 'We have to go.'

She opened her eyes as though performing a major feat. They were big and blue and slightly unfocused.

'Go where?' she asked.

'Wherever you like.'

'I need to sleep,' she said. 'I haven't slept in forty-eight hours. Not really.'

He blinked. 'No wonder you're flaked,' he told her. 'I'll drop you back to your room.'

'Yeah. Good idea.' She smiled a fuzzy smile. 'Thanks.'

'Let's go,' he said.

He helped her to stand up and then slid his arm around her waist. She rested her head on his shoulder.

'You're nice,' she mumbled. 'You are really. For a tosser of a man.'

Grace and the rest of the Golden Girls were at the table

nearest the door. Patrick smiled briefly as he walked by them and Phil gave him a lascivious wink and a thumbs-up sign, which made him laugh under his breath.

There'd be nothing with Mrs Scrooge, he thought. He wasn't interested in a sexual encounter with a woman as messed up and as drunk as her. The physical sensation might have been everything he wanted, but he needed more than a physical sensation. He needed to know that she cared.

He'd known, months before it all went wrong, that Verity didn't care any more. It was in the way she moved beneath him, in the way she over-exaggerated her moans of pleasure and in the way she told him, far too brightly, that it had been wonderful. He'd known but he hadn't known what to do about it.

He was useless when it came to women. Drunk or sober.

'So which room is yours?' he asked as they walked slowly along the corridor to the guest bedrooms.

'Nice rooms,' she said tiredly. 'Nice hotel.'

'Yes. But which one is yours?'

'I like the names instead of numbers.' She yawned widely 'Good idea. More intimate. Good marketing.'

'And you're in . . . ?'

'Nice views of the mountains.' She closed her eyes again. 'From all the rooms, it says on the website. Romantic hide-away. Hah!'

He stood indecisively in front of the wall sign indicating the location of the various rooms. Mrs Scrooge wasn't being any help whatsoever. Deliberately *un*helpful, in fact.

'Which way?' he asked her desperately.

'Who cares?'

In the end he brought her to his room. He steered her towards the mountainous king-sized bed with its billowing duvet and cool pillows and then he eased off her high-heeled shoes. (How on earth did she manage to walk in those when she was drunk? he wondered. In the same situation he'd definitely have toppled over and broken something. Although he would have fallen over sober. How did women manage? How?) He swung her legs on to the bed and she burrowed down into the duvet with a little moan of pleasure.

She'd wake up soon, he thought. She wasn't that drunk, just sleepy. And something would tell her that she was sleeping in the wrong bed. She'd wake up. And then she'd leave. A bit embarrassed, maybe. But she'd leave.

It was dark outside now, and so he closed the heavy drapes, shutting out the silver light of the full moon. He switched on the TV, which was showing a grainy repeat of *Morecambe and Wise*. He remembered his parents talking about them, how great their show had been every Christmas and how much they enjoyed watching it. He had vague memories of watching it himself, although he didn't know whether he'd watched original shows or repeats. He'd seen other repeats at various points throughout his life. He'd thought they were funny, but not in the same stream-of-consciousness way as people like Jack Dee. Patrick liked Jack Dee. He liked his mournful persona.

This show was funny, though, he realised. Joyful funny and not despairing funny. He couldn't help laughing. Occasionally quite loudly. He wondered if his laughing would wake Mrs Scrooge, but she lay immobile on the bed, fast asleep.

*

After nearly two hours, he left the room. She clearly wasn't going to wake up, and he didn't want to spend the whole night sitting in front of the TV keeping an eye on her. He was uncomfortable about the voyeuristic element of it. He didn't want her to wake up and see him sitting on the sofa opposite her. It would be weird.

He went into the bathroom, cleaned his teeth and splashed water on his face. He thought the noise of the running water might wake her up, but it didn't. Sleeping Beauty, not Mrs Scrooge, he thought as he glanced back at her before leaving the room. I wonder what happened to the Handsome Prince. I wonder why she hates him so very much.

They were playing charades in the drawing room off the bar. The boisterous family made up one entire team; a second team consisted of a striking woman (who Phil had earlier told him was a well-known painter) and a younger woman who was her daughter, together with the bland older couple, both of whom were wearing Santa Claus hats with flashing lights. The Golden Girls had their own team and were watching the man in the Santa Claus hat making kung-fu movements with his hands in an effort to convey the third word to his team mates.

'Ninja,' said Patrick, under his breath but loud enough for Grace to hear.

'Do you know it?' she demanded.

'Maybe.'

'In that case, join our team,' she said quickly. 'We're numerically challenged.'

He hesitated for a moment, then sat down beside them.

'Where's your girlfriend?' asked Gill.

'I don't have a girlfriend,' said Patrick.

'The girl in the red jumper?' Gill's dark eyes twinkled. 'You seemed very taken with her earlier.'

'Not really,' he said.

Carmel frowned. 'I do hope you're not toying with her affections,' she said sharply.

'Anything but.' Patrick was defensive.

'Why is she here on her own?' asked Phil.

'I don't know.'

'Same reason as you, perhaps?' suggested Gill. 'Who knows what might happen . . .'

Patrick said nothing, and Phil told Gill to mind her own business, didn't Patrick have a perfect right to be here without anyone, and sometimes other people were over-rated. And Gill said that she couldn't agree more, but that Patrick was a lovely man who deserved someone in his life, at which Grace remarked that it wasn't always easy to have the right person in your life, as they knew only too well, didn't they; what about Muireann? At which they all nodded sagely, leaving Patrick to wonder who on earth Muireann was and why they felt sorry for her.

The man in the Santa hat sat down in frustration as his team gave up on the movie title and the Golden Girls were offered the chance to steal it. Patrick said, '*Teenage Mutant Ninja Turtles*,' which was right and caused Carmel and Gill to hug him while the other team groaned.

Then it was the Golden Girls' turn to think of a title, and Patrick toyed with the idea of suggesting *The Twelve*

Lays of Christmas, but stayed silent and allowed them to go with *All Quiet on the Western Front,* even though he knew the opposition would guess it.

In the end, it was the large family who won, mainly because their wide age group meant they knew songs from many different eras, and because one of the girls was obviously a bookworm who seemed to have read everything that had ever been published, while the young boy was totally clued in on movies, including those made years before he was born.

'Fun, though,' said Patrick when the Golden Girls berated themselves for not doing better and winning the bottle of champagne that had been on offer as a prize. 'And who needs more champagne?'

'I do,' said Grace. 'It's my favourite drink in the whole world.'

Patrick grinned at her and stood up. He said that he was going to stretch his legs, but actually he wanted to go back to the room and check on Mrs Scrooge.

He opened the door gently and made his way softly into Slievemaan. There was an indent on the duvet from where she'd lain, but she wasn't there any more. Nor was she in the bathroom. She'd clearly woken and gone back to her own room. He looked on the writing desk to see if she'd left a note, but she hadn't. Bad manners, he muttered to himself. The least she could've done was say thanks.

He prowled around the room for a while, flicking on the TV then turning it off again, wondering if last year the programmes on offer had been quite as awful as they were now, telling himself that it would be better fun to be back in the bar or the drawing room playing charades and talking to the other guests.

I can't believe I'm thinking that, he muttered aloud. I don't like other people at Christmas! I prefer being on my own.

But he didn't want to stay in his room and watch TV. Nor was he in the mood to settle down with his iPad. He craved company. He couldn't understand it.

He left the room and walked along the glass corridor again. Outside, in the paved area overlooked by the dining room, there was a brazier burning. Two smokers, wrapped in warm jackets, stood nearby.

Patrick hadn't smoked in nearly ten years, but he had the sudden urge to go outside and bum a cigarette off one of them. Verity, naturally, had been horrified to hear that he'd even *tried* smoking, and had threatened him with banishment from the family home if he ever came home with the smell of smoke on his breath. Once or twice he'd thought about doing it just to annoy her, but he knew he wouldn't have enjoyed those cigarettes. He felt like having one now, though.

He stepped outside, and then he realised that he'd been wrong about the people standing near the brazier. They weren't smoking at all but toasting marshmallows from the big silver platter that had been left on a table beside the brazier, along with a big urn of hot chocolate.

'They're gorgeous,' said the woman, who Patrick now recognised as the woman in the Santa hat. Her husband had his hands cupped around a steaming mug of hot chocolate.

'Comforting,' he added.

The couple exchanged smiles. Smiles that conveyed a lot. There was a conversation in those smiles, something to do with having been together a long time and gone through life's ups and downs knowing that they would always be comforted by each other. Patrick suddenly envied them fiercely.

Then the woman smiled at him. 'It's a beautiful night, isn't it?' She glanced up at the sky, where thousands of stars pierced the blackness. 'The best things in life are free, don't you think?'

'Not exactly free,' observed Patrick. 'It's costing an arm and a leg to stay here and look at that sky. But I do know what you mean.'

'The sky will still be there when we leave,' said her husband, 'and so will our ability to look at it.'

Patrick thought that these comments were very Zen from someone who'd been wearing a Santa hat earlier.

'Well, good night,' said the man as they finished their chocolate and went back inside. 'Happy Christmas to you.'

He was right, Patrick thought, as he warmed his hands at the brazier. The night was particularly beautiful, with the ghostly moonlight reflecting off the whitened branches of the trees and the ground frost sparkling in the glow of the fire. He could be anywhere and it would still be as lovely.

And lonely.

But that was OK. He was used to being on his own. He didn't mind it.

Except maybe this Christmas.

'Mind if I warm my hands?'

He turned around.

Mrs Scrooge stood beside him. She'd changed out of the red polo neck and was wearing a dress again. This time it was jade green and reached to slightly above her knees. It was just as figure-hugging as the pink one had been. She had, Patrick thought, the ideal body although standing beside him now she seemed taller than earlier. He was looking straight into her clear blue eyes.

'Higher heels,' she said, noticing his almost imperceptible frown.

He glanced down at her shoes. Jade green too. With skyscraper heels.

He moved to give her some more room by the brazier as she shivered.

'It's minus two degrees,' he told her, nodding at the thermometer set into the wall. 'You shouldn't be out without a coat.'

She laughed. 'You sound like my mum.'

He laughed too. 'Sorry. But it's bloody cold.'

'I know.' She shivered again.

'Here.' He slid out of his jacket and draped it over her shoulders.

'Oh, no, thanks. That way you'll be the one to freeze.'

'I've warmed up with the hot chocolate,' he said. 'Want some?'

She nodded and he filled a mug for her.

'How about a marshmallow?' he asked. 'I can't vouch for how good they'll be, because I've never actually toasted one before, but it does seem like an appropriate thing to do.'

She nodded again. He speared a pink marshmallow with one of the wooden skewers and held it in the flames until a sticky, sweet and slightly burnt aroma wafted around them.

'Want to risk it?' he asked.

'Why not.'

She blew on the marshmallow a couple of times and then popped it into her mouth. Her eyes watered.

'Too hot?' he asked anxiously.

She hopped up and down without saying anything for a moment, and then nodded.

'A bit. But lovely,' she assured him.

They stood beside each other in silence for a moment, both of them gazing upwards at the moonlit sky. And then she gave a little exclamation, and Patrick followed her pointing finger even as he heard a whooshing sound in the air. The shooting star streaked across the sky in a white arc and then vanished.

'Wow,' he said. 'I've never seen one like that before.'

'Me neither. It was amazing.'

'I feel like we're in a specially designed Christmas setting,' he said. 'The fire, the chocolate, the moonlight . . .'

She laughed. 'We are. The Sugar Loaf Lodge promised us the Ultimate Christmas Experience.'

'With our own shooting stars laid on.'

'Absolutely. It was probably a firework.'

'Oh, don't say that.'

She laughed again.

'I came out to say thank you. You were very kind.'

'No worries,' he said.

'I've never done anything quite like that before,' she said.

'I've never allowed a man to take me back to his room and fallen asleep on him.'

'I didn't plan to take you back to my room,' he told her. 'I wanted to take you back to yours. But you couldn't remember it.'

'Kilmashogue,' she said. 'And I could remember it. But I had some vague idea . . . well, I didn't want to be on my own.'

'Why?' he asked.

'I admire you.' She didn't answer his question. 'You came here by yourself and you got into the spirit of it with everyone and they all think you're great.'

He looked at her in astonishment.

'Not really.'

'Yes,' she said. 'I heard them talking. The old dears especially. One of them said that you were "a lovely young man" and was bemoaning the fact that she wasn't fifty years younger.'

'Gosh,' he said. 'I didn't realise I was setting geriatric hearts aglow.'

'You're nice,' she said. "Why are you here by yourself?'

'It seemed like a good idea. What about you? Why are you here alone?'

'I wasn't meant to be.' Her words were as chilly as the night air.

'Oh?'

'I was meant to be with my boyfriend,' she said.

Hah, thought Patrick. I was right. Dumped.

'I thought it would be too good to be true, and it was.'

'Why?'

303

'He's married.'

Patrick was startled.

'And so getting away from his wife and family would've been difficult. But he promised.'

Patrick liked her, but he didn't have sympathy for people who split up other people's marriages.

'I know it was stupid of me,' she said. 'I know I was wrong to want it. But I thought . . .'

'What, that he was going to leave?' Patrick knew that his tone was harsh.

She nodded. 'I was a fool.'

He didn't know what to say. He'd judged her and he thought he was right to judge her. If the man had come to the Sugar Loaf Lodge and stayed with her for Christmas, and when – because it would be a when and not an if – his wife found out, all hell would break loose and the marriage would be in tatters and it would all be because of Christmas again.

'I hate this time of year,' he said. 'It makes people do bad things.'

'And good things,' she reminded him. 'You were good to me.'

'I helped a drunk woman, that's all.'

'You're annoyed with me.'

'Affairs,' he said. 'I don't like affairs.'

'I didn't know I was having one,' she told him. 'Not until I'd fallen in love with him. And by then it was too late.'

'So why didn't he come?' asked Patrick.

'It's Christmas,' she said simply. 'He couldn't in the end.'

He glanced at her. He could see the single tear on her cheek, glinting like the frost.

'I'm sorry,' he said abruptly. 'I have no right to moralise at you. I guess I want all husbands to be the good guys.'

'Were you the good guy?' she asked. 'Did it all go wrong for you?'

He explained about Verity and Steven and the great Christmases and how it was all messed up and how he'd spent the last few at home with the Tesco dinners and how he'd felt so like Scrooge about it all.

Which made her laugh.

'And I told you to call me Mrs Scrooge,' she said.

'Yeah. Ironic, huh?'

'I was glad you were there. I know I was shit company, but I was glad to have you beside me.'

He moved a little closer to her. It hadn't been her fault, he thought. The affair. Things happened. You didn't mean them to but they did. And sometimes you tried to put things right but you couldn't.

'What are you going to do now?' he asked.

'Probably go inside,' she replied. 'It's bloody cold, despite this fire.'

'I meant . . . you know, with the married man?'

'I've already done it,' she said. 'Before dinner. I called him at home, which I'm not allowed to do, and I told him that I wasn't making an emotional, irrational decision and that it was over.'

'How'd he take it?'

'He said, "I'm sorry, you have a wrong number" and hung up.' She allowed her breath to escape in a slow mist.

'I'm sorry too,' he said.

'Yeah, well.' Her voice was brisker. '*C'est la vie* and all that. I thought he was the love of my life, but how the hell could he be? I was fooling myself. We all do.'

Patrick nodded. 'Yup. We do.'

She looked at him, her eyes level with his, and then she took off his jacket.

'Don't go just yet,' he said. 'I . . . I need the company too.'

She slid the jacket on again.

'I'm an intelligent person,' she told him. 'I have a good job. I have a nice car. I can pay my own way. But I'm a dipstick when it comes to men.'

'Ditto,' he said. 'Me and women.'

They stood in silence again.

'Oh for God's sake!' She suddenly sounded impatient. 'Are you going to kiss me or what?'

He turned towards her, his expression one of astonishment.

'Well, here we are,' she told him. 'In the cutest, most romantic setting in the whole of the country. A living Christmas card, in fact. And I've told you that my heart was broken but I'll get on with life, and you said so was yours, and surely to God at some point we have to kiss each other.'

'Not because we're sorry for each other,' said Patrick. 'That'd be a disaster.'

'Would it?'

She was lovely, he thought. Lovely and probably fun when her heart wasn't broken, and someone who could get up again after passing out from drink and not be ratty and horrible. Which was not exactly a good thing; he didn't

306

necessarily want to go out with someone who could pack an alcohol punch, but in fairness, it was good to see someone who'd looked so shattered earlier look so bloody great now. Which obviously she did, in her shimmering green dress and her super-high shoes, her big blue eyes glinting with a sudden hint of mischief. His jacket looked good on her too.

'Wouldn't it be a bit of a cliché for me to kiss you?' he asked.

'Christmas is a cliché,' she told him. 'You'd be doing us both a favour.'

'You think?' He'd put his arm around her and was drawing her closer to him. She smelled of wood smoke and spices and burning embers from the fire.

He kissed her. She kissed him back.

It was very, very pleasurable. He realised that he'd stopped shivering.

'I like the way you kiss, Mrs Scrooge,' he said softly.

'I like the way you kiss, Mr Scrooge,' she replied.

'Patrick,' he said.

'Holly,' she said.

He broke away and looked at her. 'Seriously?'

'Yes.'

'How very appropriate.'

'How about we go inside again? I'm freezing my ass off, even if it is the most romantic place on earth.'

'Glad you said that,' he told her.

They turned back towards the hotel.

In the light of the glass corridor he could see Grace. She was looking out at them and smiling. And as he smiled back at her, she gave him a thumbs-up. Holly, who'd seen her too, started to laugh.

'They're a gas bunch, aren't they, those old dears?'

'Yes. But really nice. In fact everyone's been nice here, haven't they? The families, the couples, the friends?'

'All doing their best to have a good time even though they're being forced into it.'

'Am I forcing you into having a good time?' Patrick asked as he opened the door for her.

She hesitated. And then she looked up at him and smiled. 'No,' she said. 'You're making this a lot more bearable.'

'You're doing the same for me,' he said.

'Out of our frying pans and into the fire?' she asked.

He laughed. 'Hopefully not.'

She smiled at him. 'I came here expecting one thing . . . and now . . . well, it feels like something else entirely is happening to me.'

'Something good?'

'Yes,' she said. 'Something good and Christmassy and totally not what I was expecting.'

'Same here,' he said as he steered her underneath a sprig of mistletoe that was hanging from the roof. 'And I know it's naff to do this, and very much against my usual principles, but suddenly I feel very traditional.'

'So do I,' she said as she wrapped her arms around him.

And he kissed her again.

Epilogue: The Sugar Loaf Lodge II

It was nearly the end of January before Neil and Claire had the opportunity to draw breath. Ever since Christmas the hotel had been full: after their seasonal guests had left there had been the New Year groups, and after that they'd run their annual New Year Relax and Renew spa break, which Claire had worried wouldn't be booked out but which ended up having a waiting list.

All in all, Claire said to Neil as they stood in the garden together one afternoon, noticing that the days had already begun to get ever so slightly longer, it had been a fantastic Christmas and New Year and the guests had been prepared to spend far more money on themselves than she'd expected.

'Well, times might be tough, but everyone needs to indulge themselves now and again,' said Neil.

'They all did,' Claire told him. 'And they said such nice things on the website, too.'

Neil nodded. He'd read through the comments left by their visitors and had been both pleased and relieved that they'd been, without exception, very complimentary.

'I worried a bit after Christmas,' Claire said.

'Why?'

'Because . . . because of Louisa.'

'Louisa!' He turned to look at her.

'We all saw her,' said Claire. 'Our resident ghost.'

'I've thought about that,' said Neil. 'The atmosphere in the room was very highly charged. Georgina has that effect. Maybe we all just thought we saw someone . . .'

'No.' Claire's voice was firm. 'We did. She was there. Louisa Lachfort. My . . . my ancestor.'

'You don't know that for certain,' said Neil.

'I'm sure of it,' Claire returned. 'You know I always felt a connection to this place. And I always felt there was someone watching over us. It must be because it's part of my family history. And it was Louisa who was there all the time.'

'And now?'

'I don't know.' Claire frowned. 'I mean, I don't feel any differently about the Sugar Loaf Lodge. I still love it passionately. And I want to do the best for our guests. But will I be able to do that if she isn't around leaving notes on the computer any more? Will it all go wrong?'

'Why should it?' he asked.

'Maybe it wasn't us.' She turned to face him. 'Maybe it was her all the time. Maybe I'm crap at this and so are you and it's only because of Louisa.'

'Have there been any unexpected entries on the computer since Christmas Day?' demanded Neil.

'No.'

'And has the roof fallen in?'

'No.' She sounded puzzled.

'Claire, I don't know about ghosts, I really don't. I know

what I thought I saw, but even so . . . I'd had champagne. I was looking at Georgina's painting. I could have imagined her. Just as you could.'

'But . . .'

'And the notes on the computer – we've always been busy, Claire. One or the other of us could have left them without even realising it.'

'Not possible,' she said firmly.

'Maybe. You said there haven't been any since Christmas Day. And yet the guests are still happy and you still somehow seem to know what they want.'

She nodded reluctantly.

'So what you need to realise, Claire, is that we're good at being hotel owners. We're good at what we do. Not thanks to ghosts and histories or anything like that. Just because we work damn hard and you – you're a genius when it comes to looking after guests.'

She laughed.

He put his arm around her shoulders and hugged her to him.

'Ready for another year?' he asked as they watched the sun slide beneath the horizon in a swathe of orange and gold.

'Absolutely,' she said. They turned back to the hotel.

And Louisa, who was no longer able to interact with them now that she had joined her family on the other side, but who was still following their progress carefully, smiled as they went inside again and closed the door behind them.